24 Hour Telephone Renewals 020 8489 4560
HARINGEY LIBRARIES
THIS BOOK MUST BE RETURNED ON OR BEFORE
THE LAST DATE MARKED BELOW

Online renewals – visit libraries.haringey.gov.uk

Published by Haringey Council's Communications Unit 1149.19 • 11/15

D0552744

ABOUT THE AUTHOR

The medical career of physician-novelist Jack Chase has spanned the spectrum from laboratory research in molecular biology to clinical practice. He has served as attending physician on the infectious disease services of a number of medical schools and as director of clinical research for two multinational pharmaceutical companies.

His previous novels, *Fatal Analysis* and *Mortality Rate,* were published in multiple languages in print editions and sold throughout the world. Both are now available for the first time in e-book and trade paperback formats. His wife is *New York Times* bestselling author Katherine Stone.

Jack Chase is currently hard at work on his next medical novel.

Official website: www.medicalthriller.com

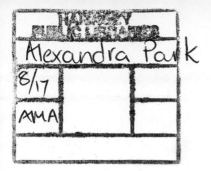

Alexandra Park

8/17

AMA

PROLOGUE

Pace Magruder stepped out into the clear spring evening and drew his first breath of non-hospital air in more than fourteen hours. He was headed for the Ritz-Carlton just down the street where the hospital guild was to hold its biggest fund-raising event of the year. A silent auction. Black tie. He'd dragged his tux to work that morning and changed after he finally finished rounds.

Pace was running late but paused for a couple moments, there on the hospital lawn, to recharge his batteries in the cooling breeze and reflect on the day's events. It had been a spectacular day in the lab. Months of research had produced a startling conclusion. The new findings would force Pace and his colleagues to dramatically alter the direction of their future research—a huge triumph for Pace's lab and yet another victory on the road to the ultimate goal, the conquest of heart disease.

The battle against that great killer would not end with today's results, nor would it be over tomorrow, but victory would come, Pace was now certain, within his own lifetime. And it was his quest for that victory, not his love of the battle, that drove Pace to the lab in the early morning and kept him there long after the others had gone home.

So as Pace stood there that night in the lee of the great hospital, he was filled with hope. It was a night conducive to hope, as spring evenings often are. It was the night on which his brief affair with super model Danica Russo was destined to begin, and a night that gave no sign of what was to come—no hint of another night, still weeks in the future, when Pace, sweat-drenched and disoriented, would awaken to a darkened hospital room, gripped by the sudden, certain knowledge that Danica Russo had killed him.

The ballroom was packed by the time he arrived— good news for the hospital guild. All the ladies were in their finest gowns, many purchased solely for this evening. It might have been a ball, the way they were dressed, but there would be no dancing. Just drinks, hors d'oeuvres, and the auction.

He glanced at his watch. Still nearly half an hour before the auction closed. Plenty of time to overbid for some item he didn't want in the first place. Pace had always argued, why go through all the expense and foofaraw of an auction? Why not just ask everybody to get out their checkbooks and do the right thing? But the professional fund-raisers claimed that an organized event would raise more money. He assumed they knew what they were doing.

Pace decided he'd head for the auction tables in a minute. But first, not being on call, he thought he'd pay a visit to one of the well-stocked bars set up at strategic locations around the room.

Danica spotted Pace as soon as he entered. She watched him hesitate at the door, then slowly make his way across the floor, greeted by nearly everyone he passed.

Danica Russo was in town on a fashion shoot. She

had gone to the benefit on the arm of a rich, older man who'd spent the evening schmoozing with other rich, older men—leaving Danica to fend for herself. Hearing the death rattle of terminal boredom, she had embarked on a search for someone, Please, God, *someone*, to talk to. When she caught sight of Pace Magruder she said to herself, He'll do *very nicely*, thank you.

He was tall, a matter of no small importance to the leggy Danica, and underneath his tuxedo she detected a rangy muscularity. He had one of those ruggedly handsome faces that render hazardous any estimation of age, but she guessed he wasn't more than forty—a good quarter century younger than her escort of the evening. Danica was instantly taken by the notion that he was a cowboy. He reminded her of that cowboy actor, Sam Elliott—a young Sam Elliot—if Sam was having a really good day.

Five minutes after spying Pace Magruder across the crowded ballroom, Danica intercepted him at the bar.

"Are you a gunslinger?"

He turned, his dark eyes deadly serious but just a hint of a smile on his face. "No, ma'am," in that quiet, resonant voice of his, raising a hand to touch an imaginary Stetson. "My gunslingin' days are done for good." He opened the jacket of his tuxedo to show that he was unarmed. "These days, I'm just an ordinary, peace-lovin' sawbones."

He offered his hand. "Pace Magruder."

"Danica Russo," she said.

"And you would be the new schoolmarm?"

"Maybe," she smiled, "when my modeling days are over."

Looking closer, Pace saw a little of what the camera saw. This was not just another beautiful face, this was a face with real ship-launching potential.

"I'm sorry," he said, shaking his head. "I'm sure I should have recognized you. Problem is, I pretty much spend my life cloistered in the hospital and the research lab. I don't get out much."

"I'll bet," she said. "What kind of research?"

"Heart stuff. If you'd like to hear an impromptu, three-hour lecture on Torsades de pointes or the bundle of His, I'm your man."

"Maybe later," she said. "Right now I'd settle for a cure for this cold I've been carrying around."

"What you need is lots of fluids," he said, offering a glass of champagne, "and plenty of bed rest."

Her notion of him as a cowboy kindled deep emotions. Pace was in fact a West Texas boy, but his people had been wildcatters, not ranchers. Their family saga was a familiar one in Texas, a roller coaster ride of soaring dreams and bitter disappointments. Pace was just ten years old when he lost both parents in an oilfield explosion. His sole inheritance was the name he shared with his father and grandfather.

The day after the funeral, Pace was shipped off to Massachusetts and into the custody of an elderly maiden aunt. He arrived with just one small suitcase, and it practically empty. But the suitcase did contain a priceless treasure—a picture, taken at the Sears, Roebuck, of a five-year-old Pace standing between two proud, loving parents. It was the only picture of his parents Pace was ever to have.

When he looked at that picture now, he saw two things. First, how happy they were. Happiness shined in all their faces. The other thing, how very young his parents were—two kids who dropped out of high school and got married, then set out to seek their fortune. They didn't need an education, you could almost hear them say it—all they needed was a little luck.

Pace didn't have an unhappy memory of their time together. Why would he, a kid with parents who were little more than kids themselves? They never had much, but they didn't need much. And they filled Pace with wondrous visions of what their future held.

Aunt Mariah, on the other hand, was a gaunt, austere woman whose concept of child rearing was a far cry from the freewheeling attitude of his parents. Pace, his grief transformed to anger, naturally rebelled, and his first years in New England were tumultuous.

School provided no respite from unhappiness. Pace was regarded as an outsider and teased unmercifully for his West Texas drawl. In self-defense, he withdrew into books, emerging only to do battle on the athletic fields. There, the taunts of classmates met with swift retribution, and he slowly earned their grudging respect.

By the time he entered Harvard the drawl had all but disappeared, but it wasn't until nearly the end of his college years that Pace began to understand that his Aunt Mariah's tough outer shell guarded a generous and loving heart.

As Pace matured and began to understand some of the events that had shaped his own personality, he wondered at the forces that might have pushed his Aunt Mariah into her life of pious seclusion. If she harbored some great hidden secret, Pace never learned it, but he would be forever thankful that she had survived his fractious youth, and that he had the opportunity, before her death, to express his gratitude and to begin to try to return her kindness.

Danica's was a very different story. While Pace Magruder's name had endured for three generations, Danica Russo's was considerably younger than she was. From early childhood, she had dreamed of becoming an actress, and from the very beginning she knew that the name Mavis Oglethorpe wasn't going to cut it. Two weeks after Mavis Oglethorpe graduated from high school, Danica Russo arrived in New York.

For nearly a year she survived by waitressing, and when the first modeling jobs came her way she viewed them only as small stepping stones toward her ultimate goal. But modeling success dawned with unanticipated suddenness, pushing her acting dreams to the side. Almost overnight it seemed the name Danica Russo was on every lip, her face on every magazine cover. Within a year, she had garnered the ultimate tribute—she became known throughout the world simply as Danica.

They were an exotic couple, Pace and Danica, as striking as they were unlikely. She was based in New York. He lived and worked in Virginia. Hers was the glamorous life of an international celebrity, his the quiet world of medical practice and research. Everyone said it wouldn't last, and everyone was right. Still, for a few short weeks that spring, they certainly turned heads everywhere they went. But as spring slipped away, so did any pretense of a viable future for the couple.

Danica was ten years younger than Pace. He hadn't been much different from her at that age. Hell, he hadn't been much different from her last year.

Still, the age difference was one of the things that kept them out of sync. Little things, like taste in music. Danica's favorites were all crash and burn. Pace couldn't relate to them. He once asked her if she liked Roy Orbison. She said, Who's *Roy Orbison*?

Danica was completely caught up in her work. Pace couldn't really fault her for that. After all, what had he been doing for the last fifteen years? Mostly living at the hospital, with an occasional fleeting relationship squeezed in around the edges.

Anne Curtis—the wife of his best friend, Brian—had once tried to talk seriously about his "problem" with women. Pace had suffered terrible losses in his life, she said. Maybe he wasn't willing to take the risk—getting close to someone. But that wasn't something Pace was eager to discuss, even with Anne. So he just laughed it off, told Anne that all she really wanted was a dependable fourth for bridge.

Pace had never in his adult life entered into a relationship with the expectation that it would develop into anything serious, and it hadn't taken long to determine that his affair with Danica was destined to be as insubstantial as all the rest. But suddenly, that wasn't enough. Now he was searching for deep and meaningful, and if that wasn't going to happen with Danica, there was no point in continuing the relationship.

Deep and meaningful? Where had that come from? Hell, the other day he'd caught himself daydreaming about what it would be like to have a son to toss a football around with or what it would be like with a daughter—staying up late, worrying, waiting for her to come home from a date. What was *that* all about?

This would be their last night together. At some level, they both knew that. Danica was waiting for him at a little Italian restaurant not far from the hospital. Rounds had taken forever. He was late. Danica had finally gone ahead and eaten without him. She wasn't a happy camper.

"Somebody figured out who I was," she said, "and then everybody in the place lined up for an autograph."

"I'm sorry," Pace said. "I can't control how long rounds go. It all depends on the patients' needs. We had a couple of new admissions who were pretty sick."

Add to that, Pace had felt absolutely drained after rounds. He'd gone back to his office just to sit in a chair and rest. It'd been getting worse for a couple of weeks, and he'd been ignoring it. Or denying it. He told himself it was just a cold, but deep down he knew it was more than that. First, he had cut out his regular jogging routine. Then he started avoiding stairs and anything else that might cause undue exertion. Now he couldn't get through rounds without having to look for some excuse to sit down.

But he couldn't ignore it any longer. He was a cardiologist for crying out loud.

His heart was failing.

"Is it hot in here?" Pace needed air. He felt claustrophobic.

"If I had another sweater, I'd put it on." Danica could get a little snippy.

"If you're done, maybe we could go outside and get some fresh air."

Standing, Pace felt light-headed, but once they were outside he began to feel better. They turned in the direction of Pace's car and immediately became aware of a commotion just ahead of them. A small crowd had gathered on the sidewalk. Pace could hear a woman's voice wailing and screaming for help, but his view was obstructed by the swarm of people milling about.

When he was close enough to look over the crowd,

Pace saw an elderly man, his face ashen, lying on his back on the sidewalk. A woman of about the same age knelt beside him screaming, "Can't someone do something? Please!"

No one in the crowd offered more than a helpless shrug.

Pace elbowed his way through the onlookers. "Has anyone called 911?"

No response.

Pace turned to Danica. "Call 911. Tell them a man has suffered a cardiac arrest and I'm beginning CPR."

By this time, Pace was kneeling beside the prostrate man, Pace's own heart problem, for the moment, set aside. "How long has he been like this?"

The elderly woman just shook her head and sobbed.

Pace opened the man's mouth to make certain his airway wasn't obstructed, then tilted the chin upward and began mouth-to-mouth resuscitation. Between breaths he tried his best to get information.

"Has he been passed out like this more than a minute or two?"

Once again, the woman shook her head—this time, purposefully. Pace felt for a carotid pulse and, feeling none, began chest compression.

"Does anyone here know CPR?" Pace yelled.

Again, no response. They were just there to watch.

Pace would have to manage by himself until the paramedics arrived. It wouldn't be the first time. But it was hard work, compressing the patient's chest 100 times per minute, only stopping after every thirty compressions for two quick lung inflations by mouth. This kind of exercise was pretty rigorous for a healthy man, and Pace was no longer a healthy man. He wasn't sure he could keep it up until the paramedics arrived. And he had no idea how much damage he was wreaking on his own failing heart.

As he tired, Pace considered giving up on the breathing portion of the CPR and just doing chest compressions. Some studies suggested chest compression alone was as good as combining it with providing breaths to the victim. But those studies dealt with lay people who, for a number of reasons, probably weren't able to combine the two steps effectively. Pace was convinced that, when CPR was administered by a practiced expert like himself, the patient benefited from the addition of ventilation. And everyone would agree that, for *prolonged* CPR, providing breaths was absolutely essential to prevent brain damage caused by lack of oxygen. So, as long as he was able, he would continue—two breaths, thirty compressions; two breaths, thirty compressions. . . .

"Does he have any medical problems?" Pace asked the wife.

"Heart," she said, seeming to regain some of her composure. "He had a heart attack a couple of months ago."

"Any medications?"

"Yes, but I can't remember the names." She once again began to sob.

Pace felt her anguish and desperately wished someone in the crowd would offer her comfort. For now, he had his hands full with the husband.

Pace heard a siren in the distance at about the same moment he realized he was in serious trouble. He could feel his own heart racing, hear his own increasingly hungry gasps for air. He was feeling light-headed again, and he worried he might pass out.

Pace's breaths kept getting shorter and shorter, the mouth-to-mouth respiration now barely adequate. The chest compression was exhausting. At any moment he would be unable to continue.

The paramedics arrived just as Pace verged on collapse. Through bleary eyes he recognized Bob Murphy, a man Pace had first trained in cardiac life support ten years ago. He'd seen Bob many times since in refresher courses. Like nearly all the paramedics, Murphy was very good at what he did.

Pace managed to get himself out of the way. They didn't need his help—even if he had been able to give it. So Pace just sat on the ground, several feet away, trying to catch his breath.

The paramedics quickly had the older man intubated and an IV running. The EKG monitor told them he was in ventricular fibrillation which they were able to reverse with a single electrical shock. They soon had a sustainable heart rhythm going and were ready to head for the hospital.

Just before they left, Bob Murphy looked up and noticed Pace's condition for the first time. "Are you okay, Dr. Magruder?"

Pace nodded yes.

"Are you sure?"

Pace nodded again. He thought he was beginning to feel less breathless.

Pace watched as the paramedics loaded their patient into the ambulance and then pulled away. He searched the crowd for Danica and found her ten feet away. She was standing there, just staring at him, a look of abject terror on her face.

PART ONE

—1—

Pace had no idea when the other person had entered the room. He knew only that someone was there, an ominous presence skulking in the shadows.

"Who's there?"

No answer.

"What do you want?"

Still nothing.

Then there was movement. A human form advancing to his bedside.

It was not until she was almost upon him that Pace realized it was a woman. She was nude. Why was he so terrified?

Her face. She had no face.

No, her face was hidden. She was holding something. A pillow. Just a pillow.

See, nothing to be afraid of.

She said, "I love you, Pace Magruder," in a smoky voice sounding so familiar.

Then she lowered the pillow, and in the first half of that split second, he recognized her. In the second half, all went black, the pillow pressed against his face with such force it felt like someone was standing on it. And he couldn't breathe.

He couldn't breathe!

He wanted so desperately to resist, to fight for his

own life, but there was nothing he could do. He was so weak . . . so weak. Life ebbed from his body.

He screamed her name, "Danica!" but without breath, his voice muffled by the pillow, no sound came. He was dead. Unless . . .

He summoned every ounce of strength remaining in his debilitated body and forced himself upright in bed. His breathing was suddenly better.

He was awake.

"What's going on, Dr. Magruder?" It was Jennifer, the new nurse working the night shift.

"Please," he said between gasps, "call me Pace."

"What's going on, Pace?"

"Nightmare."

"It's probably one of your medications."

"Probably."

"Do you want me to turn up your oxygen?"

"That's okay. I'm starting to feel better. Sitting up helps."

"Should I call the transplant fellow?"

"No, don't bother her. I'm fine."

She studied his bedside monitor. "Your heart rate's coming back down. I ran a strip at the nursing station. You were really taching."

She listened briefly to his lungs. "They sound a little wet at the bases."

"That's the way they always sound," he said, "these days."

"You're sopping wet. I'll get you a fresh gown and some pajama bottoms."

"Thank you. Extra large, if you can find them."

"These sheets are soaked too. Let's put you in a chair, and I'll see if I can rustle up a dry set."

"Thanks."

"That must have been some nightmare."

It was, Pace thought, and not a very subtle one. It had encapsulated the last three months of his life. He'd caught a cold—maybe from Danica, maybe from any one of the hundreds of other people with colds he'd been around—but at any rate, he'd caught a cold, and it wouldn't go away, and now that cold might end his life.

He'd nearly killed himself that night outside the restaurant. After the elderly man was safely in the ambulance, Pace had asked Danica if she'd mind just driving him home and leaving him there. He'd spent most of the night sitting in a chair, struggling for each breath. When the sun finally came up he called a cab to take him to the hospital. Pace told the ER physician what he thought he had, viral myocarditis—an inflammation of the muscle of the heart caused by a virus. And Pace was right. He had caught a cold, and the virus that caused the cold had infected his heart.

Hundreds of millions of people around the world catch colds each year, but only a handful of those go on to develop myocarditis. No one knows why that handful is so unlucky. The viruses that cause myocarditis appear identical to the ones that cause colds. There is no evident genetic defect that leads to susceptibility. It's one of those great mysteries of medical science remaining to be solved.

At any rate, once the virus sets up housekeeping in the heart, it is up to the patient's own body—its so-called host defenses—to cure the disease. Just as there is no medication that successfully eliminates the virus when it infects the respiratory tract and causes a cold, there is no medication that can successfully eliminate the virus from the heart. But the human body is a remarkable thing, and only the tiniest fraction of people who catch colds ever develop clinical myocarditis, and of those who do develop myocarditis, only a small subset are unfortunate enough to share the relentless downhill course Pace Magruder experienced.

One day he had a cold.

Two weeks later he was gasping for breath.

Now, he teetered on the brink of eternity.

Pace had arrived at the hospital that first morning in critical condition. His lungs were filled with fluid—pulmonary edema. His breath came in wheezing gasps. On the plus side, Pace had already figured out exactly what was wrong, and appropriate treatment was instituted immediately.

They gave him 100 percent oxygen under positive pressure and began intravenous morphine, nitroglycerin, and diuretics. His initial response was dramatic. Within hours Pace was comfortable at rest and able once again to lie flat on his back without becoming short of breath. As long as he didn't try anything too active, he felt almost normal. Within a few days, he was able to leave the hospital.

Unfortunately, his respite was brief. Over the next few weeks Pace's underlying heart condition continued to deteriorate, and, despite increasingly aggressive treatment, his overall medical condition worsened. For the last six weeks Pace's heart had been dependent on the infusion of dobutamine to maintain adequate cardiac output, and he was confined to the hospital.

Pace had spent most of his adult life in hospitals, but never before as a patient. Six weeks ago, the hospital became his home.

"Do you want me to help you get back into bed?" Jennifer had just finished with the fresh sheets.

"No thanks, I'll just sit here till Dr. Curtis comes by.

It's easier for him to examine me if I'm sitting up."

Jennifer gave her watch a long look. "It's 3:00 A.M."

"Brian's a surgeon," Pace explained. "Surgeons are early rounders."

"You need your rest."

"I'll probably nod off in the chair." But he knew he wouldn't.

"I'll turn the light out."

And there he was, like so many nights before, alone in the dark, listening to the hushed sounds of a hospital trying to get itself to sleep—the shuffling of feet in the hallway, the soft rumble of a cart being rolled by his door, the muffled voice from the hospital speaker system summoning staff to some new emergency. For company, he had the green glow of the heart monitor above his bed and the friendly little yellow light that winked at him from the machine that regulated his intravenous fluids.

His breathing was easier sitting up. How many hundreds of times on rounds over the years had he discovered his heart-failure patients sitting up in chairs, laboring to breathe, unable to climb back into bed on their own even if they wanted to?

Sometimes now, on the bad days, Pace felt too weak even to feed himself, too feeble to lift a spoon. But that's where he drew the line. No one was going to feed him. He just told them he didn't have much of an appetite for the healthful, low-everything diet they had him on.

There was only one bright note in all this gloom. His deteriorating clinical condition had earned him Status 1. Pace was at the very top of the list of those awaiting hearts for transplantation.

In the final analysis, the human heart, wondrous though it is, is nothing more than an exquisite pump.

And like any other pump, once it begins to fail, options are limited. One way to help a failing pump is to give it less work to do. In medical practice this is accomplished, in part, by removing fluid from the body with diuretics, thus reducing the workload on the heart. Other medications dilate arteries downstream from the heart to decrease the resistance the pump has to work against.

Drugs like dobutamine increase the force with which the heart muscle is able to contract and thus increase the amount of work the pump can handle. But like any other piece of failing machinery, the human heart can deteriorate to a point where only one option remains—the pump must be replaced. Pace Magruder's heart had reached that point six weeks ago.

So Pace had joined the more than 3,000 others on the list waiting for a donor heart. But only about 2,200 donor hearts would become available in the next year. Twenty percent of those on the transplant list would die waiting. Once you were designated Status 1, the only way to move up on the list was for someone else to die—either another patient awaiting transplantation, or some unfortunate soul with a healthy heart who was destined to become a donor.

From the start, Pace had played an intensely active role in his own care. He didn't want to meddle or second guess the judgment of others, but he made it clear he would participate in every aspect of the decision process. And at the beginning there had been innumerable choices to be made—which drug, what dosage, how much oxygen, and on and on. But, over time, the number of options had decreased. Therapy had been optimized. Day after day now passed during which there were simply no new decisions to be made.

Pace found it terribly frustrating. His role had suddenly grown quite passive, but so had the role of his physicians.

At this point there was only one thing left to do.

Wait.

Wait for a heart to become available.

For wakeful nights like this, Pace had his music. He slipped on his headphones and soon had Roy Orbison waxing nostalgic for a place called the Blue Bayou—a place Roy Orbison wrote and sang about, a place that Pace had never seen and maybe never existed outside of Roy's highly colored imagination.

Pace tried not to think about the donor heart he so desperately needed—not because he was afraid it wouldn't come, but because he was so certain it would.

Over the years, when his patients languished on the transplant list, Pace agonized right along with them, wanting that new heart every bit as single-mindedly as they did. But he had quickly discovered it was quite a different thing now that he was himself the potential beneficiary. He was suddenly consumed by guilt.

It was such a monstrously selfish thing to hope for—that another human being would die so that he might live.

—2—

Brian Curtis bounded in at 5:00 A.M., making rounds on all of his patients before his first surgery of the morning. He was in a very good mood, or maybe just trying to be upbeat for Pace.

"How about those Orioles?"

"They were lucky," Pace said. "If Martinez hadn't thrown the ball into the dugout in the bottom of the ninth, the Birds would have lost in regulation."

"With a little better hitting, they could be contenders."

"If they signed some new pitchers and found some guys who could play the outfield," Pace said. "That's assuming they had some infielders."

"Oh well," Brian said, "we always have the Redskins to look forward to."

It was an awkward moment, the problem with trying to be glib—like those chatty newscasters on TV who always end up saying something they shouldn't when they try to ad-lib. The football season was too far away to be very comfortable talking about it. There was no guarantee Pace would be around for football season.

"Don't even get me started on the Skins' offensive line," Pace said.

Brian smiled, taking out his stethoscope. "Why

don't you let me have a listen?"

Pace loosened his gown, and Brian carefully went through the daily ritual. He listened closely to Pace's heart and lungs, checked his neck for venous distension, then looked for evidence of peripheral edema.

"Everything seems stable," he told Pace. "How was your night?"

Pace knew that Brian would have reviewed his chart before coming into the room. He'd already read what Jennifer wrote, now he wanted Pace's version.

"I had kind of a bad dream. Probably one of my meds."

"We don't have a lot of leeway right now with your meds, Pace. There's really nothing we can stop. I wouldn't even want to lower any of the dosages if there's any way we can avoid it."

"Don't worry," Pace said. "I'm fine."

Brian was suddenly very serious. "You're not really fine, Pace. I know that you know that. Things just aren't going as well as we'd like."

"You know what I meant," Pace said. "There's no reason to change any of my drugs."

"I want to talk to you about something, Pace, and I want you to think about it. Let's not decide anything now. We'll talk again when I come back on evening rounds."

Pace had a pretty good idea where this was heading.

"I think it's time to consider a mechanical bridge," Brian said.

Pace had been expecting this. The mechanical bridge was the last potential temporizing measure before transplantation. It wasn't permanent, it just bought you time—days, weeks, sometimes even months—while you were waiting for a donor heart to become available. The "bridge" was actually a remarkable mechanical pump. Calling it a bridge reminded everyone it was meant to be temporary, holding out the hope of something beyond.

The theory was simple. The heart is a pump. When it fails, why not simply insert a replacement pump? What could be easier? Man has been building pumps for centuries. Okay, man's pumps are not quite as elegant as nature's, but then man hasn't been at it quite as long.

"I keep thinking that a donor heart will come through any day now," Pace said.

Brian gave him a thin smile. "I know you do. We're all praying for that. But you're a big guy who just happens to have Type O blood."

Brian was gently reminding Pace that the two most important factors in matching the donor heart to the recipient—body size and blood type—both worked against Pace. Someone with a body as large as Pace's needed a donor heart big enough to meet that body's demands. That meant a larger than average donor.

And the problem with Type O blood is that—even though it's the most common blood type—patients with Type O can receive hearts only from Type O donors. All other patients can accept hearts from Type O donors and at least one other blood type in addition to Type O. Thus, patients with Type O blood can receive hearts from a smaller percentage of potential donors. Consequently, on average, they spend more time waiting on the transplant list.

So, in order for Pace to receive the transplant he so urgently needed, someone had to die, and that someone needed to meet certain very strict criteria. The odds that would happen were less favorable than either Pace or Brian liked to admit.

"A bridge would get you out of this room," Brian reminded him. "Hell, it'd get you out of the hospital."

Pace nodded. That was the most appealing aspect of the new left ventricular assist devices. They attached the pump to the apex of the heart, entirely enclosed in the chest, and you wore an external battery pack that supplied electrical power to the device. You could walk around, go shopping—almost like a normal person.

But Pace couldn't free himself of the notion that the pump was a step in the wrong direction. He started to say as much, but Brian stopped him.

"Don't say anything now, Pace. I'll be back this evening, and we'll talk again. I just want to leave you with some facts you already know. Maybe I've been remiss up to now, treating you like the colleague and friend you are rather than emphasizing what is, for now, our most important relationship—doctor and patient. Since I knew that you knew all the facts, I didn't lay them out for you as I would have for a patient who didn't happen to know more about cardiology than I did. But we don't have that luxury anymore. Now I want to be certain we each have the same set of facts in front of us.

"Pace, we're out of options. There's nothing more to be done medically. Surgically, I'd give you a new heart this afternoon if I had one, but I don't. I believe we'll get one eventually, but we can't count on that happening any time soon. The only way we can help you now is with the bridge. At this moment your heart function is adequate to keep you alive as long as you don't do anything foolish—like trying to move from your chair to the bed without assistance. In terms of receiving the bridge, right now, you're an acceptable surgical risk.

"But we both know that could change at any time.

Tonight, tomorrow—even this afternoon—you could slip into fulminant heart failure. If that happens, the surgery becomes much riskier, the chance of success much less. I don't want to operate under those conditions if we can avoid it, and we *can* avoid it."

Brian gripped Pace's shoulder with his left hand and took Pace's right hand in his. "That's the truth with the bark on, Pace, right out there for both of us to see."

Pace nodded.

"I'll see you this evening," Brian said, "after I finish in the OR."

Brian hadn't meant it as a challenge, but as soon as his friend left, Pace started eyeing his bed, gauging the distance from the chair he was sitting in—pretty certain he could make it if he put his mind to it. He had been sitting for a couple of hours. His breathing was easy. He felt fine.

Pace had his IV pole for support. He grasped it firmly with his right hand then slowly raised himself from the chair. Nothing to it.

He took a couple of steps and felt dizzy.

One more step, and he knew he wasn't going to make it.

But he hadn't lost all his common sense. Pace wasn't going to compound his problems by passing out and banging his head on something. With the meager assistance of his now feeble grip on the IV pole, he slowly eased himself down to the floor. He stayed there, on his hands and knees, panting for air, desperately hoping no one would come in and find him—at least be spared that humiliation.

After several minutes he began to recover. On hands and knees he made his way to his bed. Then, after resting again, he managed to slowly climb into bed, once again totally exhausted.

Back in bed, he soon felt better. Brian was right, for now he was okay, as long as he didn't try anything crazy.

Pace worried about the pressure he'd put on Brian—having his closest friend as his transplant surgeon. Pace couldn't imagine anyone else playing that role, but he worried it was unfair to Brian. They had discussed it, in the beginning. The only real alternative was for Pace to seek care in another city. Neither of them wanted that. So Brian had accepted the responsibility, and the issue had never come up again. Until today.

Pace glanced at the clock. Not even six yet. He had at least twelve hours to worry about what he was going to tell Brian.

It was after 7:00 when Brian finally reappeared. He looked tired. He'd undoubtedly earned it.

"How was your day?" he asked.

"Same old, same old," Pace said. "How was surgery?"

"Long." Brian pulled his stethoscope out of the pocket of his clinic coat. "Lean forward and let me have a listen." He painstakingly repeated the examination routine.

"Everything seems stable," he told Pace. "Just a few râles at the lung bases."

"Then I expect you'd better get going," Pace said. "I imagine you've got sick people you need to see. Or, if you're cutting out early tonight, Anne might appreciate a visit."

"Speaking of Anne," Brian said, "we were at a gallery opening the other night and happened to run into Danica. She said she'd been doing some bathing suit layout down at the beach. Anyway, she asked about you, seemed very concerned. Anne thinks you're shutting Danica out."

Pace shook his head. "Danica and I had a few good times together. It was fun, but it was never serious. She may feel a little guilty about my getting sick, but that's nothing to build a relationship on."

"A heart transplant is a pretty tough thing to get through alone."

"I'm not alone, Pace said. "Half the medical school comes by here every day."

"That's not the same thing."

"I'm fine, Brian."

Brian shifted gears. "What are your thoughts about the bridge?"

Pace didn't hesitate. "It's not for me."

Brian didn't look surprised. "Can you tell me why?"

"Partly because I think it's a step in the wrong direction, and partly because I don't want to get stranded on a mechanical device. A guy my size, my blood type, you know as well as I do, Brian, a donor heart may *never* become available—not in time. And you can't stay on the mechanical pump forever. I don't want to end my life that way, on a bridge to nowhere. I'd rather take my chances with my own heart."

"But you know the bridge can buy you a lot of time. It can mean the difference between life and death."

"I've made my decision, Brian."

Brian started to say something else, but Pace wouldn't let him.

"Enough," Pace said. "Now go find someone who's *really* sick and requires the services of a semi-competent surgeon."

Alone again, Pace brooded over his plight. He

hadn't really made a decision. He was pretty sure Brian had recognized that.

Maggie Pearson, the clinical psychologist assigned to the transplant team, would undoubtedly tell him he was experiencing cognitive dissonance—the holding of two diametrically opposed beliefs at the same time. On the one hand, he didn't want the bridge because a donor heart would become available at any moment. On the other hand, he didn't want the bridge because that wasn't how he wanted to die, on the mechanical pump.

So which is it, Pace? What do you truly believe? Are you gonna get that new heart tomorrow, or is it never going to happen? It was a question he had to deal with. Soon.

In the meantime there *was* one consistent thread in his thinking. No matter what, Pace didn't want the bridge. That needed to be etched in stone. And there would be no deathbed conversion on the issue—no changing his mind at the last minute when he was in florid heart failure and about to die, when the chances of his surviving the surgery were nearly zero. He couldn't do that to any surgeon, let alone his best friend.

—3—

She was a pretty girl, Francine Lovett, though not perhaps the first you'd notice in a crowd. She was small and had a tendency to let her hair fall down over her face, obscuring her pretty features. And her clothes were all wrong. She naturally gravitated to outfits that tended to hide—rather than show off—her slender, athletic frame. It was her upbringing that was to blame. She'd been brought up to believe it was spiritual things that mattered, not the material or the physical. And her folks had warned her of the perils of the big city. Wouldn't they just die if they could see her now—sitting in a bar, all alone, hoping to meet a man!

She'd been in the city nearly a year now, working as a secretary and trying to improve herself. The first rule she set, no nicknames. She was Francine, not Francy, not Fanny, and never, ever did she want to hear the name she'd given herself as a toddler—Fancy! Her parents still called her that, like she was still three years old.

For a while she'd thought about changing her first name altogether, but, in the end, she had decided that Francine was perfectly okay for an adult name. What she needed to concentrate on was her new *last* name. She was absolutely determined that when she got married she was going to have one of those female *power* names. She'd tried a few on from men she knew at work. Names like Francine Lovett Hughes. Mr. Hughes was her boss' boss—old and married, but a *great* name. Or, how about Francine Lovett Michelson—a guy who worked in the mailroom and had actually asked Francine out? She didn't have time to wait for him to work his way up the corporate ladder, but another terrific name.

The bar was still mostly empty, something Francine should have expected this early on a Saturday evening. The truth was, she'd been planning her little adventure all week, and she'd been fully dressed and ready to go three hours before she finally left her tiny apartment. She'd been sitting at the bar, nursing her champagne cocktail, for nearly another hour. The bartender had told her not to worry, they had more champagne in the back. She could go ahead and drink her champagne cocktail. For ten dollars, Francine believed she was entitled to take a little time with her drink.

One guy had come in who looked a little bit interesting. Their eyes had met briefly as he came through the door. Francine had smiled—ever so slightly—but he quickly turned away. Her smile had apparently been a little *too* subtle.

He was wearing a suit and looked like a businessman, which was *exactly* what Francine had in mind. She heard him order a martini—her idea of a businessman's drink—and then she watched as he approached a couple of girls at the other end of the bar. They looked like trash, that pair, and her businessman didn't spend much time before moving off by himself.

He had a full beard, and Francine wasn't ordinarily a beard person, but this one was neatly trimmed and kind of, well, elegant. She wondered if it would scratch or maybe just tickle a little if they, well. . . if they, well, you know—she blushed at the thought.

Over the last twenty minutes or so, Francine had caught him staring at her a couple of times. She didn't risk another smile, but she didn't exactly scowl at him, either. When he finally started to move toward her, she nervously gulped down the last of her champagne—a big mistake because now she had nothing to pretend to be doing while she felt his eyes roam all over her.

"Can I buy you a martini?" he asked.

"Sure," she said. "Thank you."

"Vodka or gin?"

Francine wasn't sure what he meant by that. Hadn't she just said she would have a martini?

"Anything's fine," she said. He was standing so close to her that Francine found it extremely awkward to look him in the eye.

He ordered two very-dry martinis. Even Francine knew that *very dry* was the sophisticated way to order martinis.

"Raymond Ford," he said.

Francine was still thinking about the martinis, and at first it didn't register that he was introducing himself.

"I'm sorry?" she said.

"I'm Raymond Ford."

"Oh, I'm Fancy Lovett."

She was instantly mortified. Had she really said that? "Nearly everybody calls me Francine, though."

"Francine," he said, "that's a very pretty name."

Francine felt herself blush down to her toenails. "Are you a businessman?" she asked.

"I'm in computers," he said.

36

Computers! Imagine that. Francine knew you had to be awfully smart to be in computers.

"Are you in business?" he asked her.

"Sort of," she said. "Just starting. Office supplies. My boss, Mr. Earl J. Monroe, is expected to be named district manager any day now."

"So that will mean a nice promotion for you."

Not exactly, Francine thought, but no point in going into all of that.

When the martinis arrived, Francine didn't have a clue how she was supposed to deal with the olive. She watched as he popped his into his mouth and washed it down with a gulp of his drink. She did the same— only not such a great big gulp. The martini was strong but surprisingly good.

He offered a toast. "To business."

They clicked glasses, and she managed to spill part of her drink into her lap. Before she knew it, he was trying to blot the stain from her dress. Francine didn't know *which* was more embarrassing, the spill or Raymond Ford blotting around in such a personal area. She felt herself turning even redder.

Up close, he looked quite a bit older than she had guessed from across the room. He kept dabbing the napkin at her lap without the slightest hint of embarrassment. Francine could see that she would have to do some growing up and become a whole lot more sophisticated if she was going to make it in the big city.

"You must have spilled half your drink," Raymond said. "Go ahead and toss down the little bit you've got left and I'll order us another round."

She did as instructed. By the time they'd finished the next round, she was beginning to feel much more comfortable with Raymond. She tried *Francine Lovett*

Ford and didn't mind the sound of it.

When she asked Raymond more specifically what he did with computers, he gave her some vague response about consulting work. She worried that maybe he didn't think she was smart enough to understand what his work entailed, but—other than that—he seemed very respectful. She liked the way he was careful to call her Francine, in spite of her misstep early on.

Francine went off to the ladies' room, and when she returned there was a fresh martini waiting for her at the bar.

She was about to say she thought she'd already had enough when Raymond asked, "Have you eaten dinner yet?"

Well, she hadn't had anything all day except a bowl of cereal for breakfast. "Not really," she said.

"Why don't we finish these and then head over to Chez Larry?"

Chez Larry! Just about the hottest, most expensive restaurant in the whole city.

"You can get reservations for tonight?"

"No problem. I'm a regular."

Wow, was she going to have a story for the girls at the office on Monday. She bet that even Mr. Earl J. Monroe had never been to Chez Larry.

Francine drank her last martini a little too fast, but they were beginning to taste kind of funny anyway. By the time they got to his car, she was beginning to feel pretty wobbly.

"Nice car," was about all she could manage to say.

After that, events became increasingly blurred—so much so that Francine Lovett would thankfully have no awareness of the sudden and violent ending of her much too short life.

—4—

Despite his experience as a physician, Pace had, like most people, always pretty much taken his own good health for granted. He had tried to take care of his body—the only time it had ever received any sustained abuse was when he played college football. At Harvard. If you called that football. Now, confined to a hospital bed, sometimes with hardly enough energy to raise his head off the pillow, it was difficult for Pace to recognize this frail, debilitated body as his own.

He decided he was suffering from the phantom doctor syndrome—a condition analogous to the well-described phantom limb syndrome. In the phantom limb syndrome, patients who have undergone the amputation of a limb often continue to sense its presence long after removal. Following the amputation of a leg above the knee, for example, the patient may continue to feel pain in the absent foot.

In Pace's case, it wasn't just his leg that was gone, it was his entire physician persona. He had not yet adjusted to the fact that the former Pace Magruder, that vital young physician earnestly attending to his patients' every need, was now little more than a lingering phantom. His abrupt transmogrification from physician to patient had lent his life a surreal quality, a sensation that was only heightened by the visitation he was about to experience.

The apparition at the foot of the bed was snowy-haired and gowned in white. Pace had the notion it was God Himself having descended for the sole purpose of summoning him into the hereafter. But would God wear spectacles? An interesting question. Pace began to see the figure as a portly archangel. After all, who was Pace that God should trouble Himself . . .

Reality no longer maintained the sharp boundaries that had previously been so reliable. The edges of dreams were now often blurred, sleep and wakefulness hopelessly jumbled.

"I hope I didn't awaken you."

The apparition had spoken. Pace's dreamworld began slowly to melt away. The venerable C. Boyd Edington had deigned to pay a visit.

"How are you, Dr. Edington?"

"Oh, I'm fine. How are *you*?"

Pace shrugged. "I don't think I'll make the Olympic trials this year."

Edington managed a sympathetic smile. "I understand you're at the top of the transplant list."

"Always good to be number one."

Edington indicated a chair beside the bed. "May I?"

"Of course," Pace said.

Edington was not being—for him—unusually solicitous. This was his normal manner—ever considerate, ever cautious. He was extraordinarily adroit in matters political, a prime reason for his having endured as chairman of the department of medicine for more than two decades. The fact that he was a brilliant clinical investigator and had written hundreds of scientific papers—many of them seminal—had also not hurt his career.

Still, despite all of Edington's accomplishments, Pace regarded him as a primarily political animal. Pace was not beguiled by the courtly manners and cherubic appearance. Tales of Edington's ruthlessness were rife in the medical school, and it was said Edington could insert the dagger so artfully that you were out of his office and halfway down the corridor before you felt the pain between your shoulder blades.

After all these weeks it was unlikely that Edington's first visit to Pace's hospital room was a purely social call. The chairman wanted something. Pace felt more than a little apprehensive as to what his motives might be.

Edington removed his glasses and polished them with his tie—a classic stalling maneuver. Pace began to worry that Boyd Edington must be bearing grave news indeed.

Finally, the chairman found his voice. "I understand you're still involved in the lab."

The lab? Was that what this was all about? Edington needed the space for someone who could be more productive? Surely not even Edington would stoop that low. You could at least wait till my body's cold, Pace wanted to tell him.

"Obviously I can't go down there anymore," Pace hated being distanced from the center of activity, "but the team comes up here. We review results together and plan the future direction of our research."

The chairman nodded absently.

"We have some very important projects under way," Pace said. And that was an understatement.

Edington seemed not to hear him.

"Something has happened, Pace. It is, in a sense, serious, and you need to know of it, but it's not something you should worry about."

Edington retreated once again into his own thoughts. Pace had no idea what he was up to.

"Do you know a man named Thomas Wolfe?" Edington asked.

"The writer?"

"I don't believe so. Actually, he was a patient. No, not really even a patient. He suffered a cardiac arrest and you resuscitated him at the scene. It was at about the time your illness began."

"I expect I do know who you mean," Pace said. "It was the night I finally admitted *I* had a serious medical problem. I never did get any follow-up on the man. Did he die? He seemed awfully precarious at the time."

Edington shook his head. "No, he survived, but he's had a rather stormy course, neurologically speaking."

"I'm sorry to hear that." Pace remembered the elderly, anguished wife. It sounded as though her burden had not been lessened over the last few weeks.

Edington once again removed and polished his glasses. He finally came to the point.

"Mrs. Wolfe has filed suit on behalf of her husband. She's alleging negligence on your part and seeking ten million dollars in damages. It's covered, of course, by your insurance through the medical school, and the school's attorneys will represent you. I imagine they'll want to speak with you when you feel up to it. You could, of course, choose other representation, but then you would also have to bear the cost."

Pace felt himself slipping back into that dreamworld again. Edington was making no sense. Someone might well try to get ten million dollars in a wrongful death suit, but Pace had *saved* Wolfe's life— at no small risk to his own.

"But I thought you said Mr. Wolfe survived."

"She's charging wrongful life. They're saying you were negligent in attempting to resuscitate her husband, that you should have known he had already suffered irreversible brain damage."

"But the first question I asked was how long had he been out. His wife said it had just been a minute or so."

"She says she told you that it had been several minutes—maybe as many as ten."

"No way," Pace said. "There were witnesses."

"I'm sure you're right, Pace, and you should try not to let this upset you too much. I'm sorry to have to bring this news to you, but the suit has been filed and must be responded to. The lawyers came to me, and we decided it would be best for me to talk to you. From now on though, you should just let the lawyers handle it."

The night of the resuscitation seemed to belong to a different era—so much water had flowed over the dam since then. But Pace had a very clear memory of asking the woman how long her husband had been down.

What about witnesses? Pace thought. He had sent Danica to call 911, so she probably didn't hear him ask Mrs. Wolfe, or hear the woman's answer, but how about all those other people who were standing around with their hands in their pockets? Would any of them remember anything? How could he ever find them if they did?

Pace felt a drop of perspiration roll down the side of his face. He hoped he didn't have a fever. An active infection would be an absolute contraindication to transplantation. If a heart did become available—no matter how perfect it was for him—if he had an infection, he would be passed over. The heart would go to the next name on the list.

Pace would have to wait while the source of his fever was sorted out and treated. Then he'd go back on the list and wait for a *second* heart to become available. And if it did, he could finally have his transplant. And if Pace survived that, there was a woman out there who wanted to sue him for ten million dollars for saving her husband's life.

Pace was beginning to feel like he'd stumbled through the looking glass and plunged headlong into the world of the absurd. The more he thought about it, the more ridiculous it all seemed. He began to sense a rogue and alien emotion welling up deep inside him— an emotion so totally inappropriate he almost didn't recognize it.

But then he was smiling. And then his shoulders began to shake. And then he was laughing uncontrollably. It was all just so *totally* ludicrous.

C. Boyd Edington's natural reserve and well-developed sense of propriety demanded restraint, and his first reaction was an incredulous stare. But the absurdity of the situation was not lost on him, and the mood proved contagious. Before long, Edington had his head thrown back in laughter and tears running down his cheeks.

—5—

Courtney Bond was in no mood to be jerked around by some homicide detective who thought he was God's gift to comedy and most likely believed that the DA's office—or at least the investigation and prosecution of capital crimes—was no place for a woman. Half these guys, one minute they were putting you down and the next minute they were trying to get you into the sack. She was thirty years old and had been an assistant DA for more than five years now, and they were still hazing her like it was her first day on the job.

Courtney didn't recognize the name of the cop who called, but she had a pretty good idea what he looked like—*Homo erectus*. She wondered if he'd discovered fire yet.

The phone was already ringing when she opened her office door that morning. "Hello, Courtney, this is Detective Marks, homicide. I've got a guy here I think you might want to interview."

Courtney's first thought, "Detective," what an unusual first name. But there was no point in making an issue of it. He was Detective Marks. She was Courtney.

"I'm due in court," she said. "Is it urgent?"

"I've been trying to get you for over an hour. You must have had *some* night last night."

She could just about see the guy leering on the other end of the line, hamming it up for his buddies. "I had an accident on the way to work. Some kid ran a red light and hit me broadside."

"You don't have a chauffeur? I thought everybody up on twelve had a chauffeur."

That was a shot at the DA, Tommy Jacobs, not at her—at least not *directly* at her. Tommy was the only one who had a driver.

"I'm not on twelve," she said. But of course Marks already knew that. "What was it you wanted, Detective?"

"It's about the Lovett case. This guy may have some important information."

The problem with sex crimes investigations—one of the problems—was that you got all these creeps crawling out from under various rocks who wanted to come in and talk about the crime. They didn't have any information. All they wanted to do was talk dirty for a while—sort of an in-your-face obscene phone call. The cops thought it was funny to send them up to talk to her.

"What's his story?" Courtney asked.

"Like I said, he's got information. I'd rather not get into it over the phone."

"Look, Marks, I've got a ton of paperwork on my desk and a full day ahead of me in court. I don't have time for games."

"No games, Courtney. Like I said, I think it might be important."

"Okay, send him up. If he can be here in fifteen minutes, I'll talk to him." If this turned out to be some kind of practical joke, she was really going to come down hard on this funny-boy Marks.

"His name's Dean Arnold. He's on his way."

Arnold turned out to be this big, strapping blond-haired kid who looked like he was probably in his early twenties. He reminded Courtney of a guy she'd dated in law school who'd gone through college on a rowing scholarship. He'd looked like he could have rowed the QE2 across the Atlantic.

Courtney offered her hand. As her flesh touched Arnold's, she fervently hoped he wasn't about to tell her some creepy story, one that would make her feel like she could never get that hand clean again.

"I'm Courtney Bond, Mr. Arnold. Let's see if we can find a place for you to sit."

Her tiny office was always overflowing with paperwork, a chronic state of chaos that mirrored her frantic work life. But it wasn't quite as disorganized as it appeared. The stacks of folders on her desk were all active cases. The ones piled on the two metal visitors' chairs all had letters or reports that needed to be dictated. The folders on the floor were recently closed or suspended cases that, experience had taught her, might at any moment flare up and acquire renewed urgency.

She cleared the folders off the nearest chair and placed them carefully on the floor, taking note of where she put them so they could be quickly recovered as soon as the chair became vacant. When she had Arnold seated, Courtney settled in behind her desk and brought out the legal pad she always kept handy.

"Okay, Mr. Arnold," she said, "I understand you have some important information regarding the Lovett case."

Arnold squirmed uneasily in his seat. Maybe it was just that the standard-size chair cramped his oversize frame. Maybe it was something else. Finally he said, "I think I know who the murderer is."

"Well," Courtney said, "that would certainly fall into the category of important information." She waited for Arnold to pick up the narrative, but he seemed uncertain. So Courtney asked, "Who?"

"Ted Long."

Courtney dutifully wrote down the name. "And why do you suspect Ted Long?" This was like pulling teeth.

"I saw him leaving the scene, speeding away in his car. I mean, I didn't think anything about it at the time. Then I read about the murder in the paper. It said the body had been dumped in Stevens Park. That's where I saw Ted."

"Lots of people use Stevens Park, Mr. Arnold. That's what it's there for. What makes you think this Ted Long was involved in the murder?"

Arnold sort of shrugged and sank down a bit in his chair. "It was late at night—the night of the murder. And he was driving fast. It looked like he was running away from something."

"What time was this?"

"A little before midnight."

The time was about right, but other than that it all looked pretty thin to Courtney.

"Ted Long's the kind of guy," Arnold said, "who's capable of doing that sort of thing. Murder, I mean. And rape."

"Has he been in trouble before? Any convictions?"

"I doubt it. Ted isn't the type who gets convicted."

"What does that mean?"

"He's Edward Jackson Long, Jr."

That got Courtney's attention. "*Senator* Edward Long's son?"

Arnold nodded.

That would explain why Detective Marks was so eager to unload Arnold on the DA's office. This case was about to become a real political hot potato. "How is it you happen to be able to recognize the senator's son?"

"We went to school together—high school."

"He's a friend of yours?"

Arnold shook his head. "I don't think anyone would ever accuse us of being friends."

"Bad blood between you?"

"Kid stuff," Arnold said. "Nothing serious, but we were never friends."

Courtney studied the notes she'd jotted down so far. "You said you saw Ted Long 'leaving the scene.' What did you mean by that?"

"I don't understand."

"How close to the actual crime scene was Mr. Long?"

Arnold seemed suddenly nervous. "Oh, I don't know where the *exact* crime scene was. Like I said, I just read in the paper that the body was dumped in Stevens Park. Ted was leaving the park when I entered."

Courtney shifted to some neutral, factual questions—Arnold's full name, address, phone number, and so forth.

"That's my parents' address and phone number," Arnold said. "I'm not in school this semester. When I go back, I have one more semester before graduation."

"Are you working while you're out of school?"

"I help out at my dad's shop. He owns a printing business."

"Why aren't you in school this semester?"

Arnold once again looked unsettled. "I had a little problem. I was accused of something I didn't do. It was sort of agreed that it would be best for me to sit out a semester."

"Agreed by whom?"

"The dean of students and me."

"What were you accused of?"

"It was nothing. I'd really rather not talk about it. This isn't about me. I just came here out of a sense of duty, to tell what I know. I thought it might be helpful."

Courtney nodded encouragingly. "We always appreciate citizens' coming forward." She gave her notes another scan. "You said Ted Long is the kind of guy who is capable of rape and murder. What do you base that on?"

"There have been stories of sexual assaults that Ted's father has used his money and influence to hush up. I know a girl he groped one time. He was drunk. She was terrified."

"Were charges filed?"

"No. She just wanted to forget about it."

"What is her name?"

Arnold hesitated. "I'd have to ask her for permission before I could tell you."

Courtney decided there was no need to press the issue at this point. It was time to ask the question that had been hanging in the air since the interview began.

"How did you happen to be entering Stevens Park at midnight?"

"People hang out there. It's a place to meet. I was just driving around."

"Were you alone?"

"Yes."

"Did you meet anyone in the park? Can anyone verify that you were there?"

Arnold shook his head.

"Did you know Francine Lovett?"

Again, Arnold shook his head.

Courtney reviewed her notes one last time. She had about all she needed for now.

When she arrived at her office this morning, Courtney didn't have a single name of anyone who had been at the park when the body was dumped. Now, if Arnold was telling the truth, she had two—Arnold and Ted Long.

She would run both names and see if the computer coughed up anything interesting. And she'd take this to the DA before approaching the Long kid. Detective Marks wasn't completely stupid. And neither was Courtney. She wasn't about to walk out on *that* limb and start sawing—not without running it through channels first.

Courtney stood up behind her desk, and Dean Arnold immediately popped up out of his chair. She didn't know if he was being gentlemanly or just eager to get the hell out of her office. She offered her hand one last time.

"Thank you for coming by, Mr. Arnold. Like I said, we always appreciate citizens who are willing to come forward with information. I'm certain I'll think of some more questions later. I'll contact you when I do."

As she watched Dean Arnold head out the door, Courtney wondered if she'd just shaken the hand of a rapist and murderer.

—6—

Courtney's day in court had gone on and on, ending with protracted arguments in the judge's chambers. It wasn't until after six that night that she finally headed up to the twelfth floor to check in with DA Tommy Jacobs.

Alice was there, as always, her desk guarding the way to Jacobs' door. Alice was worth at least two assistant DA's, easy. With Alice out front, a chimpanzee could run the office.

Alice Franklin was sixty-ish with gray hair pulled back in a French roll and stylishly delicate eyeglasses. She had a quiet elegance about her. She was prim and proper and tough as nails when she needed to be. And she was doggedly loyal to Tommy Jacobs.

"Go right on in, Courtney, he's expecting you."

"Thanks, Alice."

Courtney gave a knock on the double oak doors, then let herself in. Jacobs was on the phone. He waved her to a chair.

The DA's office belonged to a bygone era. The dark wood paneling seemed extravagant by today's cost-conscious standards. And it was huge. Reportedly, only the mayor's was larger. You could fit a dozen offices the size of Courtney's into the same space.

One wall was glass, the obligate commanding view

of the city. The other walls were covered with photographs, dozens of them—Tommy Jacobs shaking hands with mayors, governors, businessmen—anyone who was anyone who had come within his reach. She hadn't previously noticed just how many of those photographs contained the handsome, smiling face of Senator Edward Jackson Long.

Courtney had no idea how Jacobs would play this. She'd long ago given up trying to predict his reactions. He would sometimes move very aggressively on a case. Then later, when confronted by a second case with a seemingly identical set of facts, he'd show virtually no interest whatsoever. Courtney understood that what appeared to be whimsy was anything but. Even though she couldn't always decipher the process, she had no doubt Jacobs' actions accorded with some personal master plan. Tommy wasn't capricious; he was calculating. And above all, Tommy Jacobs was ambitious.

Rumor had it that Tommy was about to cash in— either try for higher political office or move into a cushy partnership in one of the city's big legal firms. It occurred to Courtney that, whichever way Tommy was heading, no one was better positioned to grease the way than Senator Edward Long.

She had no idea where Jacobs would come down on the investigation of Ted Long. You could flip a coin. For her part, Courtney didn't have a clue whether Ted Long was a rapist or a choirboy, and at this point, it didn't matter. The information Dean Arnold had brought to her had to be investigated. End of discussion. She didn't want to go to war with Jacobs, and she didn't want to go behind his back; but she'd do whatever she had to do to get to the truth. There was no other way to do her job. It was a matter of personal integrity. It was a matter of public trust.

"Sorry," Jacobs said, hanging up the phone, "it was one of His Honor's political consultants. They've somehow gotten the idea that I might be interested in running against the mayor next time." Jacobs smiled.

Courtney smiled back. His Honor could rest easy. Tommy would be shooting a lot higher than mayor.

"I just need a minute," she said. "Something has come up in the Lovett case."

"Well, it's about time. Something good, I hope."

"I'm not sure," Courtney said.

Jacobs got out of his chair and opened a window. Courtney knew what that meant. At least he was considerate enough to open the window.

"Do you mind?" He pulled a cigar from an inside pocket of his coat.

She shook her head. While he was lighting up, she wondered how many weeks of her salary it would take to pay for the suit he was wearing. And he owned closets full. No one was quite certain how he afforded them on *his* salary.

But he looked good in those suits. Jacobs dressed for the job he wanted, not for the job he had. Courtney had read in some magazine that that was what you were supposed to do. He had a handsome, honest-looking face that photographed well for campaign posters. And he was big, well over six feet. They say that size always plays well on the campaign trail.

When she had his attention again, Courtney told him why she was there. "A young man named Dean Arnold came by my office today."

Jacobs shrugged. Was the name supposed to ring any bells?

"Arnold said he happened to be driving by Stevens Park at about the time we think Francine Lovett's body was dumped. He wanted to let us know that he saw Ted Long driving out of the park."

Jacobs blew a cloud of smoke out the window. "The Senator's son? Edward, Jr.?"

Jacobs never ceased to amaze her. "The same."

"What about Arnold? Is he credible?"

"We don't know much about him. He seemed okay, but he could be a nut. Or a killer. Or a nut *and* a killer."

"You run his name through the computers?"

"Not yet. I've been in court. I'll do it tomorrow."

"Run Long, too."

"Do you know anything about the Senator's kid?"

Jacobs thought about that. "Just rumors. Junior might have been a little wild—left some messes around that Daddy had to clean up."

"He have a record?"

"I seriously doubt it." Jacobs sucked thoughtfully on his cigar. "Arnold talk to anyone but you?"

"A homicide detective named Marks sent him up to see me."

Jacobs went back to his desk and wrote down the name. "Courtney, keep this under your hat and report back directly to me. I'll see that Marks gets the word too. If this Arnold's just a crank, there's no point in dragging the Long family through the headlines."

"No problem," she said. For now, it looked like Tommy was coming down on the side of the angels. Maybe he was just being a stand-up guy, or maybe he figured that tying the Long family to a grisly murder wasn't such a bad thing for Tommy Jacobs—politically speaking—especially if he was thinking about a move to Washington. Of course the political wind could change direction without warning, and Tommy was likely to change right along with it.

"I understand you had a little problem on the way to work."

Tommy heard everything. It was widely believed that Alice was his primary source.

"A kid ran a light and smacked into me."

"He have insurance?"

"Luckily. He seemed like a nice guy. Just had his mind somewhere else at the time. When I handed him my business card, he almost cried."

"You need a lift? I'd be happy to drop you somewhere."

That was another thing about Tommy, he tended to get a little amorous in private. He had a new young wife, but the story going around was that she no longer met all of his needs. It was best to avoid situations that had the potential to become awkward.

"No thanks. I'm meeting my dad. We're gonna leave my car at a body shop he knows." Courtney got up to leave.

"Remember," Tommy said, "let's keep this quiet."

"Sure," she said.

When she called her dad, Courtney apologized for running so late. Not to worry, he said. He was glad to be able to help.

And she knew it was the truth. He loved her, sure, and he'd do anything for her, but he also loved projects. Everything was an adventure. And it wasn't just since he'd retired and her mom had died. He was always like that.

The address he'd given her wasn't in the greatest area. Dark was closing in and all the shops were closed. The people loitering about were what you might charitably call opportunists. She saw them every day in court. This was not a good neighborhood to have car trouble in, run into some lowlife she'd sent away for two years—three years ago.

She finally found the body shop and pulled up behind her dad's Acura sedan. He jumped out and surveyed the damage that had been done to her car. Dad was looking pretty sporty in his crew neck sweater and loafers. He was in terrific shape for a guy of sixty. The close-cropped, salt-and-pepper hair was the only thing that hinted at his age.

"That guy really hit you," he said.

"Lucky I was in Mom's Buick. If I still had my old Beetle, I'd probably be in the hospital right now." She hadn't been certain, when her Dad offered it—a big Buick Park Avenue—but she liked the fact that it had belonged to her mother.

Courtney climbed out of her car and gave her father a hug.

"Did you bring the note?" he asked.

She reached back in and grabbed the envelope off the seat. The note was addressed to Stan, the guy her dad said owned the shop.

Meanwhile, her father was kneeling at the back of the car, searching for the magnetized key holder he'd hidden for her. She'd quickly forgotten it was there.

"In a couple more years," he said, "these cars won't have any metal left for a magnet to grab hold of."

He handed her the key to put in the envelope, then went over to the ten foot tall chain-link fence that secured the body shop's parking lot. The portion that served as a gate was secured with a chain and heavy-duty padlock. He gave the lock a yank. It didn't budge.

"Why don't you go around front and slip your note through the slot," he said, "while I figure out where to leave the car."

She did as he asked, and when she returned the

gate was standing open. He held the padlock in his hand. That was Dad. Courtney didn't ask how he did it. She was a little worried his actions might have constituted a felony.

She pulled her car onto the lot, and when she was done her dad locked the gate just like they'd found it. He gave the padlock a yank just to make certain it was properly closed.

"Let's go get something to eat. There's a place a couple of blocks down that grills a pretty good steak."

"How do you know a place in this neighborhood?"

"I used to come down here once in a while."

"To meet your friend Stan?"

He smiled.

The restaurant blended right into the neighborhood. You could drive by a hundred times and never notice it. The neon sign advertised good food and beer on tap. The brand that was mentioned had probably paid for the sign. The interior was as rough as the exterior. The waiter greeted her dad like it was the third time he'd been there that week.

While they waited for their steaks, her dad explained the insurance business to her.

"The company that insures the guy who hit you will send an adjustor to Stan's shop to assess the damage and figure out how much they have to pay. Stan will do the same thing. They'll probably agree, and that will be it. Stan will do the work and the insurance company will pay for it. If there's a problem—which means the insurance company is trying to weasel out of paying for something—you may have to take it somewhere else to get another bid. But that doesn't happen much anymore. The body shops look up all of the parts on computers. They know how much they cost and how much the insurance company will pay.

"The adjustor will write a check to cover the cost of the work. The check has to be signed by both you and the body shop before it can be cashed. When Stan has your car ready to go, all you do is go down and inspect it. If you're satisfied with the work, you sign the check and leave with the car.

"The only thing to watch for, an older car, the insurance company may want to declare it a total loss. You get a check, they get the car. They'll claim it's cheaper than fixing it. Don't let them pull that. You'll never be able to find a car anywhere near as good as that Buick for the cost of repairing it."

Courtney listened attentively. If she asked her dad how he came to be such an expert on insurance, he'd say something like, Oh, years ago I sold some insurance. Or, Oh, I used to do accident investigations. He was one of those guys, if you came to find out that what he'd really been doing all these years was working for the CIA, you wouldn't be too surprised. For as long as she could remember, Dad had described himself as "an investor."

He was right about the steaks. They did a good job on them. And her dad could eat. It was a wonder he could stay so fit and trim. Oh, I go down to the gym a couple of days a week, spar with the number two contender for the world heavyweight crown.

"You seeing anyone?" he asked.

"No one special."

"You ever hear anything from the rower?"

Her dad and Karl had really hit it off. Her mom, too. Everybody loved Karl. Her dad had actually taken up sculling for a while.

"I heard from Karl at Christmas. He thought he was about to make partner, and he was thinking about getting engaged." All of which her dad already knew.

"The only reason Karl would tell you he was 'thinking about' getting engaged would be to see if you were still interested."

"Well I'm not. Karl's a terrific guy, but he's not the one for me."

"You deserve someone special."

"I'll find somebody, sometime. You can't force something like that to happen. Meanwhile, how are you and Amanda getting along?"

She'd been encouraging her dad, with her mom gone four years now, that it was okay for him to see someone. No reason he had to be alone. He'd resisted, but for the last few weeks he'd been telling her about the Widow Johnson. She sounded nice.

"I'm afraid that might be over," he said.

"I'm sorry. Anything I can help with?"

"I doubt it. She was really into kinky sex."

"Dad . . . "

"I mean a woman who weighs more than two hundred pounds."

"Dad . . ."

"You'd think she'd try to be a little genteel about things."

"Dad!"

"What?"

"There is no Widow Johnson, is there?"

"I have wonderful memories of your mom, sweetheart. That's all I need."

7:30 in the evening, almost exactly forty-eight hours after she'd met her dad at the body shop, Courtney found herself in a place she didn't really want to be—the backseat of Tommy Jacobs' car. The insurance company had approved a rental until her car was fixed, but Courtney hadn't had a chance to pick it up. Meanwhile, the body shop thing had developed a small complication.

"Big news," she told her dad on the phone.

"What's that, sweetheart?"

"Stan sold the shop."

"Uh-oh," he said. "Who to?"

"Some guy named Dave."

"Dave who?"

"Apparently he doesn't have a last name. I don't either. He calls me Courtney at least once in every sentence. Nice to meet you, Courtney. Is this your car, Courtney? You've got quite a lot of damage here, Courtney. But you know, Courtney, when we take the doors off, we'll probably find a lot more, Courtney. By the way, Courtney, how'd you get your car onto our locked lot?"

"They get the same training the used car dealers get," her dad said. "Using the first name implies a personal relationship. That way you feel comfortable, and you know you won't get cheated—since you're already such good friends. Other than that, how did the place seem?"

"Okay, I guess. How would I know?"

"Did the insurance adjustor show up yet?"

"Dave left a message at my office. He said the insurance guy had been in and they agreed on everything. They were going to go ahead and start the work."

"How long did he say it would take?"

"When I talked to him yesterday, he said about a week."

"Well," her dad said, "I wouldn't bet the ranch on that."

So when Jacobs announced they had an eight o'clock meeting at Senator Long's house, Courtney had no real choice but to accept the ride he offered. They had Jacobs' driver, Roland, for a chaperone.

From Courtney's perspective, the investigation hadn't gotten anywhere since Dean Arnold walked out of her office two days earlier. The computer search had come back negative on both Arnold and Ted Long. She was suspicious that Jacobs knew more than he was sharing, but that was the way things worked. The DA asked questions, he didn't supply answers. Courtney didn't even know how this meeting at Senator Long's house had come to be scheduled. Who had initiated it? Were Jacobs and Long on the same team?

Jacobs was sort of splayed out on the backseat in a thinking pose. Courtney hugged the door on the opposite side. So far, he'd behaved himself.

"Did you find out," Jacobs asked, "why the Arnold kid got suspended from school?"

"The school wouldn't give me anything over the

phone, but I got the impression they'd respond to an official letter. Besides, whatever happened is likely to be common knowledge on campus. When we start interviewing Arnold's friends and fellow students we're sure to hear at least one version of the story."

"Anything new at all?"

"Zilch. No other witnesses. No other leads."

"Any more idea about what Francine Lovett did the day of her murder? Where she might have been? Who she might have seen?"

"Nothing. People who knew her at work knew nothing of her private life. People who lived in the same apartment building only knew that she was a quiet, pleasant young woman. The family doesn't seem to know much either. She had told them about a boyfriend, but it doesn't check out. It looks like she may have just made him up to please her folks." There was a lot of that going around.

They drove in silence for several minutes, then Jacobs said, "When we get there, it's probably best to let me do most of the talking. I've had some dealings with the senator over the years. He may feel more comfortable talking to me."

Courtney didn't place the senator's comfort high on her list of priorities, but she kept her own counsel.

As they drove on, they gradually left the older, more congested city center behind and entered an area of well-spaced, larger residences. The Long estate had once sat well outside the city limits, but decades of urban sprawl had changed that. The mansion had long been a local landmark, dwarfing as it did its already upscale—but far less majestic—neighbors.

A winding drive took them to the front door of the pillared antebellum main house. An assortment of Mercedes, Range Rovers, and Porsches was gathered out front. To Courtney it felt like they were pulling up to some swank country club, not a private home.

The door was opened by the senator himself, wearing a crisply starched shirt and a red silk power tie. The usual suit coat had been eschewed in favor of an elegant, shawl-collared cardigan—the great man perfectly capable of letting his hair down and being "just folks" at home.

Senator Edward Long was every bit as handsome in person as on TV. He was tall, not slender, but certainly not fat. His silver hair was combed back away from his face so as not to hide any of its glory and to give full effect to those piercing black eyes. His greeting of Jacobs was effusive.

"Tommy! So good to see you. You shouldn't be such a stranger. How's Ellen?" The senator cupped Jacobs' right hand in both of his.

Jacobs said that his wife was well. Then he introduced Courtney. Long became once again fulsome.

"Courtney—may I call you Courtney?—I've certainly heard wonderful things about you. I'm so pleased to finally make your acquaintance. Everyone says what a bright future you have in front of you."

"You're very kind, Senator." She opted not to ask who "everybody" was.

They were standing in an immense entry hall dominated by an imposing double staircase. The floor was slate. The walls were painted wood. Oil paintings hung everywhere. They looked large and dark and old. Mostly of somebody's ancestors—probably not Long's. They didn't suit Courtney's taste, but she knew she'd be astounded at what they were worth.

Long ushered them into an equally vast living room. "Where we can talk comfortably," he said.

As they entered, three well-dressed men rose from their seats. Courtney instantly recognized Robert Horvath and Lawrence Faye—arguably the two most powerful attorneys in the state. They had recently merged their two large firms into a new legal giant—Faye, Horvath. The presence of either man could be an overbearing influence in a room chock-full of lawyers. That Long could command the appearance of both at a spur-of-the-moment, informal meeting in his home was a naked display of raw political power. Horvath and Faye were there to serve notice that Long was not a man to be trifled with.

And it occurred to Courtney that there might just be another message being sent. One that Jacobs was certain not to miss. It had to do with his prospects after leaving the DA's office. A future election would be difficult to win without the support of Senator Long. Against Long's active opposition, victory would be impossible. On the other hand, if a private law practice was Jacobs' goal, there was no more prestigious name than Faye, Horvath.

Courtney didn't recognize the third man. He was as fastidiously dressed as the others, but he was physically smaller. His hair was combed forward to counter a receding hairline. He looked too old to be Edward, Jr.—which immediately raised the question in Courtney's mind, where the hell was Ted? Wasn't he the one they'd come to see?

"Tommy, you of course know Bob and Larry," the senator said. "And I believe you've met my chief of staff, Chuck Styles." There were general greetings all around, and then Long introduced Courtney, "The brightest young attorney in Tommy's vast galaxy of bright young attorneys." Then Long offered coffee, tea, or something stronger. Everyone settled for coffee.

Seeing Long, Horvath, and Faye standing side by side, Courtney was impressed by how similar they were—about the same age, each well over six feet in height, all elegantly dressed. The three of them all cut from the same bolt of cloth, all from the same club. Styles was the odd man out, the peon who, like Courtney, worked for a living.

When at last everyone had coffee and was seated, their convivial host rendered his first acknowledgment that their little gathering was anything other than purely social. "So, Tommy, how can I be of service to you?"

"As I mentioned on the phone," Jacobs said, "we just need to speak briefly with Edward, Jr. He may have—without even realizing it—witnessed activity related to a serious crime. He may be able to provide evidence important to our investigation."

"What is this crime you're referring to?" the senator asked.

"Is Edward, Jr. here?" Jacobs responded.

Long gave his shoulders an apologetic shrug. "Ted has been traveling the last couple of days. He's been out of state, but he was supposed to return this afternoon. I still expect him at any moment, but I have no way of contacting him. I'm sorry for the inconvenience."

Jacobs immediately rose from his chair. Courtney did the same. "We really need to speak with your son, Senator. I had hoped to do that informally, but perhaps that won't be possible. Thank you for your time."

Tommy had finally revealed himself. Courtney was sorry she'd ever doubted him.

Senator Long was instantly on his feet. "Please sit down, Tommy, Courtney. I assure you I had every expectation that Ted would be here, but even in his absence we may be able to be helpful to you."

Jacobs hesitated a long moment, then took his seat once again. Courtney followed suit.

"We would of course be eager to hear any information you might have that might be helpful," Jacobs said.

"That's the spirit," Long said. He paused momentarily to organize his thoughts before plunging forward. "You know what a small legal community we have in this town—in this state, for that matter."

Jacobs may have given a barely perceptible nod.

"At any rate," the senator continued, "it has come to my attention that this Arnold boy has been making certain accusations regarding the Lovett murder."

"The Lovett murder is under active investigation," Jacobs said. "Of course I cannot comment on any aspect of the case."

"Fair enough, but I know what I know, and that Arnold boy has always born a grudge against Ted—no one has the slightest idea why."

"We just need to talk with Ted," Jacobs said. "I expect we'll be able to clear this up very quickly."

The senator began nodding his head in aggressive agreement. "I believe we probably *can* clear this up, right here, tonight—even without Ted." He made a sweeping gesture with his right hand, palm up, an indication to his chief of staff that the floor was his.

All eyes were fixed on Styles. He noisily cleared his throat.

"The senator mentioned to me what Dean Arnold was up to, that he had even gone so far as to suggest Ted could be a suspect in the Lovett murder. At first my only thought was that it was ridiculous to even suggest that Ted could do such a thing. At that time I had no knowledge of any of the facts of the case, and we had no way to contact Ted because he was out of town. But after talking with Senator Long, I happened to read a newspaper account of the crime and realized immediately that on the night of the murder, Ted was with me. He was never anywhere near that park."

The eyes now turned to Jacobs. "Could you tell me specifically when you were with him?"

"All evening. He dropped by my apartment, and we fixed something for dinner. Then we talked until long after midnight."

"Is this typical," Jacobs asked, "for the two of you to spend an evening together like that?"

Styles shook his head. "No. Very unusual. But Ted had some questions. He's been thinking about beginning a political career, and he wanted to talk about getting a staff job on the Hill. His father is able to give him one point of view—from the top—and he wanted to hear from someone who had worked his way up through a number of staff positions."

Jacobs turned to Senator Long. "Were you aware of this at the time?"

"I was aware that Ted was thinking about trying to obtain a staff position in Washington. I didn't know he had such a long talk with Chuck. For the record, I was in Washington on the day in question."

Jacobs took a few moments to digest all of this, then said, "We'll still need to touch base with Edward, Jr. when he returns, but the information you've provided is very helpful."

With that, Jacobs and Courtney rose from their chairs for the last time. They all shook hands and exchanged farewell pleasantries. As he showed them to the door, Senator Long had one last thought.

"I am certain it has occurred to you," he said, "that

the Arnold boy has as much as admitted he was at the scene of the murder."

—8—

I'm dying, Pace thought.

He repeated the words over and over in his mind in an effort to force himself to admit the reality and abandon false hope.

He said it out loud. "I'm dying."

To a disinterested observer, this might not have appeared to be a startling insight, but, for Pace, it was an epiphany. He had always understood, in the abstract, that his heart condition was a potentially fatal one. That was why he was on the transplant list. But everyone knows that, sooner or later, death will come calling. Death is intrinsic to the human condition. It is, for each of us, only a matter of time. What had changed for Pace was that he now believed, for the first time in his life, that his own death was imminent.

It was the middle of the night. Night was always the hardest time, and this was his worst night yet.

He awakened severely short of breath. His room was dark. It always took him a minute to get his bearings, to remember where he was. He needed air.

He was lying flat in bed. No, not really flat. He could never do that anymore. The head of his bed was raised. But it wasn't enough.

Pace used all the energy he could muster to get

himself sitting up with his legs dangling over the edge of the bed. He leaned slightly forward, his breathing rapid and shallow, patiently waiting for whatever was going on to pass. See, Pace, there you go again—telling yourself that this will pass. One of these times it won't. And that will be the end. You need to accept that, Pace. You're dying.

What he really wanted was to crawl over to the window, somehow get it open, and breathe the cool night air. But that wasn't vaguely within the realm of his current physical capabilities.

"Why didn't you push your call button?"

It was Jennifer, his nurse, scolding him for not letting her know he was in distress. Pace just shrugged. Speaking required too much effort.

"I'll call the transplant fellow."

Pace wanted to stop her, but she was gone before he could make a sound. There wasn't anything anyone could do for him. He was dying.

The transplant fellow arrived within minutes. Her name was Ruth Golden. This was her second year studying with Brian. He called her his Golden Girl. She had a brilliant mind and remarkably skillful hands and she was the only person in the hospital who'd done a stint in the Israeli army. Brian wanted desperately to keep her on staff after she finished her fellowship, but she was planning to return to Israel.

Pace was already feeling better by the time she arrived. At least he could talk.

"I hope they didn't get you out of bed, Ruth." Pace was being facetious. He knew there wasn't any chance a transplant fellow would have an opportunity to sleep on call.

"My date will get over it," she said. "What's going on with you?"

71

"I was dreaming about popcorn. I think I probably had too much salt."

She studied his medication chart. "I have a nearly irresistible urge to change *something*."

"Everything's already maximized," Pace said. "There's only so much you can do."

"I'd be happy to give Brian a call if you'd like."

"Please don't. My breathing's already a little easier."

"Just let me have a listen."

Ruth did the obligatory physical exam, knowing what she'd find, and finding it. "You're about the same as when Brian last examined you."

Pace nodded.

"I've got a few minutes before I have to get back to the ICU if you want to talk about anything."

"Thanks," Pace said. "I'm fine. You better get back to your date."

"I wish," she said. "Call me if there's anything I can do."

"Thanks." But there wouldn't be anything she could do, not if she didn't have a spare heart in her hip pocket.

Pace had already ruled out two potential temporizing measures. The first was the implantation of the mechanical pump, the bridge, to assist his failing heart. The second was intubation, the placement of a plastic tube down his throat and into his upper airway to permit his lungs to be mechanically ventilated by a respirator.

Pace's future now held only two possibilities. One was transplantation. The other, death.

Until today, he had been buoyed by the sanguine expectation that a donor heart would become available in time. This morning he suddenly understood how ridiculously Pollyannaish he'd been. A man his size, with his blood type, stood little chance of getting a new heart. Certainly not in the days, at most the couple of weeks, he had left. It was time for his thoughts to turn away from empty dreams. It was time to face reality.

Pace wasn't afraid of dying. His years as a physician and his weeks as a patient had given him a very clear picture of what his death would be like. What he regretted, of course, was the loss of his future. He wasn't sorry about the way he'd lived his life, but he recognized he'd spent most of it building toward a future that was not to be. All of those years spent in the lab and on the wards were not a goal in themselves. They were meant only to establish the basis for the achievement of the ultimate objective.

Only a few short weeks ago, it had not been unreasonable for Pace to hope that, during his lifetime, victory over heart disease would become a reality. His life's dream had been to make a significant contribution to that victory. Instead, he would become yet another of the countless victims.

His life story, in many ways so very different from that of his parents, had turned out fundamentally the same. He'd spent his short time on earth in pursuit of a dream that was never to be his.

But his parents had accomplished something he had not. They had become a family. Another part of Pace's life that had been spent in anticipation of a future that was not to be. There had always been, it had seemed, plenty of time to think about getting married.

In this though, there was a mixed blessing. Pace had missed the joys of true love and children, but he'd also avoided the pain of leaving them behind.

He glanced at the clock. 4:00 A.M. Only an hour or

so before Brian would drop by.

Maggie Pearson, the clinical psychologist assigned to the transplant team, was waiting for Brian when he came out of Pace's room.

"You're here early," he said.

"I've got meetings all day. I'm just trying to see some patients while I can. How's Pace?"

"About the same. He had a pretty tough night."

"Did you talk to him again about the bridge?"

"I didn't hit it very hard. I think Pace has made up his mind. At some point, we have to accept that."

"Do you have any idea why he feels so strongly about it?"

"Not really," Brian said. "As you know, some patients just can't cope psychologically with the idea of depending on a mechanical pump 24 hours a day. It's a deep-seated, personal thing. Some patients won't even consider a transplant.

"With Pace though, I think it's a little different. He's come to believe that a new heart just isn't in the cards for him. He doesn't want to end his life on the pump. It's hard to argue with that."

"Is there anyone he opens up to?" Maggie asked.

"Not as far as I know."

"Why does he think he has to deal with all this totally on his own? Why does he have to be such a big, strong, stoic *guy*?"

"Because that's who he is," Brian said. "Maybe it's because that's what he's had to do since he was a kid."

"Or maybe," Maggie said, "it's just because he's a man."

Brian managed a weak smile. "I'm afraid that may be part of it too."

Maggie began shaking her head. "And that music he

plays all the time. I don't think Pace is depressed, not clinically anyway, but that music sure depresses the hell out of me."

"The Roy Orbison? Actually, if you listen to the words, it's fundamentally hopeful. Kind of remarkably so when you hear the story of Orbison's life. Pace was telling me about it. Orbison's wife died in a motor vehicle accident. He lost two kids in a fire. And Roy himself died relatively young."

"Oh?" Maggie said. She was beginning to detect a familiar thread.

"Heart disease," Brian said. "He might have been a transplant candidate."

"Oh God," Maggie said.

When Maggie entered Pace's room, he gave her a feeble wave. She felt her heart sink. They'd been friends too long for her to have any hope of objectivity. The big strong man she knew had become so thin and frail.

"Hi, Pace." She walked over to take his hand. "I heard you had a difficult night."

"I had a little trouble breathing, but it's better now."

"I guess they've pretty much maxed out your medical therapy," she said.

Pace nodded.

"If you let Brian implant a left ventricular assist device, you'd not only feel better, you'd also be buying the time you need."

"That's a closed subject, Maggie. I've made up my mind."

"Would you like to talk about *why* you're so dead set against it?"

"A new heart is really a long shot now. You know that, Maggie. I don't want to die on the pump."

"I don't know how many times I've heard you tell patients they should go onto mechanical assist—just until a heart becomes available."

"I try to recommend what I believe is best for a given patient. I supply the information. *They* make the decision."

"It's just a bridge, Pace. It's not permanent."

"It's only a bridge if a donor heart materializes. Otherwise, it's permanent."

"Damn it, Pace! You're running out of time!" She felt the beginnings of tears in her eyes.

Pace managed a slight smile and gave her hand as strong a squeeze as he could generate.

"I'm sorry to put you through this," he said. "We're just too close to each other to be as objective as we should be."

"We don't want to lose you, Pace," she said.

"We don't always get what we want," he reminded her.

—9—

On the phone Courtney told her dad that things weren't going quite as smoothly as she had hoped at the body shop.

"They still can't tell me when I'll get my car back."

"Hell, they've had it two weeks," her dad said, "and they promised it would only take one."

"There's some part on order. Dave says it's beyond his control. All he can do is wait."

"Did Dave say what the part was?"

"Yeah. I wrote it down." Courtney pulled a pad out of her purse. "It's the floor pan mounting bracket."

"How about you let me take you to lunch tomorrow?" her dad said.

"I won't have much time."

"That's okay. We'll go someplace you haven't been before."

Another adventure, she thought.

Her dad was double parked, waiting for her when she walked down the steps of the city building. He was wearing his best suit.

"Dad, I really don't have time for anything fancy. Just a quick sandwich or something."

"Oh, the suit," he said. "The suit's for something I have to do after."

"What?"

"You'll see."

He drove her to a place a few blocks away. She had been by the restaurant a hundred times. It would have never entered her mind to go in. There was an open parking place right out front. Like they were saving it for them. That's what going places with her father was like.

"Try the lobster bisque," he said.

"They have lobster bisque here?"

"Like you wouldn't believe."

And he was right. The best she'd ever had. Hands down.

"Anything new on the Lovett case?" her dad asked.

"Not a thing."

"The Long kid turn up?"

"Not so far."

"You got a search out for him?"

"It's not that kind of deal, Dad. He's got an ironclad alibi. We'd like to talk to him, but we can hardly call him a suspect."

"Pretty hokey if you ask me. The suspect's alibi is from a guy who works for his father."

"That hasn't escaped our attention, Dad."

"You think Jacobs is on the up and up?"

"What do you mean?"

"You think he's in Long's pocket?"

She shook her head. "It certainly didn't seem like it when we were out at the senator's house."

"I've been thinking, what if they just put on that little dog and pony show exclusively for your benefit?"

"I'm not following."

"Out at the senator's house. Nobody's on the record about anything. No witnesses except the guys Long controls—including, maybe, Jacobs. They blow a little smoke in your direction, and the investigation just quietly dies."

"There's been a murder, Dad. No one's going to forget that."

When they were done eating, her dad said, "I've got a quick errand to run. Won't take ten minutes."

He drove straight to the body shop.

"What are you up to, Dad?"

"Gonna get your car out of hock."

When they went through the front door, Dave was standing behind the counter. He gave them a big smile.

"How can I help you folks?"

"Hi, Dave," her dad said. "Of course you've met Courtney here. I'm Brock Schroeder, her attorney. Can you believe that? Even lawyers have lawyers these days." He handed Dave a business card. "Anyway, Dave, we're here to check on Courtney's car, see when it's gonna be ready."

Courtney was thinking, Brock Schroeder? Attorney?

Dave smiled patiently. "Like I told Courtney over the phone, she could have the car tomorrow if we had the part we needed." He began to speak very slowly, like he was talking to a four-year-old. "See, we're waiting for something called the floor pan mounting bracket. As soon as that's in, we do the paint job and we're done."

Her dad looked crestfallen. "But, Dave, you promised Courtney the car would be done in a week. And, Dave, it's already been two!"

"That was seven *business* days, and there was never any promise. How long it takes to get parts is something that's beyond our control. There's a disclaimer right here on the counter." He pointed to a piece of faded paper under the glass. "On these older models, we sometimes have to order parts from Detroit. That can take weeks."

Her dad was scrutinizing the fine print under the glass. "Kind of small print, Dave. I'm not sure the courts would hold that this was an adequate disclaimer. But anyway, Dave, it doesn't matter. This is your lucky day!"

He reached into his suit pocket and pulled out something that looked, to Courtney, vaguely automotive.

"Here's the mounting bracket for the car, Dave."

"We can't use just anything. They have to be certified parts."

"Here's the invoice, Dave. Call the supplier if you have any questions. Or, even better, Dave, go and talk to the supplier in person. You must do business with them all the time. They're only a couple of blocks down the street."

Dave didn't look too happy.

"So, we'll be by tomorrow at five o'clock to pick up the car, Dave."

"I can't have it by *tomorrow*!"

"You just told me you could, Dave, if you got the part."

"The paint shop is a little backed up." With the sheepish tone of a man caught in a lie.

"Okay, Dave, then just mount the floor pan and we'll take the car unpainted. I'm surprised you'd want to do that, the painting being such a high margin business, but that's up to you. We'll just have another shop do the paint job."

"You can't do that," Dave said. "The insurance check is right here in our safe. Courtney has to sign the check before we'll release the car. And the check covers the paint job."

"No problem, Dave," her dad said. "She'll sign the check over right now, and we'll take the car. You can refund the painting charge back to the insurance company."

"I won't do that."

"That's up to you, Dave, but I'd be careful. You charge a big insurance company for work you didn't do, they're likely to get upset. I'd say they'd probably sue you. Probably never do business with you again. Ouch. Hell, I'm just a hack civil attorney, so I wouldn't know, but Courtney here is an assistant district attorney. All she does all day is prosecute, prosecute. What do you think, Courtney, a deal like that, could there be criminal charges?"

Courtney shrugged. Could be.

"So, what'cha think, Dave? You think you can get the car painted by tomorrow night, or you want us to just go ahead and take it right now?"

Dave thought they could get the work done.

Back in her dad's car, he explained things to her.

"This is what they always pull, these body shop guys. They never want to turn away business, so they promise you'll get your car in a week or so, but, times like these, they're so busy they don't have a prayer of getting the job done. Then, when you call up, Where's my car, they tell you there's some part on order. It's out of their hands. Then they just finish the work on a schedule that suits them. A lot of them operate that way."

"But where did you find the part?"

"Like I told Dave, down the street. I just went on the Internet, located the part. I picked it up this morning before I met you. Cost me ten bucks, meaning the supplier made seven or eight bucks on the deal.

"The point is, the mounting bracket was readily available and Dave knew it. He just has more work than he can do, and he was putting your car off so he could finish some car he'd promised another customer a month ago."

"You think I'll really get my car back tomorrow?"

"I'd say so. I think we have Dave's full attention."

—10—

Sheriff John Wade Dash was in no mood to deal with the discovery he was about to make. First off, he shouldn't even have been out here, cruising county back roads in the middle of the night. If God had meant for sheriffs to be doing this kind of work, He never would have created deputies.

Of course, it was the deputies—or rather the shortage thereof—that were the crux of the problem. These days, deputy sheriff was just one small step on a career path that quickly led to bigger and better things. Kids would graduate from high school, do their two-year hitch in the army, then hire on as deputies. Two years later—when you were lucky if you'd gotten *one* decent year's work out of'm—they were applying for jobs on big-city police forces or looking into some kind of private investigative work. Right now, Sheriff Dash had only one deputy who'd been on the force more than three years, and he had four vacancies he'd been trying to fill for months. So far, the only applicants he'd had were girls, and he wasn't about to start down that road.

So that was why John Wade Dash was out driving around in the dark of night instead of relaxing at home in front of a nice warm fire with a bottle of good bourbon to keep him company. On the brighter side, one of the qualities Sheriff Dash most admired in a fine bourbon was its portability. If God hadn't meant him to have a slug or two of bourbon while he was out on patrol, He wouldn't have created hip flasks.

Just now, Sheriff Dash—bored and fortified with a substantial quantity of the aforementioned elixir—was playing a game of chicken with himself, trying to see if he could get his Ford Crown Victoria police interceptor up to 100 before he had to brake hard for the blind curve just ahead, and hoping to God that some hapless deer, or—worse yet—some errant cow, didn't chance to wander into his path. It was this last possibility, the dreaded bovine eventuality, that caused the sheriff to back off the accelerator a little sooner than he otherwise might have, and allowed him to merely notice the evidence of the previous accident rather than joining the other vehicle in the depths of the ravine.

The curve was famous locally. Attempting to negotiate its sharp bend at high speed had become a rite of passage for area teenagers. Every few years some unlucky youngster would make a fatal miscalculation and end up at the bottom of the ravine or wrapped around a tree trunk somewhere along the slope.

Dash carefully brought his cruiser to a halt, then turned his flashers on and backed to a point well beyond the accident scene. He then drove slowly forward, his headlights on high beam, searching for any clues as to what might have happened. The first thing he noticed was what was missing—no skid marks, no evidence that the driver had hit his brakes before leaving the pavement.

The next obvious finding was what he'd already spotted on the fly—the major disruption of roadside vegetation at the point where the vehicle and the pavement had parted company. Dash pulled off the road and shined his searchlight down into the ravine. There was a car down there, about halfway down the slope, and it wasn't just some old derelict. That much was certain. The motor was still running.

Dash didn't have much choice in the matter. There was no way to avoid climbing down into the ravine and having a look. He took one last grateful pull from the hip flask, then grabbed his big Mag flashlight and headed down.

The incline was steep and Dash was no mountain goat. Time and again he lost his footing. At one point, landing on his rear end, he just sat there wondering what was to stop him from climbing back up out of the ravine, jumping into his car, and heading off. Who was to say he'd ever even been at the accident scene in the first place? *What* accident?

But in the end he started back down—more because he refused to be beaten by that stupid hill than from any sense of duty or moral obligation. When he finally made it to the spot where the car had come to rest, Dash was glad he'd taken that extra swig of bourbon. The scene was about as grisly as any he'd ever come across.

The car was one of those sporty coupes they called "muscle cars" when Dash was a kid. The easiest way to make a car fast was to combine a big engine with a light body. The result was a car that could very easily get out of control, especially with an inexperienced driver at the wheel. One look told Dash this was one driver who had had all of the experience he was ever going to get.

There was a sizable hole in the windshield. It looked as though the driver's head had gone nearly all the way through the glass before some countervailing force had pulled it back inside. The head had probably been bludgeoned and slashed coming and going. The injuries to the cranium were obviously massive and mortal. The driver's disdained seatbelt hung limp and useless behind his left shoulder.

Dash reached across the steering wheel to turn off the engine and made two additional findings. First of all, there was a female passenger in the car. She was slumped forward at the waist, restrained by her seatbelt. Second, with the engine off, Dash heard faint, intermittent gurgling sounds coming from the driver. He was still breathing, barely.

Dash made his way around to the other side to check on the passenger. She was unconscious, but she was breathing.

He gently tugged on her right shoulder, pulling her torso upright. She registered no complaint. Her deep, sonorous respirations continued without interruption. It sounded for all the world like she was snoring—like she was sound asleep. She didn't look to have a scratch on her.

Dash gave her shoulder a slight shake and spoke in a raised voice. "Ma'am," he said. "Ma'am!"

With that, the young woman pulled away from his hand and said, "Leave me alone." The words were badly slurred.

This was a syndrome Sheriff John Wade Dash instantly recognized—one with which he had had a great deal of firsthand experience—acute alcohol intoxication. She appeared to have completely escaped injury, presumably through the intercession of the patron saint of drunks, cats, and whatever else is graced with nine lives.

Dash flashed his light around the interior of the car.

There were no more passengers, but a glint of metal caught his eye. He carefully opened the passenger-side door and reached across the young woman to retrieve the object wedged under the driver's right leg. His hunch was right. It was a gun. When he pulled it out, a man's leather wallet came with it.

The gun was a .38 caliber snub-nosed revolver. From force of habit, Dash sniffed the barrel and checked the cylinder for spent cartridges. It had recently been fired, three shots.

When he checked the wallet he found twenty crisp, new one hundred dollar bills. Two thousand dollars. The two kids in the fancy car, the money, the gun, all that added up to just one thing as far as John Wade Dash was concerned—drugs. He'd bet a year's salary you'd find cocaine residue on those bills. Of course that wasn't quite as wild a bet as it sounded. These days, *most* hundred dollar bills that had been in circulation for any length of time had detectable cocaine residue.

All this caused wheels to begin turning in the sheriff's head. There probably wasn't much record of this money anywhere. No one was likely to come forward and say, Yeah, that two thousand bucks was mine—from a drug deal. In the end, the money in the wallet would just be gobbled up by some level of government and do nobody any good. What Dash was thinking, maybe he should just un-discover this little accident. Keep the money—thank you very much—but let somebody else find the accident tomorrow, or the next day, or whenever. He would be two thousand dollars richer, and no one would be any the wiser.

It sounded like a pretty good idea to Sheriff Dash until, almost as an afterthought, he checked the wallet for identification. Then his plans underwent an abrupt change.

Dash recognized the young man's name, and the address looked right too. The sheriff's night had just gotten a whole lot longer and a hell of a lot more complicated.

That brain-dead body behind the steering wheel belonged to Edward Jackson Long, Jr.

—11—

Daylight had come and Dr. Joan Bennett's twelve-hour shift in the emergency room was, theoretically, nearing its end. *Theoretically*, she could now dump everything onto her daytime replacement. But if she did that, he would be so bogged down trying to learn about the patients she'd been treating all night that he wouldn't be free to deal with the next emergency that came through the ER door. So Joan would need to hang around for a few hours and give him a hand.

It had been one of those nights. Their small hospital tried to serve the needs of an entire county. Sometimes—just like in big cities—everybody seemed to get sick at the same time, and the system got overwhelmed.

Nights like this awakened memories of her mother's dreams for her. Joan's mother had been that one mother in a million capable of being disappointed by a daughter's decision to become a doctor. Joan was supposed to have been an actress. That's why she'd been named Joan in the first place.

"But, Mother," she had argued, "if I become an actress, the first thing I'll have to do is change my name."

"*Why?*" Her mother just didn't get it.

"Because, Mother, there's already been an actress

89

named Joan Bennett."

"But you don't look a thing like *that* Joan Bennett," her mother said. Joan might as well have been speaking Greek. "What would you change it to?"

"I was thinking maybe Gwyneth Paltrow."

"No one will ever be able to remember an odd name like that," her mother assured her.

Last night, just after midnight, two very concerned parents had shown up in the ER with their eight-year-old daughter. She was in status asthmaticus, a life threatening respiratory crisis. The little girl had a history of asthma, but had never before been so seriously ill. She could hardly breathe. When Joan listened to her chest, she could scarcely hear air moving at all.

Fortunately, the youngster had a gratifying response to therapy. Unfortunately, her insurance was with an HMO that had reluctantly agreed to pay for her ER care, but refused to approve admission to any hospital other than their own. Joan told the administrator at her hospital, "Here's what we'll do. Have them put in writing that they'll pay for the ER care. Have them fax you a copy. When you get that, call them back and tell them she's still much too sick to travel to their facility. Tell them that it would be criminally negligent to transfer her, and that I've made a note to that effect in her chart. Then tell them they have a choice. We can keep the girl in the ER where she will receive expert but *very* expensive care, or she can be admitted to the hospital under the care of one of our able pediatricians. That would save them a great deal of money, but it's up to them."

That did it. The HMO blinked. They approved the admission. Joan was just waiting for the pediatrician to arrive so they could sit down together and review the patient's management before she went upstairs.

About the time Joan began to square away the little girl with asthma, an elderly man—an inpatient on one of the hospital's wards—had a cardiac arrest. Since Joan's responsibilities included responding to in-house emergencies, she left the ER to direct the resuscitation efforts. Then she admitted the man to the intensive care unit located immediately adjacent to the ER.

By the time she returned to the emergency room, Joan had a young man with a broken arm and a couple of patients with skin lacerations to deal with. It was at about that time that she heard about the motor vehicle accident victims that were on their way, so she called an orthopedist to come in to set the arm and prevailed upon him to suture the skin lacs—since he was already here. He was a pretty good sport about it.

The first of the MVA victims to arrive was a young woman who had not yet been identified. Sheriff Dash followed the ambulance and arrived at about the same time as the Jane Doe. Joan instantly noted that Dash and the victim smelled like they'd just come from the same party.

The medics had quite appropriately worried that the Jane Doe might have sustained an inapparent spinal injury. She arrived strapped to a body board that immobilized her head and spine—an effort to forestall possible further injury. Joan examined her carefully. The girl appeared to be neurologically intact with no evidence of significant trauma. Joan was inclined to agree with Dash's assessment—nothing wrong with the patient that a little time and a lot of black coffee wouldn't cure. Still, Joan ordered spinal x-rays and continued observation with frequent neurological checks.

The Long boy arrived about ten minutes after his passenger. Because of his obvious, severe injuries, the process of extracting him from the car had been painstakingly slow. The paramedics had intubated him at the scene, providing an airway so the patient's otherwise agonal respiratory efforts could be assisted mechanically.

But with one look at his horrific head wound, Joan knew there was nothing she could do for him. The neurological exam revealed no evidence of cortical brain function. Any brain cells that might somehow have survived the initial trauma, had subsequently succumbed to asphyxiation. A few minutes without proper oxygenation causes irreparable damage to the human brain. Long was now well past the point where medical science had anything to offer. But other vital organs are less sensitive to oxygen deprivation than the brain. Even though there was nothing Joan could do for Ted Long, there might still be something the senator's son could do for someone else.

"Is he a donor?" she asked Dash.

The sheriff wore that perplexed look that Joan's mother so often displayed.

"On his driver's license," Joan explained, "has he consented to having his organs donated?"

Dash reached into the large Manila envelope he was carrying and pulled out a worn, leather wallet. Joan noticed that it was brimming with cash.

Dash found the driver's license but didn't seem to be making any headway on the answer to Joan's question.

"Let me see if I can find it," Joan suggested. There it was, right where it should be—yes, consent for organ donation had been given. "Have you notified the next of kin?"

Dash shook his head.

"Obviously, when you talk to the family on the phone, you'll need to judge how much to tell them and when. From my initial assessment, I am comfortable saying that the patient has sustained a severe head injury and that there appears to have been extensive damage to the brain. Survival is not expected."

Joan's words sounded harsh and coldly clinical, but the reality was, if anything, even more grim. For all practical purposes, the young man had died when his head smashed through the windshield. The brain damage was obviously that severe. The fact that his heart was still beating was largely irrelevant.

Dash just stood there, staring blankly, as though he hadn't heard a word she said.

"If there's nothing else, Sheriff," she said, "I've got a lot of work to do."

"Unless *you* want to talk to the family," he said.

"If they have questions, I'll be happy to try my best to answer them. Just have them call me. But there's no way I can take time away from my patients right now to try to locate Mr. Long's family."

With that she turned her attention once again to her patient. Even though Edward Long was already brain-dead, very aggressive medical management would be required to preserve various vital organs for transplantation. She needed to call in a neurologist to confirm her assessment that the patient had indeed suffered fatal, irreversible brain damage. And she needed to contact Life Force, the organization that maintained the regional transplant registry and coordinated the matching of donated organs with the patients who needed them.

Aggressive and meticulous medical management of the donor is a critical element in successful transplantation. Careful attention must be paid to blood pressure, oxygenation, cardiac function, metabolic balance, temperature regulation, and myriad other issues in order to preserve organ function prior to removal. In addition, the donor's medical history must be reviewed and a variety of tests performed to exclude underlying diseases that might either effect organ function or, as in the case of an infection or a malignancy, transmit a disease process to the transplant recipient.

For now, there was no one but Joan to manage everything that had to be done. Her night on call kept growing longer and longer.

—12—

Joan had just left Long's bedside in the ICU, thinking she could safely duck out for a few minutes to get herself a cup of coffee, when she saw them coming down the hallway. *Heard* them, to be more precise— the sheriff and whoever the hell the other guy was, yelling at the sheriff from two feet away. It didn't require any great amount of feminine intuition to know that this new guy, the screamer, had something to do with her new ICU patient. But he wasn't the father. *Everyone* knew what Senator Long looked like, and this guy wasn't Senator Long. Joan didn't see any family resemblance whatsoever.

But she wouldn't have to wonder for very long who the man was. He and the sheriff were headed straight toward her, the little guy still yelling at the sheriff, "This is *not* going to happen! Let's get that straight right now. This is *not* going to happen!"

When they reached Joan, Dash stopped. The other man walked on for several steps before realizing that the sheriff was no longer keeping pace. When he turned, Dash nodded toward Joan. "She's taking care of the senator's son," Dash said.

The little man was beside himself. "I told you I want to speak to the *doctor* in charge of his care, not some . . . some *nurse!*"

"This is Dr. Bennett," Dash said. "She's in charge." Then, turning to Joan, he said, "This is Mr. Styles. He's the senator's chief of staff."

Joan offered her hand. Styles ignored it.

"Has Ted been pronounced dead?" Styles asked.

Joan shook her head. "The neurologist agreed with my clinical impression that brain death has occurred, but he recommended we get an EEG. Depending on what that shows, we might try to do a CT scan, but that would be difficult for all kinds of technical reasons."

"So, what am I supposed to tell Senator Long—just cool his heels and wait for you to get around to doing some tests?"

Joan was thinking she had already had just about enough of this arrogant little twit, but she managed to control herself. "I suggest you tell him what I've told you. Or you could ask Senator Long to call me here at the hospital. I'd be happy to answer any questions he might have."

"Senator Long is on Air Force One accompanying the president to the European monetary summit. He can't just pick up a phone and give you a call."

Joan shrugged. "All I can do is make myself available. I would have thought Air Force One would have all kinds of communication equipment."

Styles fixed his beady little eyes on her and gave her his version of a hard stare—but he didn't say anything.

"Meanwhile," Joan said, "we'll be supporting the patient fully and performing tests in anticipation of the possibility that he will become an organ donor."

Now Styles began shaking his head violently. "No way!" he shouted. "The senator's son is not going to be cut up and have his vital organs removed like he's some kind of lab rat."

"Keep your voice down, Mr. Styles. This is a hospital." Joan was about to just walk away, then changed her mind. "Are you saying that you have power of attorney in this matter—that you have authority to direct this patient's medical care?"

"I'll be talking to his father. He will *not* permit this to happen."

"I'd be surprised at that," Joan said. "I've personally heard the senator speak out on behalf of organ donation programs. Besides, the patient is not a minor, and his driver's license clearly indicates his desire to donate. I'm no lawyer, but I would assume that—unless there is compelling evidence to the contrary—a court of law would order us to follow the patient's clear intention."

Styles just stood there, seething.

Joan decided to shift to a more neutral subject. "Do you know anything about the patient's past medical history? Any illnesses he might have had in the past?"

"Not much," Styles said.

"Has he had HIV infection or has he ever abused intravenous drugs?"

"Of course not." Styles was indignant at the suggestion.

"Has he ever had any communicable disease that you are aware of?"

Styles shook his head.

"Has he ever had hepatitis?"

Styles immediately leaped onto that one. "Three or four years ago he had hepatitis. I'm certain of that."

"What kind?"

"I think it was his liver," Styles said.

Joan suppressed a smile. "They often identify the kind of hepatitis with a letter—usually A, B, or C. Hepatitis C used to be called nonA-nonB hepatitis."

"I think it was C."

That could be a problem, Joan thought. Or Styles could be lying—or simply misremembering. "When you talk to the senator, please ask him to provide any past medical history that he has knowledge of. Or, if there's a physician I could talk to who knows his son's history, that would be very helpful."

Styles didn't look like he was predisposed to be helpful.

"Look, Mr. Styles," Joan said, "I know what a difficult time this is for anyone who is close to the senator's son. I'm sorry for that, but all I can do is, well, all I can do."

Without another word, Styles turned and stomped off. Dash set off after him. In addition to everything else she had on her plate, Joan now had to contact the hospital's lawyers for advice on how to proceed.

She was more than a little surprised when, twenty minutes later, Styles and the sheriff tracked her down at Ted Long's bedside in the ICU. Suddenly fawning and apologetic, Styles said he had contacted Senator Long on Air Force One. The senator was, of course, devastated, but had no objection to organ donation—if it came to that.

—13—

For Pace, the days had long since ceased to be distinguishable. Confined to his hospital room, to his bed, there was a pervasive sameness, not only to the days, but even the hours. Time was marked only by the change of nursing shifts and the rounds of the medical and surgical teams assigned to render his care. He envied them, these happy, healthy people with lives that extended beyond the hospital's walls.

As the reality of his death loomed ever more imminent, Pace was all the more resolved to meet his end with stoic dignity. He reminded himself that he was fortunate to have no wife whose heart would be broken by his passing, no children to be condemned to a fatherless childhood. Even the loss of his own parents, the great tragedy of his own childhood, seemed now a blessing in disguise. Had his parents survived to their normal life expectancy, they would soon be mourning the loss of a son.

His medical care had been excellent. He could fault it on only one count—the relentless cheerfulness with which it was administered.

Pace was not given to self-pity, but he was a realist. And as he prepared to meet his death, a wistful yearning began to grow within him, a desire for tranquility and solitude.

Pace began to dream of dying at home.

He wanted to spend the time he had left—perhaps a few days, maybe just a few hours—in serenity and seclusion. Some animals did that. Sensing the end was near they took themselves off to some quiet place to meet death alone.

Pace resolved to notify Brian of his intention to leave the hospital AMA—against medical advice—a decision that would remove all professional and ethical responsibility from Brian's shoulders, and, Pace hoped, might also relieve at least some of the emotional strain that Pace had placed on his dear friend.

Pace waited for Brian's second visit of the day before relating his news. He didn't want to dump any new worries on Brian just as he was heading off to the operating room.

"I've been thinking about this for quite a while now, Brian. It's time for me to go home."

Brian shook his head emphatically and used his most serious doctor's voice. "That's just not a very good idea, Pace. There's no way I could let you do that."

But Pace was determined. "I know it's not what you'd recommend. I'll sign out AMA. It's a personal decision I've made. I've thought this through very carefully. It's time."

"Just do this for me, Pace. Stay in the hospital a couple more days. After that, if you still want to leave and nothing's changed, you can go home with my blessing."

Pace shook his head. "I'm planning to leave tomorrow morning. Two days from now, I may not be able to manage at home."

"That's precisely the point, Pace. You can't make it

on your own."

"I'll have a nurse come by to check on me."

"That's just not enough."

"I want to die at home, Brian."

Brian Curtis studied his old friend, then made a decision. "I've got some news. There's a heart available. I was just notified a couple of hours ago. You're second in line. That's why I didn't want to mention it. I know what a devastating disappointment it can be to come this close and not get the heart. But if whoever's number one on the list doesn't take it, the heart is yours."

Pace took a deep breath. He knew that Brian hadn't yet revealed the whole story. The availability of a Type O heart big enough to meet the demands of Pace's large body was a rare event. There was only one reason why the guy ahead of Pace on the list wouldn't jump at the opportunity. There was something wrong with the donor heart, something potentially quite serious.

"It's a high-risk heart," Pace said. It was a statement, not a question.

Brian nodded. "There's a history of hepatitis C in the donor."

Pace understood the implications of Brian's words. The donation of organs from patients with hepatitis C was controversial because of the risk of hepatitis C developing in the recipient. Acute hepatitis C tended to be mild, but could be more severe in a transplant patient. At the very least it would complicate the post-transplant course. But the real problem was *chronic* hepatitis C. It could lead to cirrhosis and even cancer of the liver. Hepatitis C was no picnic.

"What do you recommend?" Pace asked.

"The good news is, it's a local heart. We wouldn't

even need to send a plane. And the donor is young and was apparently healthy prior to sustaining fatal head trauma. He was an unrestrained driver in a motor vehicle accident."

Pace winced at that—the tragic story that was the flip side of his own good fortune. A young man struck down in his prime. How would Pace learn to live with that?

The part about the heart being local really was good news. It was important to keep the time between removal of the donor heart and transplantation as short as possible. In no case should more than six hours elapse. If the donor heart was far away, it was standard practice to hire a private jet to go get it.

"My vote is," Brian said, "if the heart is offered to us, we take it and run."

Pace managed a smile for his old friend. "Then I guess it's unanimous," he said.

—14—

Less than an hour later, the call came through from the coordinator at Life Force. Brian Curtis took the call himself.

"The other patient has declined the heart," the lady from Life Force said, "so we're able to offer it to your patient, Magruder."

Brian didn't hesitate. "We'll take the heart. How soon can we do the harvest?"

"That's not clear yet. Because of the hepatitis history, there haven't been any takers so far for the other organs. We're still working our way down the lists."

Ideally, a single donor might provide organs to several recipients. This is especially true in the event of head trauma, and it is sometimes possible to harvest a heart, two lungs, a liver, two kidneys, and a pair of corneas from one donor. Other sought-after organs include the pancreas and even bone. Since the supply of each of these organs is always inadequate to meet the desperate need, a major goal of an organization like Life Force is to insure that not a single potential donor organ is wasted.

"How's the donor doing?" Curtis asked.

"It's been a little rocky. Initially the donor had profound hypertension and tachycardia, but now we're dealing with the opposite."

"He's herniating," Curtis said, almost to himself.

Typically, following severe head trauma, the pressure inside the patient's skull increases and that causes the release of powerful chemicals called catecholamines. These catecholamines cause elevation of both blood pressure and heart rate. This process is often referred to as "catecholamine storm."

Subsequently, if the pressure increase inside the skull is great enough, the brainstem may be forced downward through the small opening at the base of the skull. This herniation is rapidly fatal if not quickly relieved.

Proper management of the donor during the period prior to the harvesting of organs is a very tricky business. To prevent organ damage, proper blood flow and oxygenation must be maintained. Complex issues arise involving fluid and electrolyte balance, temperature regulation, control of blood pressure and heart rate and rhythm, and even hormonal balance. Even in expert hands, the task could prove daunting. Brian Curtis knew that a small, rural hospital was unlikely to have staff experienced in the highly esoteric science of donor maintenance.

"How's the local medical staff holding up?" Curtis asked.

"So far, they've been terrific. A Dr. Bennett was on call in their ER last night, and she's essentially stayed on and assumed total responsibility. She couldn't be better, but she must be nearing exhaustion—especially now, with the donor so unstable."

Brian had heard enough. "I'm going to go ahead and send our team. Obviously, we won't go ahead with the harvest until we have your okay, but meanwhile we can provide some expertise and relief."

"I was hoping you'd say that."

"The other thing," Curtis said, "that I'm sure you've considered, if there are no takers for the other organs very soon, we'll have to go ahead and harvest the heart. Obviously, we'd all like to see as many organs utilized as possible, but it would be a shame if we lost the heart while we were waiting for takers for the other organs—takers who might *never* materialize."

Brian had put his full team on standby notice as soon as he'd been told that a heart might become available. Now it was a simple matter to place them in motion. The group sent to harvest the donor heart would consist of five people—two surgeons, an anesthesiologist, a pump perfusionist, and a scrub nurse. They would take with them everything they needed—from surgical instruments to the Igloo cooler used to transport the donor heart. They would depend on the other hospital for virtually nothing.

Once Brian had the retrieval team under way, he headed back to Pace's room. Remarkably, his patient was asleep. Under normal circumstances, Brian wouldn't have bothered him.

But he approached the bed, Pace opened his eyes. He looked expectantly at his old friend.

"The heart is yours," Brian said. "I've sent Al Becker with a team to go have a look. As you well know, there could still be some problem with the donor heart that will prevent us from doing the transplant, but based on everything we know now, all systems are go."

Pace nodded. He'd been this far before with patients of his own and then been devastated to find out that some detail had been overlooked, and the donor heart was, for some reason, not acceptable.

"I'm going to transfer you to the ICU," Brian said,

"so we can tweak your meds and make certain you're in optimal shape for surgery."

It was an emotional moment for the two old friends, and Pace wasn't certain he could trust his voice. He offered his hand, then managed to get out, "Thanks, Brian, for everything."

—15—

Under the circumstances, Pace found the bustle of the intensive care unit strangely reassuring. It was a place very familiar to him, albeit from a quite different point of view. For *Dr.* Magruder, the unit had always represented the absolute pinnacle of modern medical science, and his own brutal transformation from physician to patient had done nothing to alter that assessment.

The ICU staff were all smiles and encouragement. They eagerly accepted what Pace would not yet permit himself to believe—that this new heart would soon be his.

He was a man whipsawed between two competing visions of reality—the one he'd just come to accept, that he was going home to die, and this seductive new version, the one that offered the return of his purloined future. Pace had found peace only a few short hours ago, and he was reluctant to abandon the serenity of that place for what might prove nothing more than a sadistic illusion.

He remained peculiarly detached, floating somewhere above the body in Bed Two that everyone referred to as Pace Magruder—a general unwilling to commit his emotional resources lest they be decimated by the unleashing of yet another new reality.

Pace dozed off and awakened to find Brian standing at his bedside. Brian was slowly shaking his head, but he had a smile on his face.

"You're certainly the most relaxed pre-transplant patient I've ever seen," Brian said. "How are you feeling?"

"The breathing's a little easier. I think the extra Lasix helped."

"Al Becker just called in," Brian said. "It's a good heart."

Pace either misunderstood or was unwilling to understand. "They've seen the clinical data, the EKG, the echocardiogram? They're all good?"

"Al's way past that, Pace. The team's in the OR. They've opened the chest and examined the heart. Pace, it's a *good heart*. We're a go."

Once again unsure of his voice, Pace nodded to show that he understood.

The moment had arrived. The moment he had refused to allow himself to hope for. He would get his transplant, a chance at a future.

Pace was reeling from an emotion he couldn't label. Every nerve ending in his body was charged and demanding release. If he'd been a crier, he would have cried. If he'd been a hugger, he would have hugged. A healthy Pace might have gone for a good, hard run. But this Pace, the ICU Pace, could only nod.

"It looks like the heart will be the only organ donated," Brian said, "so things are going to begin to move very quickly."

Once again, Pace nodded.

Usually, multiple organs were donated. In that situation, the cardiac surgeons would open the donor's chest and examine the heart and lungs, then step back and allow other surgeons to remove the kidneys, pancreas, liver—whatever they were after. The heart and lungs were removed last, so that appropriate perfusion and oxygenation could be maintained to the other organs until they were removed. It was a shame that, because of the history of hepatitis C, only the heart would be harvested, but it certainly made things a lot easier for the cardiac surgeons.

"So, everything's in place." Brian paused briefly as though lost in thought, then said, "I guess that's it. You know the drill as well as I do. Any questions?"

Pace was still struggling to find his voice, but he held out his hand.

"Thanks," Pace said. It might or might not have been audible.

"So, next time you see me," Brian said, "you'll be in the recovery room sporting a new heart."

"See you then," Pace whispered.

With that, Brian was off, leaving Pace to his own thoughts. Pace *did* know the drill. He'd been here many times in the past with his patients.

Now that Al Becker's team had accepted the donor heart, the next step would be to cross clamp the aorta and begin the actual removal. Cross clamping the aorta halted the circulation of blood to the donor heart. From that moment onward, it was a race against the clock. Without circulation, the cells of the donor heart were deprived of oxygen. Without oxygen they would die. It was only a matter of time. The magic number was six. It was considered unwise to attempt a transplant if more than six hours would elapse between the moment the donor aorta was cross clamped and the time when circulation would be reestablished in the recipient. When the heart must travel long distances and be transported by jet, precise time estimations include taking into consideration the effects of headwinds and tailwinds. Not a minute can be wasted.

Pace knew that his new heart was not far away, so headwind and tailwind calculations weren't relevant in this case. Still, careful coordination was necessary so that as little time as possible would elapse. Communication would be maintained between the donor and recipient surgical teams to insure that, when the donor heart finally did arrive in the operating room, Pace's body would be ready to receive it.

The recipient's heart—Pace's heart—would not actually be removed until the donor heart was considered "available." The definition of "available" varied somewhat from hospital to hospital and even from case to case depending on time constraints. Some surgeons required the donor heart to actually arrive in the operating room—or at least in the recipient's hospital—before removal of the recipient's heart. Others argued that this requirement wasted valuable time. If you waited that long, you'd have the donor heart just sitting in an ice bath in the OR waiting, its cells dying, while surgeons removed the recipient's heart. Such wasted time could well mean the difference between a successful transplant and a catastrophe. Brian Curtis took the latter view and tended to begin removal of the recipient's heart when he was notified that the ambulance containing the donor heart was within fifteen minutes of arriving at the hospital. When the donor heart reached the OR, the patient's chest was ready to receive it.

Pace had dozed off once again when Bud Alexander, the anesthesiologist, came by to check on him one last time and order the administration of Pace's pre-op sedation. They talked only briefly, then Pace was sent off to a chemically induced dreamland.

There was no place in the world where Brian Curtis was more at home than the operating room. There was literally nowhere he would rather be. For as long as he could remember, he had no other dream than to become a cardiac surgeon. Now, his main goal in life was to continue to be a cardiac surgeon for as long as fate allowed.

He had been asked if he thought his friendship with Pace Magruder would be an obstacle to his medical objectivity. Brian had said, No, that's not a problem. He believed that then, and he believed it now. Looking down at the operating field he saw only a chest prepped for surgery. The patient was otherwise not identifiable.

"What kind of music are you in the mood for today, Brian?" It was the circulating nurse. Brian was already scrubbed and ready to go.

He gave her a look. Surely everyone in the hospital knew what they'd be listening to today.

"Just kidding," she said.

A moment later they were listening to "Pretty Woman," a song Roy Orbison had written and sung long before it was re-popularized by the movie. A nice, upbeat tune to get them started.

Brian made the long, sternal incision just as he had hundreds of times in the past, moving carefully but quickly. Then he cut through the sternum using the oscillating surgical saw specifically designed for the task. All went well. Just the usual bleeders to tie off or coagulate with the electrocautery blade.

Then, as if on cue, the call came through from Al Becker's team. Al estimated they were now fifteen minutes away from the hospital. Brian began the dramatic process of actually removing the heart Pace had been born with.

Even a surgeon of Brian's experience could not help being shocked at the condition of Pace's heart. Massively dilated, its walls paper thin, the heart might at any moment beat for the last time. The wonder was that it had somehow managed to keep Pace alive this long.

Brian's concentration was intense. He didn't even look up for twenty minutes. When he did, he noticed the clock.

"Would you give Dr. Becker a call on his mobile phone," he asked the circulating nurse, "and see what's holding him up?"

Five minutes later she reported back. "I've dialed the number several times. There's no answer."

Brian shook his head. "Somebody probably forgot to check the batteries on the damn phone."

Fortunately, this wasn't one of those times when they had to worry about all the things that could go wrong with air travel—the weather, airport congestion, and so forth. Pace's new heart was coming solely by ambulance.

"They probably got stuck in traffic," Bud Alexander said.

Meanwhile, Brian continued the work of removing Pace's diseased heart. When the donor heart arrived, they'd be ready for it.

He had Pace on the bypass pump and the old, failed heart completely removed when the circulating nurse returned. Roy Orbison and k.d. lang had just launched into their haunting duet rendition of "Crying." The nurse seemed worried and hesitant.

"We just got a phone call," she said. "There's been

an accident."

It wasn't just her words that devastated Brian. It was the look of mortal terror in her eyes as she stared into the operating field and saw the irrevocable, the empty cavity where Pace's heart had been.

PART TWO

—16—

Although others, on hearing the story of Pace Magruder's life, might well have counted him unlucky, this would never have been an opinion Pace would have shared. The loss of his parents at such a tender age had been a grievous and incomprehensible blow, but the same fate that destroyed his family had subsequently delivered him into the capable, caring hands of his Aunt Mariah, and Pace had—in the fullness of time—come to appreciate the elemental, formative role she had played in his life. Pace had understood that his had not been the first childhood to be so bereaved, and he was grateful he had not shared the fate of so many orphans who found themselves adrift without so much as a guiding hand to warn them of the treacherous rocks and shoals that threatened from all points of the compass.

His most recent trial, the devastating heart infection that delivered him to death's door, was succeeded by a postoperative course benign beyond even his surgeon's fondest dreams. From his first waking post-transplant moments, Pace could feel the difference his new, healthy heart made. There was a vigor, a vitality, he hadn't known for months. His body was becoming once again the coiled spring of his youth—that well of boundless energy constrained only by the limits his mind chose to place upon it.

On the second postoperative day, Pace sat in a chair beside his bed. By the fourth, he rode a stationary bicycle in his hospital room. Ten days later, he was home.

Even infection and rejection—the twin dark clouds that hover ominously over any transplant procedure—were, for Pace, only tiny smudges on a distant horizon. And the dreaded hepatitis C infection—the "risk" in Pace's high-risk donor heart—even that never materialized.

It was only after he'd been discharged from the hospital that Pace first got wind of the paralyzing moment in the OR when the operating team was notified there had been an accident involving the donor heart. Even then it was only by chance that he heard the story. Pace was back at the hospital for some tests and decided to drop by the cafeteria for a bite to eat. He happened to sit near a table where an OR nurse was loudly recounting the incident to a group of colleagues. Pace was lost in his own thoughts and had only the vaguest awareness of their conversation. He would never have connected it to himself had one of the nurses not noticed him and made an almost comical attempt to silence her friend.

After some investigation, Pace casually broached the matter at one of his frequent dinners at the home Anne and Brian Curtis.

"I understand," he said, "there was a little excitement in the OR you never told me about."

"Not really," Brian said. He had this I-don't-have-a-clue-what-you're-talking-about look on his face.

"The car accident," Pace said. "The donor heart."

"Oh that. It was nothing. A little fender bender right outside the front door of the hospital. Al Becker just walked the heart up to the OR."

"I heard it was ten blocks, and Al did it on a broken ankle. I seem to remember him, after my surgery, hobbling around the hospital in a cast. He told me he broke it playing tennis."

Brian gave Pace a bemused shrug and quickly changed the subject. "You think the Redskins are ever gonna get their act together?"

That night turned out to be one of those difficult ones Pace still had. Nothing like what he experienced in the hospital, but enough to remind him he wasn't yet back to normal.

He tossed and turned and could never quite get comfortable. And he was nauseated, a reaction to the fistfuls of pills he had to take to prevent his body from rejecting his new heart.

When morning finally came he had no appetite for breakfast. He dutifully took his medication and set out for a walk around the neighborhood—part of his ever-escalating exercise regimen. Even for someone as highly motivated as Pace, it was sometimes difficult to stick to the program. It got pretty boring. What Pace needed was a partner, and he was about to get one.

Pace hadn't made it to the corner before Max fell in beside him.

"My name's Pace. What's yours?"

Max turned his head and gave Pace a look, but other than that, he just kept walking.

"Not much of a talker, huh?"

Max just kept walking.

Pace stopped. Max stopped.

Pace started on. Max continued right along beside him. Max was heeling—his way of letting Pace know that Pace had been adopted.

Max was a rather gaunt and bedraggled and of indeterminate age and breed. He was big. You wouldn't be surprised to learn he was a cross between a golden retriever and a St. Bernard. His coat was a reddish with black around the muzzle and paws. He had a thoughtful expression and dark, caring eyes. The tag on his collar identified him as Max, but contained no other information.

The dog looked like he hadn't had a decent meal in some time. Pace worried that Max might have been on his own for a while.

Pace walked; Max remained steadfastly abreast. When Pace turned onto the walkway that led to his front door, Max stayed at his side.

Pace pulled open the screen door, and Max looked up hopefully, making deliberate, direct eye contact and wagging his tail for all he was worth.

"Sorry, Max. Time for you to go home."

Pace went inside, closing the door behind him. Max curled up on the welcome mat. He didn't appear to be going anywhere.

Pace waited fifteen minutes, then checked on the dog. He was still there. He waited another half hour before checking again. Max was on the mat, looking up at him, wagging his tail. Three hours later, when it was time for another of Pace's scheduled walks, Max once again fell in beside him. After their walk the scene repeated itself at the front door. Pace remained resolute, but he did fill a bowl with water and set it out for Max. The dog drank gratefully.

A couple of hours later, Pace finally felt like he might be able to eat something. He fixed a plate for himself, and filled another one for Max at the front door. Max certainly seemed appreciative. When he'd cleaned the plate, Max nosed it toward Pace's foot—his way of letting Pace know that he could use another helping of everything.

After he'd polished off a second plate, Max lay down, put his head between his paws, and gazed up plaintively at Pace. It was a shameless ploy, clear evidence of Max's instinctive understanding that the road into the living room wound directly through Pace's heart.

"Okay," Pace said, "but if I take you inside, the first thing that's going to happen is you're going to get a bath."

Pace opened the door wide and made a sweeping motion with his right hand. Max was instantly on his feet and through the door. Pace followed the dog inside, turning his back only briefly to lock the door. When he turned back around, Max was gone.

Pace heard an odd, rhythmic sound emanating from somewhere upstairs. He couldn't imagine what that dog had gotten into already.

Pace found him in the bathroom, standing in the tub. As Max swished his tail back and forth it struck the sides of the bathtub and made a loud clunk each time it made contact.

"You're somebody's dog," Pace said shaking his head. "And that somebody is probably missing you an awful lot right now. As soon as we get you cleaned up, we'll start trying to figure out where you came from."

But there were to be no responses, either to Pace's newspaper ads or to the notices he posted at the grocery store and the hospital.

"I guess it's just going to be you and me," Pace told Max, "a couple of gimpy old confirmed bachelors, trying to get along as best we can."

That appeared to be okay with Max.

—17—

It was an idea Courtney had been brewing since the death of Ted Long—or rather, since she'd *known* of the death of Ted Long. His body was cremated long before anyone in the DA's office even knew he was dead.

"I want to get a court order, Tommy, to compel the hospital to release any blood or tissue specimens they may still be holding from the Long case, so we can check Long's DNA against the evidence from the Lovett crime scene."

They were in Jacobs' cavernous office on the twelfth floor. Courtney had asked for the meeting. Judging by the sour expression on Tommy's face, he wasn't buying what she was selling.

"What's the point?"

"To solve the Lovett murder. To finally be able to close the case. Maybe to provide a little closure for an emotionally devastated family."

"Do you mind?" Tommy asked.

He was headed for the window. A cigar was coming out. There would be the obligatory pause in their conversation until he finally got the thing lit.

"Look," Tommy said between drags to get his cigar going, "I understand all that. I *sympathize* with it. But from a practical point of view, we'd stir up a lot of trouble for no real benefit. Ted Long is dead. If he's guilty, he'll never harm anyone again. Besides, with the Arnold kid taking off the way he has, he's still the number one suspect."

It was hard to argue with that. "Still," Courtney said, "I don't like the way they rushed Long's body to cremation. They knew we wanted to talk to Ted. They knew we would have been interested in his DNA."

"It was all perfectly legal," Tommy said. "Ted Long was not an official suspect. And cremation was perfectly natural given the condition of the body."

He took a long, appreciative draw on his cigar. "I don't see the point in putting Senator Long through any more. You should have seen him at the funeral. He was beside himself with grief."

"You were at the funeral?" Courtney was astounded. When had *Tommy* learned of Ted Long's death?

Jacobs was already shaking his head. "Not really a funeral. The memorial service. It was six weeks after the accident. The body was long-since cremated."

"I still want to get the court order."

Jacobs put his foot down. "No. No court order. This office is short on personnel and short on money and we're not going to expend precious resources trying to convict a dead man."

As far as Tommy was concerned, that was that.

But Courtney was already conducting her own behind-the-scenes investigation. She had driven out to the site of the accident. Then she had tracked down the young woman who'd been in the car that night with Ted Long. So far, Courtney's inquiries had produced more questions than answers, but she wasn't done yet.

What Tommy didn't know wouldn't hurt him.

This Dr. Bennett lived way to hell and gone out in the sticks. Courtney had asked if she could meet with Dr. Bennett at her home, being pretty cryptic, telling her only that it was a very sensitive legal matter. Bennett had seemed hesitant at first, but then said okay, how about Saturday?

It was a farmhouse—not too big a surprise given the location—white clapboard with dark shutters that were either black or darkest green. Everything about it was immaculate. And the yard was spectacular. Lots of flowers and big old oaks.

As Courtney pulled up the drive the front door opened. A tall, dark-haired woman walked toward her car.

Courtney climbed out and offered her hand. "Hi, Dr. Bennett, I'm Courtney Bond."

"Please call me Joan."

She had soft, gentle eyes and a winning smile. Courtney immediately liked her. "What a lovely home you have."

"Thanks. Actually, I can't take any credit for it. My husband's responsible for everything."

The inside of the house was completely unexpected. Lots of unusual pieces of furniture—what Courtney would call "modern"—not at all the traditional things she anticipated. There were paintings everywhere. Mostly abstract and, well, "modern."

"You have quite a collection," Courtney said.

"My husband's an artist. They're all his work. Theoretically they're for sale, but I have a lot of trouble parting with them."

"I can see why. He has enormous talent."

The two women were immediately comfortable with each other. Joan was a few years older than Courtney, and it wasn't difficult for Courtney to imagine herself in a similar situation in a couple of years—still with her career, but married.

"Do you have any children?"

Joan shook her head. There was the briefest hint of sadness in her eyes. "You?"

"Someday," Courtney said. "So far I haven't even managed to get married."

Joan offered tea, and they exchanged some more small talk before getting down to business.

"I'm sorry I couldn't be more forthcoming on the phone," Courtney said. "Like I said, it's all quite sensitive. It concerns Edward Long, Jr. I understand you were on duty the night of the accident."

Joan's eyebrows arched on hearing the name. "That was a night I won't soon forget."

"What I'm about to tell you is quite confidential. I hope you'll regard it that way."

Joan nodded.

"Ted Long's name has surfaced on the periphery of another matter. It's the type of situation where a sample of his DNA would be useful in clearing his name. But to obtain the sample, a court order would be required. If we do that, the media will have a field day. Ted Long's name will be dragged through the headlines and associated with a crime he may have had nothing to do with. Frankly, there's some disagreement in the DA's office about whether it would be worthwhile to put the senator's family through such an ordeal."

Joan had heard enough. "Let me make one thing perfectly clear. If you have the idea that I might be able to somehow surreptitiously obtain a specimen for you, that is something I will not do. There's a reason a court order is required."

Courtney felt terrible she'd been so misunderstood.

"*Of course* I would never ask any such thing. Believe me, I'm an officer of the court, and I take that very seriously. I don't violate the law and I don't ask anyone else to.

"In a nutshell, here's the deal. I don't have a clue if the hospital even has a specimen suitable for DNA analysis. If I make a formal inquiry, I might as well have gotten a court order. There's no way it would stay quiet. Everyone would want to know why the district attorney's office is interested in Ted Long's DNA.

"On the other hand, if I go through the court, that will immediately become a matter of public record, and it may be all for nothing—if the hospital doesn't even have a suitable sample available.

"And there's one other thing, a personal problem I have. My boss, the DA, doesn't really want to go forward on this. To get a court order, I'd have to put a lot of pressure on him. I'd win in the end, because I'm right about this, and he wouldn't want the public to find out he resisted me. It wouldn't look good. But he'd make me pay for it. That's for sure. I might as well start looking for another job. If it comes to it, that's something I'm willing to do—quit my job. But I'd really hate to go to the mat on this thing only to find out it was all for naught—that there's no suitable specimen at the hospital.

"So here's what I wanted to ask. I thought that you, as the attending physician, might be able to casually inquire as to what's lying around the hospital lab without drawing a lot of attention. Once I know what's there, I can act accordingly."

Joan gave a relieved smile. "That," she said, "I can do."

Monday afternoon Joan called with her news.

126

Courtney returned the call that evening after court.

"There's nothing," Joan said.

"Nothing?"

"I checked with pathology, the chemistry lab, the hematology lab, everywhere I could think of. No one has anything. There *are no* specimens."

"Does that surprise you?" Courtney asked. "I mean, is that typical?"

"No," Joan said, "it's not typical at all. It's very peculiar."

—18—

That dog had a clock in his head, and every three hours an alarm went off. And every three hours, unless Pace had turned in for the night, Max would nuzzle Pace's leg or his hand or whatever body part Max could find to nuzzle, and they would set off on another walk. Over the weeks and months the fitness of both man and dog steadily improved. Soon they were jogging instead of walking. And even that wasn't enough for Max who spent additional endless hours romping with other dogs and chasing down balls Pace threw for him.

Pace's new heart—unlike the old one—had no dietary restrictions. He could eat an entire bag of potato chips all by himself if he wanted to, although Max encouraged him to share. Pace had essentially no limitations in his performance of normal, everyday activities. In short, Pace didn't feel "totally disabled." Yet that was how he was classified at the medical school—retired, with total disability benefits. Pensioned off.

A year earlier, confined to his hospital room and struggling for breath, Pace had reluctantly accepted the advice of friends, faculty members, hospital administrators—just about everyone he talked to. They had convinced him that retirement offered benefits otherwise unavailable to him. And of course all this was done with a wink and a nod. Really nothing more than a formality, they said. When the time came, it could all be quickly undone. Pace could come back to work as soon as he was ready. So he signed the papers. And with that signature, Pace was no longer a salaried member of the medical school faculty. He became a retiree with only his life's savings and his disability insurance to support him.

But it wasn't about the money. It was all about his research. He was itching to get back to it. Sure, he dropped by the lab from time to time, but it wasn't the same. Pace was an outsider now. He felt like he was imposing on his former colleagues. They always acted delighted to see him, but they had work to do, and Pace wasn't really a part of that anymore. He couldn't rid himself of the notion that he was in the way.

Brian had cautioned him not to rush into anything. Pace said, "Hell, Brian, it's been nearly a year. I'm going stir crazy."

So Pace planned to make an appointment with Boyd Edington and see what could be worked out at the medical school. It was time to rejoin the faculty and get back to work. It was time to un-retire.

But he knew that merely returning to work would not quell the restlessness he felt deep within. There was something else, a haunting question that dogged his days and invaded his dreams.

It was the kind of thing Maggie Pearson had always wanted to go on and on about before his transplant. It was the kind of thing Pace had openly scoffed at, a question he could never have imagined could become, for him, nearly an obsession.

Pace owed his life to the transplanted heart now beating within his chest. Pace Magruder, the cardiologist—the pre-transplant Pace Magruder—would have regarded that heart with the objective eye of a physician-scientist. On the macroscopic level, it was a pump fashioned out of muscle. Microscopically, it was a collection of highly specialized cells and tissues—intricate in their complexity, wondrous in their functionality, but still nothing more than cells and tissues. Except for certain obvious medical concerns related to such issues as rejection and infection, it didn't matter one whit where Pace's new heart had come from.

But that was precisely the question that now preoccupied his mind. Contrary to all his expectations, Pace was unable to simply accept his new heart as an anonymous act of fate. With every beat it reminded him of its presence. With every beat it called to him. He was not the first man to possess this heart. It had known another life before his. And much to his own surprise, that other life now mattered deeply to Pace. How had it been lived? How had it ended?

He broached the subject cautiously with Maggie Pearson. She at least had the grace not to say, I told you so.

"I sometimes wonder," he said to her, "about the person who had this heart before me."

"That's perfectly normal," Maggie said—very nonchalantly.

"I owe him so much. There ought to be some way to express my gratitude."

"You wrote to the family. I'm sure they understand." Maggie was referring to the customary letter sent by the transplant recipient to the survivors of the donor. It was forwarded by the transplant coordinator. From the perspective of the recipient, the donor and his family remained anonymous.

"That's so little," Pace said, "compared to what I received."

Maggie had been through this a hundred times before. For someone who was really into all of these touchy-feely aspects *pre*-transplantation, she had surprisingly pragmatic ideas as to how they should be addressed *post*-transplantation.

"What you're feeling has a name, Pace. It's called guilt. Here you are doing wonderfully well and thinking about going back to work, and there's only one reason—someone else died. And you're a very moral person, and naturally it occurs to you that this is not a totally equitable situation. You're alive and well and happy and the other guy is dead. And probably, the better you feel, health-wise, the guiltier you feel."

"I'm sure that's part of it," Pace said.

"What you have to remember, Pace, is that the donor did not die for you. He didn't get up one morning and decide he wanted to donate his heart. That's not what happened. What happened is, he suffered a fatal event. He died—all on his own. You didn't kill him. You didn't cause him to die. I'm not saying that his making his heart available was not a wonderful, generous thing. I'm just saying that it's nothing you should feel guilty about."

"I understand all that, Maggie. It's just that I really feel the need to do something—something more concrete—to express my appreciation. That's all."

"And you're thinking about doing a little investigating to find out who the donor was, maybe look up his family?"

Pace responded with a slight shrug of his shoulders.

"That's not a good idea, Pace. That's why we go to such great pains to keep the donors anonymous."

"I wouldn't abuse the access I have here at the medical school, Maggie. If I did any investigating at all, I wouldn't use hospital records."

"That's not the point. The point is, it's just not a good idea. It's not good for you *or* for the donor's family."

"I'd be careful. The last thing I want to do is cause any more unhappiness for the donor's family."

Maggie took a deep breath, then she reached for Pace's hand and held it tightly. "Pace, I'm advising you—as a friend—please don't do this. Please, just leave it alone."

Tommy had asked her to come up to his office to discuss some cases. He'd been doing a lot of that in the months since the Lovett murder, asking Courtney's opinion on cases she wasn't otherwise involved with. As usual, she wasn't sure what Jacobs was up to.

"There's a new wrinkle in the Cowley situation," Tommy said.

Lamar Cowley was a small-time gangster and dope dealer the DA's office had liked for a whole slew of crimes over the years. Despite dozens of arrests, Cowley's sheet showed no convictions.

This time, Cowley had been arrested for armed robbery—mostly because he was spotted in the vicinity of the crime, and it was the kind of thing he did. The identification had been tenuous at best, and no one was very hopeful of a conviction. Then, all of a sudden, Lamar copped a plea. Everyone assumed he was taking the fall for someone higher up in his gang, but nobody was shedding any tears for Lamar.

"Let me guess," Courtney said, "you've found the guy who really did the stick-up."

"It's better than that," Tommy said. "I think we can get Lamar for the murder of a rival gang member."

"So what's the problem?"

"Lamar would have to have been in two places at

once. The murder occurred at the same time as the robbery he's already copped to."

"So the plea gives him an alibi," Courtney said. She'd heard it all now. "Still, I think a jury'll see through that."

"You're probably right. But his attorney's going to have a lot of fun with this."

"Who's he got?"

"Irv Shorn."

"Get ready to read about it in the papers," Courtney said.

"I can see it now," Tommy said. "Irv is going to call prosecutors as witnesses for Lamar. They'll have to testify to their good faith belief that Lamar had done the robbery. Old Irv'll claim that they didn't care *what* they convicted Cowley of just so long as he was convicted of *something*."

Which isn't all that far from the truth, Courtney thought.

"It's not the kind of laundry you like to have hanging out during an election," Tommy said.

Against all expectations, Jacobs was running for reelection.

"This isn't for public consumption, Courtney, but this is the last time I'm running for DA. Two more years and I'm out. Schwartz is leaving right after the election."

Mike Schwartz was Tommy's chief deputy. They'd been together for years.

"I'd like you to move into Mike's spot, Courtney."

She was stunned. "Tommy, thank you. I don't know what to say."

"You don't have to say anything. You've earned it. You're the best I've got. Let's keep it between ourselves for now. We'll announce it after the election when Schwartz makes his announcement."

"Where's Mike going?"

"Faye, Horvath."

Why wasn't Courtney surprised?

"Of course, all this will put you in position to run for my job in two years. You're young, but you're well qualified. You've made a substantial name for yourself. If everything lines up politically, I'll be happy to throw my support your way."

If everything lines up politically.

"Thanks, Tommy. I'd be honored to serve as chief deputy, but this is all a little too sudden for me to have any thoughts about being DA. I'm flattered, of course, but that's a big jump into the political arena. I've never been there." She wasn't certain she would ever want to be.

"No hurry. You'll get a taste of politics as chief deputy. At that level, it's not just the law. You always have to have your political antennae out. Everything you do has ripple effects in the community. Whether you move forward on a case often involves political as well as legal judgment. The Lovett case is a good example."

Uh-oh.

"I know my decision not to request a court order didn't satisfy the legal purist in you. I understand that. I respect that. But I still believe mine was the correct judgment."

Tommy arched an eyebrow. "I also know that you did a little investigating on your own a few months back. That's fine, too. You did it quietly, tried to keep it off everybody's radar screen. It's just that when politics is involved, it's awfully hard to keep things quiet."

How the hell had Tommy found out about her little

trip? Courtney decided not to deal with that directly.

"All the specimens from the Long case are missing. The hospital can't account for them."

"I understand that," Tommy said.

"Somebody took them. It's likely that Senator Long was involved."

"That's certainly possible. What does that tell us?"

"It suggests that Ted Long was a murderer and that the senator knows it."

Tommy nodded. "And there's nothing we can do to hold Ted Long accountable, is there?"

Tommy was right about that.

"And if some specimens were stolen from a hospital way out in Howard County, well beyond our jurisdiction, there's nothing we can do about that either, is there?"

Courtney would have to think about that one.

—20—

The poets have always ascribed to the human heart a host of attributes having nothing to do with its role as a pump. The heart has been alleged to be everything from the wellspring of romantic love to the repository of the human soul.

It is perhaps then not particularly astounding that a certain mystique has grown up around cardiac transplantation, and it has been widely claimed that, during these procedures, much more is transplanted than a mere physical organ—that some portion of the donor's psyche is transmitted to the recipient as well.

Patients often report remarkable personal transformations that occur in conjunction with the receipt of their new hearts. They describe new insights and interests. Dietary habits may suddenly undergo a radical change with the patient now craving exotic or even previously disliked foods. Some patients have even reported the acquisition of new knowledge—specific facts—which they could not have possibly been aware of before transplantation. And, in many of these cases, heart transplant recipients have come to believe that these newly acquired tastes, attitudes, and ideas were those of the donor and were simply transferred to the recipient along with the donor's heart.

As a cardiologist caring for transplant patients, Pace had heard all the stories. But he was not persuaded. For him, this was the stuff of *silly science*. He was especially critical of attempts to legitimize the idea by applying terms that suggested *real* science. "Cellular memory" was one term that had gained a certain currency. Proponents of the cellular memory theory argued that individual cells of the heart could harbor knowledge that could be transplanted. Whenever the theory was espoused in his presence, Pace had a tendency to ask, with as little sarcasm in his tone as he could manage, why it was no one ever talked about cellular memory when livers and kidneys were transplanted. Could it be that patients took a somewhat less romantic view of those organs?

But with patients, Pace was ever respectful and considerate. When they raised these paranormal concerns, he told them these were areas in which science had few answers, and, depending on the particular needs of a given patient, he referred them either to a member of the clergy or to Maggie Pearson.

So when Pace himself grew restless in the weeks and months after transplantation, when he began to detect those first dissonant notes arising from someplace deep within his being, he did not look to *silly science* for an explanation. It was only natural, he reasoned, to have some degree of curiosity regarding the provenance of his new heart. And what sort of man would he be if he felt no sense of gratitude for the generosity of the donor and his family, or if he failed to seek a means, however token, to repay some tiny portion of the great debt he had incurred? It was a perfectly understandable human response. There was no need to invoke some parapsychological explanation.

Pace understood that he was treading on forbidden ground. So far as he knew, all cardiac transplant units had the same policy. They tried to maintain a firewall between the donor's family and the recipient. It was a seldom disobeyed rule, and Pace had not really expected Maggie to endorse his intention to violate it. But he did not require her approval. His mind was set.

It had been years since Pace Magruder had stepped inside a public library. From the time he entered medical school, his research needs had always been met by the resources of medical libraries. The information he needed was nearly always to be found in a recently published scientific journal, almost never in a book. The time required to write and publish books meant the information they contained was likely to be at least three years old—on the day they were published.

So Pace had anticipated the musty, creaky public library of his youth. He discovered instead a fresh, modern building that was a beehive of activity. Kids were everywhere. There were racks filled with paperback books—unheard of when Pace was young. They even had videos to check out. And the bright-eyed young man with the flowered shirt and ponytail was a far cry from the stern, elderly female—a dead ringer for his Aunt Mariah—who had been the archetypal librarian of Pace's youth.

"May I help you?" the young man asked.

"I need to look through copies of the *Herald-Dispatch* from about a year ago," Pace said, "if they're available. I'm looking for events that occurred on a specific date. I can't do that on their Internet site."

"No problem. Just follow me."

Pace expected to be led to a stack of moldering

newspapers in some far-off, dimly lit corner. Instead, the librarian went to a nearby computer terminal and popped in a CD.

"Do you know how to search a CD for what you want?"

"Sure," Pace said. Well, he was pretty sure. . . .

The librarian left him to his search, and Pace quickly got the hang of it.

He had firmly decided he would not use hospital records or impose on colleagues to identify the donor. In truth, he didn't think either would be necessary. When Brian first told Pace that a heart might become available, he had said it was a local heart and that the donor had been killed in a motor vehicle accident. Pace knew the date of the accident. It had to be the day of his transplant, or at most a day or two before. He essentially had everything *but* the donor's name. Pace figured the newspaper would give him that.

And it did. The story appeared below the fold on page one.

"Edward Jackson Long, Jr., the son of Senator Edward Long, died Tuesday of injuries sustained early that morning when the car he was driving veered off of the road and into a ravine. The accident occurred on Morgan Pike in rural Howard County. An unidentified passenger in the car was treated at Howard County Hospital and released.

"At the time of the accident, Senator Long was traveling with the president's party aboard Air Force One en route to the European economic summit. He is expected to return from Europe immediately. Tragically, the senator's wife, Miriam "Sunny" Long, also died in an automobile accident—nearly a decade ago. She was the former Miriam Burke, of the Richmond banking family. Edward Long, Jr., who was known as Ted, was their only child.

"The hospital released a statement from Dr. Joan Bennett, the attending physician, which said only that Mr. Long was pronounced dead at 4:00 P.M. Tuesday, and that death had been caused by massive head injuries.

"Mr. Charles Styles, the senator's chief of staff, remembered Ted Long as a wonderful, caring young man and the light of his father's life. 'Ted was planning a career of public service,' Styles said. 'He had hoped one day to follow in his father's footsteps, to serve both the state and the nation that he, like his father, loved so dearly.'

"Edward J. Long, Jr. was 21 years old. Memorial arrangements have not been announced."

Pace felt a lump in his throat. He had not expected to be so shaken. "Donor" was such a cold, clinical term. It stirred little emotion. But the donor now had a name, and a life story—however brief. Only twenty-one years, such a short time to live.

The fact that the donor was the son of the much-admired senator also had an effect. Edward Long was now serving his fourth term. His face was familiar to everyone, and because of the intimacy of television, he wasn't just some vague, distant figure. You felt like you really knew the man. If you bumped into him on the street, the natural impulse would be to reach for his hand and greet him warmly.

For Pace, the discovery rendered all the more poignant the events surrounding the donation of his new heart, and galvanized his need to do *something* to demonstrate his profound gratitude.

He couldn't yet be absolutely certain that Ted Long had been the donor. But Pace was pretty sure he knew how to find out.

—21—

Pace decided it would be easiest just to catch her at the end of her shift, so he called ahead to be certain he got the timing right. He arrived at the Howard County Hospital ER a little after four in the afternoon. Joan Bennett was hunched over a desk reviewing an EKG rhythm strip with a man who appeared to be in his early fifties—undoubtedly the doctor who was coming on duty to replace her.

Joan was filling him in on a case that was spilling over into the next shift.

"He's an eighteen-year-old kid who says that every once in a while his heart 'just starts to run away,' by which he means it beats very fast. When he came to the ER today, Judy took his pulse and said his rate was at least 150, but by the time she got the leads on him and ran an EKG, he was in normal sinus rhythm. So we didn't get to see what his tachycardia actually looked like.

"But here's his full EKG," she pulled it out of the patient's ER chart, "and it's certainly not normal."

Pace walked up behind them and read the EKG over Joan's shoulder. The ER doctors were so totally absorbed in studying the EKG they didn't notice his presence.

"I'm sure," Joan said, "that this is a syndrome we

should recognize. Any ideas, Rick?"

Rick shook his head.

"The PR interval is about .1," she said, "and there's this funny doohickey on the upstroke of a very wide QRS complex. There's a name for this, Rick. We just need to put our heads together . . . "

Still unnoticed, Pace nodded silent encouragement from behind.

Then Joan had it. "Wolff-Parkinson-White!"

"Good girl," Pace said.

Rick looked around first, his features reflecting a reaction somewhere between uncertainty and annoyance.

Then Joan looked up. "Pace!" She jumped to her feet and threw her arms around his neck.

"Rick Wells," she said, "meet Pace Magruder, the world's smartest cardiologist."

The two men shook hands. "Joan never was much of a judge of intellect," Pace said.

"Actually, Rick, I shouldn't even be talking to this guy. I was the only girl in the entire medical school he didn't ask out. I was crushed."

"You weren't crushed," Pace said. "You were married. How is the old painter anyway?"

"He's fine. His career has really taken off. You wouldn't believe what his work is selling for these days."

"Of course I would. I offered him a thousand dollars for a painting back in med school."

Joan shook her head. "You know what he wanted, Rick? He wanted David to do a *nude* painting. I'll let you guess *who* Pace wanted to be in the picture."

"And it had to be done realistically," Pace said. "I wasn't going to pay a thousand dollars for one of his abstracts, one you couldn't tell if it was a picture of

Joan or maybe just a bomb had gone off in a paint factory."

"Incorrigible," Joan said. "Anyway, Pace, what should we do with our case of the day?"

"How symptomatic is he?" Pace asked.

"Every month or two he feels the tachycardia. It lasts less than an hour—probably a *lot* less—and it's never caused any other symptoms."

"It doesn't sound like you need to start him on therapy today," Pace said. "If you can get him in to see a cardiologist right away, the cardiologist can follow him and make the therapeutic decisions. The patient needs electrophysiological studies and probably will be a candidate for radiofrequency catheter ablation. These days, surgery is rarely required."

"Sounds like just your kind of case," Joan said. Then, her voice softening, "Are you back seeing patients?"

"Not yet," Pace said. "But soon."

"Let me get one last patient squared away, Pace, then I'll let you buy me a cup of coffee."

Twenty minutes later they were in the hospital cafeteria, off in a far corner so they could talk.

"I heard about your transplant, Pace. You certainly look like you're doing wonderfully well."

"From what I understand, you more than just 'heard' about it. It sounds to me like I have you to thank for being alive."

Joan gave him a small smile. "At the time, I didn't even know you were sick. We just had a potential donor, and then it turned out that Brian Curtis was the surgeon who accepted the heart. Later, when I heard that you had been transplanted, it was pretty easy to put two and two together. The donor was such a big kid, and that's of course exactly what you needed—a big heart. I didn't know for certain, but I assumed you were the recipient. It made me very happy to feel I might have been able to play a small part in that."

Pace felt slightly devious, approaching Joan this way. He would never have asked her directly about his heart, but, one by one, she was filling in the blanks. The heart had come from Howard County. Brian was the accepting surgeon. Even the name of the donor was all but proven. Pace would get to that.

"I can't get over how terrific you look, Pace."

"I was a pretty sick puppy before the transplant, but since, I've had nothing but smooth sailing. Even the hepatitis C thing never materialized."

Joan shook her head. "That's too bad," she said, then she immediately realized how that sounded. She reached across the table and touched Pace's arm. "I'm sorry. That sounded awful. What I meant was, because of the concern about hep C, we didn't get takers for any of the other organs. That's really a shame. With 120,000 Americans waiting for organs, we can't afford to waste any."

"Well, at least you do have one very grateful recipient. I read your name in the news accounts of Ted Long's death, and I wanted to come and personally express my gratitude."

"Just doing my job, Pace. Same as you would have done."

"The newspaper said Senator Long was out of the country. That must have complicated the consent procedure."

"Actually, Long's chief of staff did show up at the hospital and initially tried to block the donation, but he had no legal standing. Permission for organ donation had been checked off on Ted's driver's license—which wasn't a big surprise given the senator's longstanding public support for organ donation."

"Why was the chief of staff opposed to the donation?"

Joan shrugged. "I don't know for certain. He was more into giving orders than discussing things. My guess is that, with the senator unavailable, his chief of staff felt responsible—or at least feared he would be *held* responsible—for anything that went wrong. And, too, he was being shadowed pretty closely by our sheriff. I don't know if there was some legal issue surrounding the accident, some investigation that might have been worrisome from a political point of view."

"When I heard about the hepatitis C," Pace said, "I naturally thought of intravenous drug abuse, that maybe drugs had played a role in the accident."

Joan shook her head. "Not as far as I know. The routine drug screens we ran didn't show anything. Looking back, one thing does stick in my mind. When we were checking Ted Long's driver's license, I noticed there was a whole lot of money in his wallet. I just got a quick peek, but it looked like a bunch of brand new hundred dollar bills. It could have been thousands of dollars. These days, when you see a kid with that kind of cash, you always think it might be related to drug dealing. On the other hand, Ted Long came from a very wealthy family, so maybe that was just chump change to him."

"Or maybe I'll suddenly develop a taste for cocaine," Pace said.

"Pace, I'm sorry. First I tell you it's too bad you didn't get hepatitis, then I suggest you got your heart from a drug dealer. I can't seem to keep my feet out of my mouth."

Pace smiled. "It's no big deal. The truth is the truth. Besides, I've sort of become curious about my new heart's previous owner. I owe him, and you, quite a lot."

They talked for a while about old times. Joan wanted to know if there was anyone special in Pace's life at the moment. Pace told her no, only his conditioning coach. When they walked out to their cars, he introduced her to Max. The dog was sitting impatiently in the driver's seat, with a tennis ball in his mouth.

"I promised Max I'd throw a few balls for him when I came out," Pace explained.

He opened the door and threw the ball as far as he could across the expanse of hospital lawn. Max was off like a shot.

"Thanks again, for everything," he told Joan. He gave her another last hug and put her in her car. By then, Max had returned, eager for Pace to give the ball another fling.

—22—

They were in the senator's office, up on the Hill, at the end of a long, gray Washington day. Styles had been waiting for the right moment to tell him and decided now was as good a time as any.

"We got a call today," he told the senator, "from Magruder."

Senator Long had his feet up on his desk, his leather chair tilted back as far as it would go. His eyes, closed tight in a vain effort to assuage an excruciating headache, blinked open involuntarily in response to Styles' news.

"Well," the senator said, "we always knew we'd hear from him, sooner or later. I'm amazed it took this long. What did the good doctor have to say?"

"That he had just learned Ted was the donor, that he'd like the opportunity to visit with you personally to express his gratitude."

Long sighed deeply and closed his eyes once again. "Is there any way to avoid it? Couldn't we just say that the wound is still too fresh, such a meeting would simply be too much for Ted's grief-stricken father to endure?"

Styles shook his head. "I wouldn't risk leaving him dangling like that. Better to go for closure. Meet with him. Let him express his appreciation, then let that be the end of it. Finito. You're pleased that he was able to benefit from your son's gift, but you subtly suggest you're not interested in establishing any kind of ongoing relationship. *That* is something your grief-stricken heart definitely could not endure."

"I suppose you're right," Long said. "Any news from the district attorney's office?"

"As near as I can tell, there hasn't been any active investigation for months. The case isn't closed—it may never be closed—but it's just as good as."

The senator opened his eyes and looked at his chief of staff. "It *will* never be closed. You can take that to the bank. And don't ever count Tommy Jacobs out. That man is driven by a voracious ambition. Nothing makes a man more relentless than ambition. And that little piece of arm candy he brought with him that night, Carrie, whatever her name was—Bond, that one—she looked like she was cut from the same bolt of cloth."

Long brought his hands up and pressed the heels against his temples. The lancinating pain behind his eyes abated, but only briefly.

"So, Chuck, what should we do?"

"Invite Magruder up to the house some weekend afternoon," Styles said, "and let him unburden himself for a little while. Give him a chance to be grateful, but let him know that, psychologically speaking, you've moved on—reluctantly, but necessarily. Then, when the time's right, we'll do the presidential phone call routine and send him on his merry way."

"Okay, Chuck, set it up. And could you see if somebody in the outer office has a couple of aspirin?"

Pace's mind was not entirely at ease as he drove up the long, winding driveway that Saturday afternoon.

He had no anxiety about meeting the famous senator per se. In his medical practice, Pace had frequently attended the rich and famous and found them to run the gamut of human character attributes—pretty much like everybody else. In fact, as an admirer of the senator's stands on many important public issues, Pace would have, under normal circumstances, looked forward to the meeting.

But these were certainly not ordinary circumstances. The heart of Senator Long's only child was now beating within Pace's chest—the elephant in the room that neither man could ignore.

On the phone, when he first spoke with the senator's chief of staff, Pace had felt awkward, uncertain how much to say. How would they know he wasn't just some nutcase trying to get close to the senator to commit who knew what unspeakable act? But Styles had been sympathetic. He had seemed eager to bring Pace and Senator Long together. The worry dogging Pace's mind was that the senator might not share his aide's enthusiasm.

Pace was troubled by the possibility that his visit might, however inadvertently, inflict additional pain rather than provide the solace and closure Pace intended. But this concern was dispelled the moment Pace arrived at Senator Long's front door.

It opened before Pace had a chance to knock. The man in the doorway would have been recognized by most Americans, but the expression on his face was one Pace hadn't seen before. It was neither the well-known look of grim determination, nor that wide, triumphant, election-day smile. It was an expression constrained by events—the kind of look you might see on the face of a man who chanced to meet one old friend at the funeral of another. It was a look nearly identical to the one on Pace's face.

"Dr. Magruder," the senator said, extending his hand, "so thoughtful of you to come by."

"I don't mean to intrude," Pace said. "I just hoped to have the opportunity to express my gratitude in person."

"No intrusion at all. Please, come in."

He released Pace's hand and ushered him through the entry hall and into the large, elegantly furnished living room. Pace declined the offer of something to drink, and the two settled into wing chairs on either side of the fireplace. The senator did not permit an awkward silence to develop.

"First of all," he said, "I want to thank you for that thoughtful letter you sent. I keep it in my desk." He nodded toward the large burr elm desk that stood in an alcove at the far end of the living room.

"It was just a meager attempt," Pace said, "at expressing my feelings. Of course, at the time, I had no idea who the donor was."

"Of course," Long said. "Now, if it's all right with you, I'd like for you to know a little bit about Ted."

"I'd like that very much," Pace said.

"He was such a wonderful son." Long's words were accompanied by a fleeting, radiant smile. His voice wavered at first, then grew more confident. "Ted was a gifted student and a fine athlete, but it was his character I was most proud of. You couldn't ever hope to meet a more thoughtful, more caring young man."

The senator's smile returned. "I'm not trying to tell you he was perfect. He was all boy—especially in his younger days. He had his share of scrapes, just like any other kid. And his mother, God rest her soul, had a tendency to spoil him—she simply doted on the boy—and she was always showering money on him.

But that's all in the distant past. More recently—as an adult really—Ted had truly found his footing. He was destined for great things.

"Had you heard he was headed for a career in public service?"

Pace nodded. "I read that in the newspaper."

"It wouldn't have surprised me," Long said, "if one day he had come to occupy my seat in the Senate. But there would have been no reason for him to stop there. He was the kind of young man you looked at and realized that he really had no limits. He could have been president someday. There's no doubt about it."

Pace was deeply touched by the father's words. "I can't tell you how sorry I am, Senator, that he didn't have the opportunity to pursue those dreams."

"Thank you, Dr. Magruder. And, for my part, it's a comfort to know that Ted, even in death, was able to give the gift of life to a fine person such as yourself."

"There's hardly a moment that goes by that I'm not mindful of that gift. I will be forever grateful." Pace was painfully aware of the insufficiency of mere words.

"What kind of medicine do you practice?"

"Ironically enough, cardiology. I guess 'practiced' would be more accurate. When I became ill, I had no choice but to go on disability, but I'll soon be rejoining the medical school faculty."

At that moment a third man entered the living room. "I'm sorry to interrupt," he said.

"Dr. Magruder," the senator said, "I'd like you to meet my chief of staff, Chuck Styles."

Pace stood and offered his hand. "It's a pleasure to meet you, Mr. Styles. Thank you for arranging for me to meet with Senator Long."

"My pleasure, Doctor."

Then Styles turned and said something to Long that Pace couldn't quite hear. The senator immediately rose to his feet.

"I'm afraid something has come up, Dr. Magruder. The president's on the line, and of course I must take the call. It's probably about all this uneasiness in the Middle East. I don't know how long I'll be."

"I understand completely," Pace said. "You've been more than generous with your time."

"I'm glad we had this talk, Doctor. I can't say that the circumstances aren't a little difficult for me. The pain of losing Ted is still very near the surface. It always will be. Still, I'm glad we had this opportunity to meet—just this once."

"And let me say, one last time, how very grateful I am," Pace said. "If there is ever anything I might be able to do to somehow return, in some small measure, your generosity, I hope you won't hesitate to contact me."

"You're very gracious, Dr. Magruder." Long offered his hand one last time. Then Pace shook Styles' hand once again.

"You gentlemen have important responsibilities to attend to," Pace said. "I'll just show myself out."

—23—

Max was bored out of his gourd. He kept bringing his tennis ball up to Pace and dropping it on the hardwood floor, creating a surprising amount of racket in the otherwise silent house. Pace would give the back of Max's head a quick rub and say, "Not now, Max." Then Max would go lie down for a while and make loud, sonorous, sighing sounds in hope of gaining Pace's attention.

These actions comprised phases one and two of Max's painstakingly structured attention-seeking behavior. Phase three included the performance of forbidden acts—lying on the couch, helping himself to food left on kitchen counters or in accessible cabinets, etcetera. Phase four involved wanton acts of destruction—knocking over lamps, the chewing of shoes or chair legs, and other such activities that could not be ignored.

"Don't even think about it," Pace warned.

Max had been seriously put out when Pace went off to his meeting with Senator Long and didn't take him along for the ride. The brief workout he received when Pace came home was viewed by Max as woefully inadequate.

But Pace was preoccupied. He had come away from the senator's house with renewed determination to find some tangible means of expressing his gratitude. It was the kind of thing that was much too easy to put off—indefinitely—and Pace was not about to let that happen.

Pace sat himself down in front of his computer and logged onto the Internet.

His plan wasn't complicated. He wanted to learn more about Senator Long's major interests and activities, with a view toward discovering a favored charity or organization that Pace could contribute to—time, money, or both—as a means of demonstrating that his gratitude extended beyond mere empty words.

When he was online, Pace searched the term "Edward Long."

He hit "enter."

The search returned 27,856 hits. Way too many to deal with.

The hits represented the usual swarm of sources. Many were links to legitimate newspaper and magazine articles, but there were also links to the full spectrum of special interest groups, chat rooms, and personal web pages that most Internet searches returned. It was all pretty much what Pace expected to find. It also reminded him that, when you do a search under "Edward Long," the computer doesn't know you're only interested in *Senator* Edward Long. There were lots of other Edward Longs in the world.

Pace was about to recast his search using the term "Senator Edward Long" when he made a discovery that caused him to forget all about his interest in the senator's charitable activities. One of the Edward Longs who turned up in the search was the senator's son. And the context in which Ted's name arose was rape and murder.

Pace immediately performed another search, this

time using "Edward Long murder." He got a couple hundred hits that he scanned quickly, finding links to only two legitimate newspaper articles. The first was a follow-up story on the brutal rape and murder of a young woman named Francine Lovett. The story had been published ten days after Pace's transplant operation, more than two weeks after the murder was committed. The death of Francine Lovett had obviously received a great deal of attention locally, but Pace had been so ill in those last pre-transplant days he hadn't followed the news. The gist of the newspaper account was that there had been no breakthrough in the investigation. The reference to Ted Long came at the very end.

"The *Herald-Dispatch* has learned from sources close to the investigation that, prior to his recent death, prosecutors sought to question Edward Long, Jr., the son of Senator Edward Long, in regard to the crime. Prosecutors were frustrated when the late Mr. Long failed to appear for a scheduled interview. Because of his subsequent death in a motor vehicle accident, Mr. Long was never questioned in the matter."

The second article was mostly just a reaction to the first. Prosecutors were furious about the leak.

"Assistant District Attorney Courtney Bond would not comment on the investigation into the Lovett murder except to emphatically deny that the District Attorney's office was the source of any of the published information."

There was also a statement from Senator Long's office expressing indignation that Ted's name had been linked in any way to the murder. "Prosecutors had hoped that Edward Long, Jr. might have witnessed some aspect of the crime, and that he might have been able to provide information to assist their investigation. As it turned out, he had no such information. Eyewitness testimony regarding Edward Long, Jr.'s activities at the time of the crime proved unequivocally that he could not have been a witness."

For its part, the *Herald-Dispatch* reiterated that it had only reported that prosecutors had sought to question the senator's son and were frustrated by their inability to do so. The *Herald-Dispatch* stood by its story.

That ended the issue so far as the legitimate press was concerned, but the Internet is an entirely different beast. The conspiracy theorists were out in full force, claiming not only that Edward Long, Jr. had committed rape and murder, but that his father, with the assistance of various law enforcement and/or intelligence agencies, had successfully engaged in a cover-up that had obstructed the investigation.

It was alleged that, by the time the local district attorney's office learned of Ted Long's death in rural Howard County, the body had already been cremated. A subpoena had been issued, it was claimed, to compel the hospital to turn over any specimens in its possession that might yield DNA for comparison to DNA found at the crime scene. When the hospital attempted to comply with the subpoena, it discovered all relevant laboratory samples to be inexplicably missing.

Now, nearly a year later, the conspiracy buffs still refused to let go of the story. In their minds the fact that the crime remained unsolved after so long a time only buttressed the cover-up hypothesis. Much was made of the fact that Senator Long was aboard Air Force One at the time of his son's death. This was cited as clear evidence of involvement of the federal government.

Then it hit Pace.

Nowhere in any of the articles was there any mention that Ted's heart had been donated.

And that gave Pace the first spark of an idea, something he might be able to do for the senator, something tangible that might begin to repay a portion of the debt he owed.

—24—

First thing next morning, Pace called the DA's office.

"This is Pace Magruder calling for Ms. Courtney Bond."

"Who?" the woman asked.

"Courtney Bond."

"No, who's calling?"

"Pace Magruder."

"Ace?"

"No. Pace. 'P' as in Patrick."

"Oh, Patrick. And what is this concerning?"

"I have evidence regarding the Francine Lovett murder."

"One moment please. I'll see if Ms. Bond is available."

Pace wasn't too sure how much to reveal over the phone. He figured the best thing was to play his cards close to the vest. Just tell her whatever it took to get his foot in the door.

"Courtney Bond," the voice said.

Pace knew nothing about her other than her name, which he'd seen in the newspaper article, but he had a pretty good idea who he was talking to—the stereotypic long-suffering public employee. Overworked and jaded, she was probably clinging to her job by a fingernail, hoping she could hang on just a couple more years until retirement.

"This is Pace Magruder, Ms. Bond. I have some evidence regarding the Francine Lovett murder, and I'd like to come to your office to discuss it with you."

"What kind of evidence, Mr. Magruder?"

"I'd rather not go into it over the phone. It's really something we need to discuss in person."

There was a very long pause on the other end.

"Look, Mr. Magruder, I spend most of my day in court. It's very difficult for me to have any idea when I might be available. If you could just give me some idea of what your evidence is."

"It relates to the son of Senator Edward Long," he said.

Again, silence.

"I expect to be out of court by five," she said, "but I can't guarantee it. If you're willing to take the risk, you can come down to my office and wait. If I'm not there by five, feel free to either hang around and wait or just go ahead and leave."

"Thank you, Ms. Bond. I'll be there."

"Let me be sure I've got your first name right. Is it Patrick or Ace?"

It was the story of his life.

Pace arrived fifteen minutes ahead of time to find the assistant DA's door closed and no response to his knock. He took a seat on a bench down the hall and waited. And waited.

At 5:30, he decided it was pointless to stay any longer. As he walked down the hall he passed a trim young blond headed in the opposite direction. She had a briefcase in one hand and a stack of files under the opposite arm and appeared to be utterly immersed in thought. Being male, Pace's mind registered the fact that he was in the immediate vicinity of an attractive female, but if he had not happened to hear her stop and put the key in her lock, it would not have occurred to him that she was the woman he was scheduled to meet.

"Ms. Bond?"

She was by then fifteen or twenty feet away, trying to open her door with the hand that was holding the briefcase and absolutely determined to accomplish the feat without setting down the stack of files still pinned under her other arm. She glanced in his direction and threw him a sort of half smile, the kind you use if you're pretty certain you're being accosted by a total stranger, but it might turn out to be someone you should have recognized.

"Can I give you a hand?" Pace offered as he approached.

"I'm fine," she said—but the door didn't budge. She reached to give the key another turn, which gave gravity a free hand with the stack of files. She said something under her breath that was probably profane. Pace had the files before they hit the floor.

"Thank you," she said. A little more of a smile this time.

"I'm Pace Magruder," he said.

Her smile vanished. "I'm Courtney Bond."

He followed her into her office, a small room off the central hallway. She cleared a place for him to sit, then relieved him of the files he was still holding. When she took a seat behind her desk, Pace had the definite impression she regarded it as a protective barricade.

"I'm sorry to have kept you waiting, Mr. Magruder. Now, what's this evidence you've discovered?"

"I'm not sure 'discovered' is quite the right word,

Ms. Bond. Actually, it's been in my possession for quite some time."

She greeted this information with a rather weary expression. "What *is* your evidence, Mr. Magruder?"

With bright sunlight streaming through her office window, Pace was able to confirm his initial impression that Courtney Bond was an extremely good looking woman, but she seemed to have a serious attitude problem. He wasn't certain just exactly what her hang-up was, but he was beginning to believe that perhaps she wasn't the right person for him to be talking to.

"Could I just ask one question?" he said. "Is Edward Long, Jr. a suspect in the Lovett case?"

"What makes you ask that?"

"I have that impression from the newspapers and from some of what I've found on the Internet."

"We haven't named a suspect in the case. Beyond that I can't comment—except to say it's not a good idea to believe everything you see on the Internet."

Was she *trying* to be offensive? Pace was starting to get a little irritated. "I assume there is crime scene DNA that has been preserved, but I understand that none of Mr. Long's DNA is available for comparison."

"Without giving away too much, I think I can tell you that, yes, there is crime scene evidence available that contains DNA, and, as you are undoubtedly aware, Edward Long, Jr. is deceased. His body was cremated, and none of his DNA is available for testing."

"I'm sorry, Ms. Bond. I don't mean to be so mysterious. It's just that, from what I've read, I have the impression that Ted Long was, for some reason, considered to be a suspect, but that he had an ironclad alibi and couldn't have committed the crime. In spite of that, it looks like the conspiracy theorists have gotten into this thing, and I'm certain that is very unpleasant for Ted Long's family. If my DNA evidence could clear him, that would be useful to your investigation, and it would also take the weight of suspicion off the backs of his family."

"Let me get this straight, Mr. Magruder. You're offering me a sample of Ted Long's DNA?"

"Exactly."

"And how is it you happen to have come into possession of his DNA?" Her tone had gone from healthy skepticism to total incredulity.

"About a year ago, I had a heart transplant. Ted Long was the donor."

She did not appear convinced. "And, supposing that's true, how does that help us? Are you planning to just hand over your heart and let us run it down to the lab for testing?"

Supposing that's true? Pace took a deep breath. "There's a simple procedure called a cardiac biopsy. It's done routinely after heart transplantation. There are some minor technical issues that would have to be dealt with, but testing the DNA should be relatively straightforward."

Courtney was suddenly on her feet. "I want to thank you for coming in and offering to let us biopsy your heart, Mr. Magruder. I'll just run this by my superiors and see what they have to say, then I'll get back to you."

A few seconds later she had ushered Pace into the hall and shut the door behind him.

Courtney slumped back into her chair and sighed. The meeting with this Magruder character had gone just about as she had expected. With any luck she'd never hear from him again.

Every time she thought she'd seen it all, some wacko walked into her office and proved her wrong. She'd had some pretty strange offers in her career as a prosecutor, but no one had ever before offered to let her biopsy his heart!

And if that strapping fellow she'd just thrown out of her office had had a heart transplant, then she was the Queen of England. Why were the good looking ones always so weird?

She opened her briefcase and tried to get her mind back on her afternoon in court, but didn't have much success. Finally, she checked her watch, then looked up the number of the Howard County Hospital in her file.

"Howard County Hospital." The operator sounded more weary than Courtney.

"May I have the ER, please."

A few seconds later, the emergency room clerk came on the line. "ER. May I help you?"

"May I speak with Dr. Joan Bennett, please?"

"She's not on call this evening."

Courtney didn't know what she'd done with Bennett's home number. Besides, this was no emergency. "Will she be in tomorrow?"

"Yes, at 8:00 A.M."

"Could you ask her to call Courtney Bond when she has a chance?" Courtney gave the woman her office number.

"Are you a patient, Ms. Bond?"

"No," Courtney said, then hesitated, "it's a personal matter."

—25—

Pace heard the phone ringing from outside the house as he and Max were returning from a morning jog. By the time he picked up the receiver, there was no one on the line. It rang again when Pace was in the shower. He tried to ignore it, but that was easier said than done—vestigial guilt from his days and nights on call. He made a dash for the phone, sloshing water along the way.

"Hello?"

"Dr. Magruder?" her voice hauntingly familiar, but perplexingly pleasant.

"Yes."

"This is Courtney Bond—from the district attorney's office?"

"Yes." The last person in the world he expected to hear from—after she'd given him the bum's rush out of her office just the night before.

"I'd like to meet with you again, if I could—as soon as possible. I'll be tied up in court all day. Would it be possible for us to meet tonight after work? Maybe I could buy you a drink?"

The last person in the world he'd expected to call, asking absolutely the very last question he expected to hear.

"Sure," he said. "Why not?"

It had been a long time since Pace had been in a bar at six o'clock on a weeknight. The place was packed, clearly a favorite among young singles who worked downtown. Noxious music played loudly from hidden speakers.

Courtney had commandeered a booth a safe distance from the epicenter of the pandemonium. She waved him over as soon as he came through the door, then stood and offered her hand as he approached. She was wearing the kind of dark business suit that career women often wear—designed to conceal feminine curves so that their male colleagues will take them seriously and not become unduly distracted. Pace thought she had a ways to go to perfect the concealment concept.

"Thanks for coming, Dr. Magruder. I didn't realize what a zoo this place is. It was recommended by someone I trusted—up until just now. I hope you don't mind."

"It's fine," he said. "Call me Pace."

"I'm Courtney," she said. "The next thing I need to apologize for is yesterday. As you may have realized, I wasn't buying your story."

"I had that impression. Please, have a seat."

Courtney sat back down and Pace slid into the booth on the other side of the table.

"You were sort of asking a lot of questions," she said, "and at first I thought you might be with some newspaper or magazine, trying to get background for a story. Or some lawyer could have sent you around to see if we had any new leads. Then, when you started in with the DNA and the heart transplant and the heart *biopsy*, I decided maybe what you really needed was a *brain* transplant. I was ready to label you *non compos mentis*. We see just about every kind of crazy there is, just about every day. After a while, you begin to expect it."

Pace smiled. "I may be a little nuts, but everything I said was true."

"Oh, I know that now. But I've got to tell you, yesterday, I didn't believe a word you said. You really dropped a bombshell on me. To the best of my knowledge, until you came in yesterday, no one in the DA's office had any idea that Ted Long's heart had been transplanted."

"You're kidding."

Courtney shook her head. "That's what I thought, How could we possibly *not* have known? But when you think about it, it's not so terribly surprising. The Long family obviously didn't want the fact made public, and the medical community did its job—maintaining the family's privacy. The news media never got hold of it, or, if they did, a decision was made to respect the wishes of the family. It was all *don't ask, don't tell.*

"The other thing that worked against us was the fact that Howard County is outside our jurisdiction. That and the fact that Ted Long was never formally a suspect meant there never was a real investigation.

"At any rate, when you said you'd had Ted Long's heart transplanted into you, I thought. . ." She made a rapid circular motion around her ear with her index finger. "And, if you don't mind my saying it—you look more like a lumberjack than a guy with a heart condition."

Pace smiled. "It's not that kind of heart condition— not anymore." Then he said, "So why am I suddenly so much more credible today than yesterday?"

Courtney gave him a slightly embarrassed smile. "I did do a little investigating a while back, and I got to know Joan Bennett. So I gave her a call, and she straightened me out. You've got a real fan there. She said she'd be more than willing to get a divorce if you ever showed the slightest interest."

"She's a happily married lady," Pace said.

"She said that with fifteen minutes' notice, she could begin a trial separation."

A waitress came to take their drink orders, and they ended up ordering a half bottle of a California Chardonnay.

When the waitress had gone, Courtney asked about the biopsy. "Joan said she was no expert on heart biopsies, but it wasn't quite as big a deal as it sounded."

"It's not nothing," Pace said, "but it's part of the post-transplant routine. The point is, I'm going to have the biopsy anyway—to look for evidence that my body might be rejecting the transplant. So why not take full advantage of it? There'll be technical issues you'll have to sort out with whoever tests the DNA. My own DNA might contaminate the biopsy specimen, but testing laboratories have lots of experience in dealing with contamination problems, mostly in rape cases where there's always the issue of distinguishing the DNA of the rapist from that of the victim. In this case, my DNA profile can be treated as a known. It can just be subtracted out."

Courtney was suddenly very serious. "There could be some real danger in this for you."

"Like I said, I'm going to have the biopsy either way—to look for rejection."

Courtney shook her head. "That's not what I meant. We're dealing with a rape and murder. There's likely to be at least one person who doesn't want this case to be solved."

"But that's not going to be Ted Long," Pace said. "In

the first place, he's dead. And, in the second place, my understanding is that no one really believes he had anything to do with the crime. That's what got me involved, the idea that this will *clear* Ted Long. If that's within my power, it's something I'd like to do."

"I looked at some of the stuff that's floating around on the Internet," Courtney said. "And we've gotten some anonymous calls at our office. There is no doubt there's someone out there who very much wants us to believe that Ted Long was the murderer, and it may not just be the usual random crazies. If Francine Lovett's murderer is still alive, it's awfully convenient for him that we have another suspect who can never be cleared."

"Now *that* does sound nutty," Pace said. "You think someone would come after me to prevent Ted Long from being exonerated?"

"The people who commit these types of crimes aren't always as rational as you and me," Courtney said. "Let me tell you about the brain trust I was up against in court today—the Dobson brothers.

"These guys are part of the white supremacist, anti-government, survivalist, paramilitary, lunatic fringe. The only people they tolerate are the other members of their merry band. Everybody else, they hate.

"At any rate, about five years ago, these two troglodytes strolled into town to pillage the populace, and set their collective eye on a Korean immigrant named Mr. Kim who happened to operate a small convenience store. The Dobson boys stormed Mr. Kim's little store like it was Pork Chop Hill. One came in the front, the other came in the back. Both had assault rifles. Within seconds there was a full-scale firefight under way.

"When the smoke cleared, both the Dobson

brothers were down. Mr. Kim was hiding behind the counter where he'd been throughout the onslaught. You see, Mr. Kim hates guns. Never owned one, wouldn't touch one. The Dobsons had just had this fierce gun battle with each other. Nearly killed themselves."

"Those boys aren't into rape, are they?"

"They would be," Courtney said, "if they were smart enough to think of it."

"Anyway," she said, "once they were out of the hospital, the Dobsons were packed off to prison, and if it had ended there, our little story would have a happy ending. But sadly our boys' criminal careers were not yet over. About a month ago they were released. And what do you think was the first thing they wanted to do?"

Pace didn't have a clue.

"Get even with Mr. Kim, of course—that no-good immigrant foreigner who'd caused them to have to go to prison. But Mr. Kim had had enough of our fair city. He'd long since sold the store and moved west. But that didn't stop our dynamic duo. They hit the shop again, apparently not noticing that it was now a dry cleaning establishment and that the woman behind the counter—a tough old bird by the name of Olsen— was very unlikely to be even distantly related to Mr. Kim.

"The other thing that was new, Mrs. Olsen has a thing for guns. Absolutely loves 'em. Had two pistols right under the counter. And the Dobson brothers, having previously learned a costly lesson about the dangers of firearms, this time came armed with only a tire iron and a hunting knife. The minute they threatened Mrs. Olsen, she opened up with both guns. The rest was just like last time. Once the smoke cleared, both Dobson's were down and on their way back to prison.

"Of course they're entitled to a trial, and they're not about to make the same mistake they made last time—get a lawyer from the public defender's office. No way. These guys don't need an attorney. They're acting as their own counsel. They'd be lucky if they only had a fool for a client.

"Today I got to cross-examine Keith. He's the smart one, the one with the fifth grade education. The court gets to hear Keith's theory of the law, which is that he was fully entitled to seek revenge on Mr. Kim. But what, I asked, does that have to do with your attempt to assault and rob poor Mrs. Olsen?

"Keith gets this sly look on his face, like I've finally asked the question he's been waiting for—that high, hanging curve ball he can smack right out of the park. He squints at me and says, 'How'd we know she wasn't adopted?'

"That's their theory of the case—not guilty by reason of suspected adoption. Like if the Dobsons could just convince people it was reasonable for them to have believed that Mrs. Olsen was in some way related to the dastardly Mr. Kim, there wasn't a jury in the world that would convict them."

Pace could only shake his head. "I trust the Dobsons aren't going to be back on the street any time soon."

"Not unless they find a better lawyer." Courtney took a sip of her wine. "I just wanted to give you some idea of what I deal with, day in and day out, so maybe you could find a way to forgive the attitude I had yesterday."

"I understand. Medicine sometimes gets a little relentless too."

They traded a few more war stories, getting comfortable with each other. Pace decided that, down in the trenches, the practice of medicine and the practice of law had a lot in common.

They'd been talking for more than an hour when Courtney stole a peek at her watch. "I'm afraid I'm going to have to get going. I have to face Keith Dobson's closing argument first thing in the morning. It'll probably be the old standby of not recognizing the authority of the court to try them, but I haven't given up hope that Keith will treat us to one of his more novel theories."

"Good luck," Pace said.

"Thanks," she said. "I'll need a couple of days to organize things for the handling of the heart specimen. Is the biopsy already scheduled?"

"Next Wednesday."

"So I'll get back to you this week. The DA agrees that this is a worthwhile thing to pursue. If nothing else, it might eliminate one potential suspect. We appreciate your coming forward and making the offer."

"I figure it might help to unburden the senator's load a little."

"I'm sure you're right," Courtney said. "I want to apologize one last time for yesterday." She offered Pace her hand.

"Water under the bridge," he said, taking her hand.

"And I'm sorry about this place too," Courtney said. "Not really my kind of place. Not really my kind of music."

"What kind of music do you like?" Pace was intensely aware that he was still holding her hand.

"Did you ever hear of Roy Orbison?" she asked.

"When do I get to see you again?" he said.

—26—

The call from the senator's chief of staff came the following afternoon. Styles was polite but cryptic. The senator would be coming down from Washington tomorrow, could Pace possibly come out to the house for a meeting in the late afternoon?

"Sure," Pace said, "I'd be glad to."

He had not expected another meeting with Senator Long—ever. The last time they met, Long had signaled, subtly but unambiguously, that Pace's presence was simply too painful a reminder of his son's death. But something must have occurred to the senator, perhaps some lingering uncertainty that Pace could somehow allay. Pace was more than willing to provide whatever consolation he could.

Pace arrived to find several cars parked in front of the Senator's mansion, suggesting he was not to be the only guest. Pace had not even considered the possibility that Long had summoned him for purely social reasons.

He didn't know what the senator had in mind, but Pace wasn't about to let himself be put on display—here's the guy who got my son's heart; come take a look.

It was Styles who opened the door. The chief of staff seemed distant, formal.

"Thank you for coming, Dr. Magruder. This way, please."

Pace was shown into the same large living room as before. This time Senator Long was seated at the far end, behind the massive elm desk. Two tall, serious-looking men stood on either side of the senator. Long didn't bother to get up as Pace approached.

"Dr. Magruder, allow me to introduce Lawrence Faye and Robert Horvath." The two men nodded but remained implanted behind the desk. "Larry and Bob have handled my family's legal affairs for decades, and they represent the estate of my late son."

"Gentlemen," Pace said. He had no idea where this was headed, but he wasn't sensing any warm and fuzzy sentiments emanating from the other side of the desk.

"When you were here before," Long said, "I tried to convey to you some sense of how difficult the last year has been for me, to give you some comprehension of the depth of my grief. I believed then that you understood my position. I now know that you did not. Tell me, Doctor, do you have children?"

"No, Senator, I don't." What could possibly have prompted Long's dramatic change in attitude?

"Perhaps," the senator said, "that is the explanation. Perhaps one who has not had children to love can't be expected to comprehend the despair of a father who has lost a son. It's like asking a blind man to appreciate a painting. The requisite faculty is wanting."

"Senator," Pace said, "if my contacting you has caused pain, I am truly sorry. I had intended just the opposite. I had thought you might find comfort in seeing the tangible effect of your son's generous gift. If this has brought you sorrow instead of solace, all I can do is apologize once more and assure you I will never again impose on you."

The senator's face colored instantly. "But you *are* imposing on me! That's precisely the problem!"

Pace was truly mystified. "Senator, I am here at *your* request."

Finally, one of the statues spoke. It was Horvath. "It's this business of the biopsy, resurrecting all of those old, tawdry lies."

Oh. *Now* Pace understood. How the hell had Long found out about the biopsy?

"I wanted to do something to show my gratitude, Senator, in some more substantial way. When I discovered all those ugly stories circulating on the Internet, I knew how hurtful they must be. It's like the unending theorizing about the Kennedy assassination. No one ever stops to think how difficult that must be for the family. I can't do anything to help the Kennedys, but in your case I thought, I can put an end to all of that. I can stop that pain."

Long was violently shaking his head. "But all that talk had *finally* started to die down! Now you're about to start it up all over again."

Long was either in denial or he simply didn't know the truth. "I've checked out what's on the Internet," Pace said. "If anything, the discussions about your son are increasing. There's no sign whatsoever that this is dying down."

Long tried another tack. "You say you want to do something to demonstrate your appreciation. Well, here's your chance. Don't go through with this biopsy business. That's the favor I'm asking."

This was Long's most compelling argument, the one Pace was most susceptible to. And it gave Pace pause. He might have wavered had Faye not decided at just that moment to jump in.

"We'll get a court order if we have to. When Ted checked off permission on his driver's license, allowing his organs to be donated, he did so with the expectation that those organs would be treated with dignity and that his privacy would be respected." As he spoke, Faye's voice became ever louder, his tone more shrill.

"You, Doctor, are depriving him of that right to privacy, stripping his memory of that dignity. I assure you, if you go ahead with this biopsy, we will file suit. We will pursue this matter to the full extent of the law."

Making threats was not a good way to gain Pace's cooperation.

"Don't insult my intelligence, Mr. Faye. The biopsy is going to happen because it's medically indicated. It's a necessary procedure, and there's not a thing you can do to stop it. And the legal action you're suggesting would be aimed at preventing the district attorney from availing himself of important evidence in a murder investigation. There's not a court in the world that would interfere with that. Besides, we both know that such a case would never be brought. How would Senator Long explain to the voters that he wanted to deprive the state of that evidence?"

Pace turned his attention back to the senator. "I'm sorry, Senator, that it has come to this. It was my understanding that your son had an ironclad alibi, and that he could not have been involved in any way in that terrible crime. Given that, I don't see how a DNA analysis can do anything but remove a stain on his memory. I cannot for the life of me understand why you would not want that to happen."

The room was silent. There was really nothing more to say.

Pace turned and stalked out.

—27—

Pace was having a restless night. Finally, at about four in the morning, he dragged himself downstairs to talk things over with Max. The dog wasn't in such a hot mood either, still a little miffed at having been left behind when Pace drove to the senator's house the afternoon before.

Pace sat on the couch. Max lay at his feet, cocking his head as he listened intently and tried to make sense of what Pace was saying.

"You know, Max, when you're up to your waist in alligators, it's sometimes difficult to recall just exactly why you waded into the swamp in the first place."

Max sighed heavily.

Pace's only goal had been to begin to pare away the massive debt he owed. His efforts had achieved nothing but animosity.

"No kind deed goes unpunished for long," he reminded Max.

Max swished his tail.

But now there was a larger issue on the table. The only logical explanation for Senator Long's attitude was that the senator knew the DNA evidence would incriminate his son. Pace wasn't happy with this turn of events, but it wasn't something he could back away from. If Ted Long was a killer, the state—not to mention the family of Francine Lovett—was entitled to the truth.

It was perhaps understandable that Senator Long would not want his son's actions to be exposed. He might even have rationalized that, with both Ted and Francine Lovett dead, no useful purpose would be served by revealing the truth. And for his part, Pace was not overjoyed at the prospect of proving that his transplanted heart had previously belonged to a rapist and murderer.

But all of that presented no moral dilemma for Pace. He was saddened that things had turned out this way, but his course was clear, and the patently empty threats of Long's lawyers had done nothing but stiffen his resolve. Long would have to come up with something a whole lot more ominous than those hollow threats if he hoped to do anything other than simply goad Pace forward.

Pace was in Boyd Edington's office, ostensibly to discuss rejoining the faculty. Edington seemed preoccupied. He was doing a lot of the cleaning-his-glasses-with-his-tie thing.

"A small problem has arisen," Edington said. "It's about the Wolfe litigation."

"The 'wrongful-life' suit?" Pace said. "Everybody assured me it would just go away. The medical school's attorneys said it was nothing more than a nuisance suit, that it would never make it to trial. They said I was fully protected under the Good Samaritan law."

"Well, they've changed their tune. The plaintiff is alleging gross negligence.

That effectively removes your Good Samaritan status. The medical school wants to settle the suit and cut its losses."

Pace fought to keep his tone of voice even, to keep the anger he was feeling from breaking through to the surface. "That may make sense for the medical school, but it's not going to look very good on my record. It could be perceived as an admission that I committed malpractice. I didn't."

Edington shrugged. "It seems proving that may be more difficult than our lawyers originally believed. Of course, you don't have to accept the medical school's decision. You are free to retain your own lawyers and fight on, but, as you know, you would then be required to personally bear the expense. It could be very costly, and, even should you prevail legally, I doubt you would be able to recoup your costs."

"When you say 'the medical school wants to settle the suit,'" Pace asked, "who do you mean? Who is 'the medical school'?"

"Ultimately, the dean. He's the one who has to make the financial determination, with the advice of various others in the administration—as well as the lawyers, of course."

"This isn't right," Pace said. "It's not fair for my record to be marred when I've done nothing wrong."

Then, for the first time, Pace considered the setting in which Edington had chosen to raise the issue. "This won't affect my reappointment to the faculty, will it? That's not what you're trying to tell me?"

Edington once again removed his glasses and began wiping them with his tie. "Obviously, *everything* is considered, but, in the normal course of events, something like this wouldn't be determinant— certainly not in the case of someone of your stature. But the suit is a definite negative. It's the kind of thing that might tip the balance if there were other negative issues."

At first, Edington's comment went right past Pace. There simply *weren't* any negative issues in his background. But there was something in Edington's tone that left his words dangling accusatorially in the air.

"Are you trying to tell me something? Is there some 'other negative issue' I ought to know about?"

Edington answered slowly, choosing his words very carefully. "I'm simply suggesting that this wouldn't be a good time to become involved in anything controversial. No one wants you back on the faculty more than I do, Pace, and under normal circumstances there would be absolutely no question—"

Pace had heard enough. "I don't believe this! It's Long, isn't it? He's *gotten* to you!"

"Not to me, Pace, but he's been talking to others."

"This is a total joke."

Edington shook his head. "It's very serious, Pace. Senator Long is an extremely powerful man. Not only can he influence the awarding of government grants— which, as you very well know, we are absolutely dependent on—but he also has made large personal donations to the school, with the express promise of much more to come. I don't like this any more than you do, but the fact is, politically speaking, a man like Long simply cannot be ignored."

"You know about the biopsy?" Pace said.

Edington nodded.

"And you know why Long doesn't want the prosecutors to get the DNA?"

"I've heard stories," Edington said.

"I would think," Pace said, "that a pretty fair case could be made that Senator Long is attempting to obstruct justice."

"I'm no lawyer," Edington said.

"I'm not a lawyer either," Pace said, rising from his chair, "but you can rest assured I'm going to hire one."

Pace had his hand on the doorknob when he turned and fired his parting salvo. "And any faculty at the medical school who are abetting the senator's little conspiracy might do well to consider how a felony conviction might affect their careers. Medical review boards tend to take a pretty dim view of that sort of thing."

Edington looked like he'd just been told he only had six months to live.

28

Pace had no real intention of hiring a lawyer—not yet anyway—but he figured the threat might put a little starch in some backbones around the medical school. It might make Boyd Edington and the others stop and think for a minute before allowing themselves to become complicit in Edward Long's blatant attempt to obstruct justice.

For his part, Pace resolved to let the chips fall where they may. He had no second thoughts. If the DNA comparison showed Ted Long to be a rapist and murderer, so be it.

Courtney's schedule turned out to be about as hectic as Pace's once had been—before he retired. In addition to everything else, Tommy Jacobs' reelection campaign was putting extra pressure on the entire office.

So they decided to get together on Sunday afternoon—three days before the biopsy. Without thinking, Pace suggested Stevens Park. It had long been a favorite of Max. He and Pace began frequenting the park months before Pace learned of the Francine Lovett murder. Courtney said Stevens Park would be fine.

It was all very informal and low key. Hardly even worth calling a date. Still, Pace felt more than a little guilty. What right did he have to think about beginning a relationship with someone? Sure, his post-transplant course had been remarkably smooth, but there was no guarantee that would continue. He had been able to totally accept his uncertain future so long as it didn't involve anyone else, but how fair was it to ask another to take on the burden of that uncertainty?

On the other hand it occurred to Pace that a year ago he would have asked Courtney out without a moment's thought to his health—and look what happened. Tomorrow is promised to no one.

You're getting way ahead of yourself, he told himself. You're meeting a woman on a Sunday afternoon in a crowded park. Nobody's making any commitment here.

Pace arrived a half hour early to give Max a good workout before Courtney showed up. Max could be a handful if he was too wound up, and Pace did his best to wear him down. As it turned out, Max and Courtney were just fine together.

"He reminds me a lot of the dog I had when I was a kid," Courtney said, giving Max's head a good rub behind the ear. "My dog died the summer before I went off to college. I was heartbroken."

"Were you raised around here?"

"Right here in the city. My dad's family grew tobacco for generations, but Dad didn't want the farming life. He moved to the city long before I was born."

"Does your family still live here?"

"My dad does. He's all I have. Mom died a few years ago. I never had brothers or sisters."

Courtney was dressed much like Pace—T shirt, athletic shorts, and running shoes. Her blond hair was tied back in a single braid. It was obvious she was an athlete—something you might not realize, seeing her dressed in her downtown clothes. She was even more of a knockout today. Pace noticed she drew lots of glances from passing males.

"You a jogger?" he asked.

"No, tennis," she said. "It's a good workout, and it's more interesting than just jogging."

"I won't disagree with that," Pace said, "but the thing about jogging, you can do it at any time, in any weather, almost anywhere. And you don't have to reserve a court or line up an opponent."

Courtney smiled. "And *that's* the problem. With jogging, you never have a good excuse *not* to do it. With tennis, if you're not in the mood, you can come up with a dozen excuses without even trying."

"Not if you have Max for a partner," Pace told her. He gave her an overview of Max's training methods. "The place where Max falls down is diet—he'd take in a whole lot more calories than he burns up if I let him. That's our deal. He keeps me on my workout regimen; I keep him on his diet."

It was the kind of day when you realized that winter was at long last gone, that spring had finally come. The sky was suddenly blue and cloudless. There was, for the first time in months, a warming sun beating down. They walked and threw the ball for Max, then found a sun-warmed grassy slope to sit on while Max optimistically investigated a nearby clump of bushes. Pace put forward the obvious question.

"What color are those eyes?"

She smiled. "My dad always says cornflower blue— the same as my mother's—to go with my corn-silk hair. It always sounded quite romantic when I was younger."

They were quiet for a few moments, then Courtney said, "Sometimes I hear just the slightest hint of an accent in your voice. I can't quite place it."

Pace gave her an abbreviated version of his life history. "So," he said, "you could be hearing either Boston or West Texas in my voice."

"I don't think I'm hearing Boston," she said.

They talked for a while about other things before Pace asked, "Are we still on for Wednesday?"

"From my side we are, but we've got the easy part. All we have to do is collect the specimen and document the chain of custody. How about you?"

"Well, you have to remember that I get the pleasure of having the biopsy whether or not you do any DNA testing, so I'm ready either way." Pace hesitated, then asked, "Have you been pressured not to do the tests?"

"Why, have you?"

Pace nodded. "I've been told my return to the medical faculty is no longer the sure thing it once was."

"By Long?"

"Long asked me not to provide the biopsy material for testing. The part about the job came later, from someone else, but it was clear that Long was pulling the strings. To tell you the truth, it surprised me. My impression from the newspaper accounts was that Ted Long had a solid alibi—despite everything the conspiracy theorists were claiming on the Internet. But this pressure from Senator Long casts everything in a different light."

"It certainly does," she said.

"You didn't answer *my* question," Pace said, "whether you've been pressured at all?"

"Not directly. Long is too smart for that. But Tommy Jacobs got a call asking if he might be interested in a senate seat—not Long's, the other one, the one that comes vacant in two years. Without saying anything directly it was made clear that if Tommy played ball now, he would get support later. If he doesn't cooperate, he can forget about the senate and any other office he might ever think of holding."

"Long's not doing any of this because he believes in his son's innocence," Pace said.

"No," Courtney said. "He's not. And it certainly shoots the hell out of my theory of the case."

"Which is?"

She smiled. "Complicated and highly speculative and probably totally unfair to my personal number-one suspect. So, if you'll let me, I'd rather not say too much just yet. Let's see what the DNA shows."

"Mystery, thy name is woman," Pace said.

"I'm trying to be alluring," she responded.

"You're probably succeeding," he said.

29

Pace showed up at the hospital early Wednesday morning to have blood work and an EKG before Brian did the biopsy. The medical specialty of the person who actually performs heart biopsies varies from medical center to medical center and even from day to day. Brian Curtis, like many cardiac surgeons, preferred to biopsy his own patients, but other surgeons defer to cardiologists or even to the so-called invasive radiologists—whoever, at a particular center, has the most experience.

Pace was all squared away and ready to go by 9:30, a half hour before the procedure was scheduled to start. He had nothing to do but sit and wait—and freeze. It felt like it was sixty degrees in the cardiac cath suite. And that was before you calculated the wind-chill factor created by the oversized air vents.

Pace wore only a hospital gown and a pair of surgical scrub pants, and he worried he was about to succumb to frostbite. Seeking a more hospitable climate, he stepped out into the hallway and discovered a young man dressed in a down parka and looking completely lost.

Pace wanted that parka.

"Can I help you find something?" Pace asked.

The young man, portly and balding though only in

his early twenties, looked at Pace with an expression that seriously questioned whether Pace could offer any meaningful help.

"I've obviously been sent to the wrong place," he said. "I'm looking for where they do the heart surgery. I have to collect a biopsy specimen."

"Well, this is the place," Pace said.

"They do heart surgery here?" The man's face continued to convey extreme incredulity.

"Sure," Pace said. "If you go to the OR you've got anesthesia, the heart-lung machine, all those extra people. That stuff's expensive. So they do it up here, quick and dirty. It hurts like hell and there's some risk of infection, but it saves thousands of dollars." Pace offered his hand. "I'm Pace Magruder. I'm the patient."

The young man shook Pace's hand. "Howard Smith," he said. "You're putting me on."

Pace smiled. "A little. When people hear that a heart is about to be biopsied, they usually imagine something quite different from what really takes place. You're here to collect the evidence, huh?"

"For the DNA sample."

Pace glanced up at the clock, "Well, it won't be long now."

Pace introduced Howard Smith to the lab crew, saying only that Smith was there to collect a specimen. No one but Brian Curtis knew the whole story.

By the time Brian arrived, Pace was on the cath table with an IV running.

"I don't know why I'm even here," Brian said to Pace. "You've done more of these biopsies than I have."

"If you had a mirror on the cath-lab ceiling," Pace said, "like the one in your bedroom at home, I believe I just about *could* do this by myself." That brought a chorus of hoots from the staff.

Pace introduced Brian to Howard Smith. "Howard's here to collect the specimen. He's also the only person here with sense enough to dress properly for this deep freeze masquerading as a cath lab."

Howard had this bemused look on his face—obviously not convinced of the propriety of all the frothy banter.

The right side of Pace's neck was quickly prepped with Betadine and sterile drapes were placed to isolate the field. Then all was ready.

"Okay," Brian said, "here we go."

From the right side of the neck, Brian inserted a large bore needle into the internal jugular vein. A catheter was then pushed through the needle and into the superior vena cava, then advanced directly into the right side of the heart. The biggest concern was the induction of an arrhythmia—an abnormal heart rhythm—caused either by the biopsy itself or even by the mere presence of the catheter as it touched the cardiac wall. A monitor above the table gave a radiographic view of the catheter's progress, and Pace could see exactly what Brian was doing. He discovered he could watch with remarkable detachment, as though it wasn't his own heart depicted on the screen—which, in a sense, it wasn't.

"Okay, Pace, here comes the first biopsy."

Pace felt a vague, rather diffuse tugging sensation. Then his heart had a premature contraction and he felt it flip-flop, but that was all.

In Brian's skilled hands, the subsequent biopsies were equally uneventful. Twenty minutes later Howard Smith was on his merry way with the biopsy specimen and a tube containing ten milliliters of

Pace's blood. Soon after that, Pace was rolled off to the cardiology ward to recover in the requisite horizontal position.

Courtney hadn't been certain when the results of the DNA comparison would be available. She said the preliminary screening could be completed in a couple of days. It was not so much a question of the time required to perform the test, but rather the priority the lab placed on running it. And that was beyond her control.

So all Pace could do was wait. He had set something in motion that had now achieved a momentum of its own. It would run its course, Pace thought, in a couple of days—no matter what he did.

He could not have been more wrong.

—30—

Pace had expected to hear from Courtney before the weekend. He didn't. By Monday afternoon, unable to abide the silence, he called her at her office. What gives?

"The lab had some kind of technical problem with the assay," Courtney said. "They've had to rerun everything, but they're promising results by late this afternoon."

"Why don't you let me take you out somewhere for dinner?" Pace said. "I'll come by your office, and you can fill me in on the test results when I get there."

"That would be nice, Pace. I ought to be able to shake loose by six, if that works for you."

"See you then."

As Pace knocked on Courtney's door, he heard the phone ring inside. She pulled the door open and threw him a quick hello, then retreated to answer the phone.

"Sure, Alice," she said, "I'll be right here."

"That was Tommy Jacob's secretary," she said, hanging up the receiver. "They're expecting the lab to phone in its report sometime in the next half hour or so. Tommy wants me to hang around. Apparently Senator Long is coming by to get the results in person—probably wants to begin damage control as

192

soon as possible.

"Sorry about the delay," she said.

Pace tried his best to conceal his impatience. "No problem," he said.

"Let's find a place for you to sit." Courtney grabbed a stack of folders to clear a spot for him. "Someone once described my filing system as an endless game of musical chairs," she said.

When they had both settled in, Pace said, "You still think that Ted Long's DNA won't match?"

"That's my bet," she said.

"So what's this theory you have that gets blown out of the water if the DNA *does* match? It's been bugging me all weekend."

"I probably shouldn't have said anything about that, Pace. It's only speculation, and it might be difficult for you to hear."

"I'm a big boy. If it's not true, it won't hurt me. If it is true, it's probably something I'm going to have to deal with sooner or later."

Courtney nodded. "Well, first of all, if there *is* a DNA match, then Ted Long was a murderer and a rapist and that's that. But if the DNA *doesn't* match— well, I've been worried for a long time that what really happened a year ago in Howard County—what appeared to be a fatal, single car accident—was really a murder." She let the words hang in the air, waiting for a reaction.

Pace didn't see how murder could even be a possibility. "The newspaper said there was a passenger in the car—somebody who would have been an eyewitness."

"The girlfriend," Courtney said. "She was dead drunk. Her last memory was supposedly of events that occurred hours before the accident."

"Supposedly? You think she's lying?"

Courtney shrugged. "Probably not. If I had the blood alcohol level she had at the hospital, I'd be dead. I guess I'm just frustrated by the overall quality of the Howard County investigation. The local sheriff is notoriously incompetent. Ted Long could have had an arrow sticking out of his chest and Sheriff John Wade Dash might have missed it. Our office doesn't have any jurisdiction out there. The only nexus we had was the Lovett murder. That gave us the right to ask questions, but we basically had to accept whatever answers Dash gave us."

"What did the autopsy show?"

"Cause of death—head trauma with secondary brain injury. No one doubts that."

"So where's the problem?"

"The question is, what *caused* the head trauma? If we believe Dash's report, there was remarkably little damage to the car—the motor was still running when he found it—and there were no skid marks on the road. I went out to the scene to have a look. The car had long-since been removed, but you could see where it came to rest, halfway down the ravine, tire tracks all the way to it. So we know the car was never airborne. It makes you think it wasn't moving very fast when it left the road. Add to that, the passenger didn't have a scratch on her. As soon as she sobered up, she walked out of the hospital.

"So I think it's possible that someone killed Long with blows to the head, then staged the accident."

Pace asked the obvious question. "Is there a suspect—someone you think might have wanted Ted Long dead?"

"That's where it gets interesting. There's this guy, Dean Arnold, who came to us with a story putting Ted

Long at the park the night of the Lovett murder. It turns out the two had a long history of mutual animosity. I mean they really *hated* each other. So it's possible Arnold created the story out of whole cloth simply to cause trouble for Long. On the other hand, to the extent you want to believe Arnold, he's placed himself at the park that night. What's his alibi? Obviously, he doesn't have one. He admits he was there."

"So," Pace said, "you think he might have been the rapist, and he was trying to throw the blame onto Long? This Arnold guy doesn't sound too bright, drawing attention to himself like that."

"But," Courtney said, "What if somebody saw *Arnold* at the park that night? If Arnold knew he'd been seen, then all of a sudden it's not quite so stupid to come forward—he's already been spotted at the scene, so he has nothing to lose."

"Why did he kill Ted Long?"

"Maybe Arnold figured if he made Long the prime suspect and then Long died, the investigation would end."

Pace still wasn't buying the theory. "But what about crime scene DNA? Even with Long dead, it would—under any normal circumstances—still be easy to run Long's DNA against what was found at the scene."

"Maybe Arnold was stupid. It just didn't occur to him. Or maybe Arnold was a whole lot smarter than we think. Maybe he figured, by staging the accident out in Howard County, the body would be cremated before anyone ever discovered that Long was a suspect in a murder case in another jurisdiction. As a matter of fact, of course, Ted Long wasn't even a suspect. He had an air-tight alibi."

"But surely Arnold would have known that you

could always check *his* DNA if you had any suspicion that he was the rapist."

"But Arnold probably didn't believe he would ever become a suspect."

"*Did* you check Arnold's DNA?"

"No. He took off right after the accident."

"But if he didn't believe he'd ever become a suspect, why did he take off?"

She gave Pace a slight smile. "I never claimed the theory was perfect. I'm not ready to take it into court."

They lapsed into silence, then Courtney said, "There's one other thing. Ted Long had a gun when he was found. Three shots had been recently fired— according to the sheriff's report. I'm still trying to fit that little piece of information into my theory."

"What about the money?" Pace said.

"What money?"

"Joan Bennett got a peak in Long's wallet at the hospital. She said he had a big wad of cash."

Courtney shook her head. "I'd have to pull the report again, but I'm pretty certain I'd remember if there was a significant amount of cash."

Their thoughts were abruptly interrupted by the ringing of the phone on Courtney's desk.

Courtney answered, "Courtney Bond." She listened briefly, then said, "I'll be right there."

"That was Alice, Tommy's secretary," she said, turning back to Pace. "Tommy has the DNA results."

31

"Tommy's office is up on twelve with all the other bigwigs," Courtney said. "Where the great views are. We can take the elevator."

They walked the length of the long corridor, then turned left into an alcove that housed a bank of elevators on either side. Courtney pushed the call button, and within seconds an electronic chime announced the arrival of the elevator. When the doors parted, they suddenly found themselves face-to-face with Senator Edward Long and his chief of staff.

Had Pace been alone, he would have been tempted to turn away and wait for the next elevator—let the Senator make the ride up in peace. But Courtney didn't hesitate.

"Good evening, Senator, Mr. Styles," she said stepping into the elevator.

Pace nodded to both men. Styles nodded back, his expression noncommittal. The senator regarded them with silent fury. Long had the look of a man on the verge of violence, a man whose emotional state loomed so close to critical mass that even the slightest additional stress might detonate a massive reaction.

When the doors opened on twelve, Long charged out.

"It's to the right, Senator," Courtney said.

Long didn't pause. He didn't look back. "We know the way," he said.

Long turned right as he left the elevator. At the main hallway, he turned left.

Courtney turned right at the main corridor. Neither she nor Pace said anything or even peeked in the direction Long and Styles had taken.

Pace was immediately struck by the stark contrast between Courtney's cramped cubbyhole and the district attorney's wood-paneled, plushly carpeted outer office. Paneled double doors on the wall opposite the entrance undoubtedly led to the sanctum sanctorum. A fastidiously dressed, gray-haired woman sat at the desk that guarded the double doors.

"You should have been home hours ago, Alice," Courtney said.

"Well, you know, Courtney, the work of the wicked and all that."

"This is Dr. Pace Magruder, Alice."

Pace and Alice exchanged greetings, then Alice said, "You're to go right on in, Courtney."

"Senator Long is right behind us, Alice," Courtney said as she moved toward the double doors.

In fact, Long and Styles arrived just as Courtney disappeared into Jacob's office.

Alice was instantly on her feet. "Good evening, Senator. Mr. Jacobs will be with you in just a minute. Please have a seat. Is there anything I can get you? Coffee? Tea?"

The Senator said nothing. Styles shook his head and whispered, "No thank you."

Both men remained standing. So did Pace.

After an endless minute or two, Alice's phone buzzed. She picked up the receiver and listened only briefly before replacing the receiver and once again rising to her feet.

"Senator Long, please go on in," she said as she moved to open the door.

Long hurried through the doorway without a word, leaving Pace and Charles Styles standing together in the outer office. Styles wore a mild expression. He did not appear to be possessed by the same rage that consumed his boss. Pace took the opportunity to lighten his own load a little.

"I don't know what the DNA comparison showed," Pace said, "but no matter what the results, I hope Senator Long can come to understand that this is not at all what I had envisioned. I thought this would be a simple way to prevent any more unfair tainting of his son's memory."

"I believe, in his heart, the senator already understands that," Styles said. "He loved his son very much, and all this has been agonizing for him. In time, he will begin to heal."

Pace was relieved to hear Styles discuss the issue in such a rational, civil way. "When you think it's appropriate, Mr. Styles, please tell him once again how very grateful I am. I doubt the senator fully understands how close to death I was. The chances of a donor becoming available who was my blood type *and* my size—well, the chances weren't very good."

Just then the door to Jacobs' office flew open and Courtney emerged. Behind her, in clear view through the open door, was the seated figure of Senator Long, hunched forward, sobbing inconsolably.

Courtney spoke first to Styles. "Please go on in, Mr. Styles."

As soon as Styles was out of the room, she turned to Pace. "There was no match, Pace. There's no DNA, or any other credible evidence, linking Ted Long to the rape and murder of Francine Lovett."

PART THREE

32

They were in a small trattoria, not far from Courtney's office. Pace was trying to make sense of what they'd just witnessed.

"When I saw Senator Long sitting there, all slumped over in his chair and crying, I naturally assumed the DNA had matched, that the evidence proved his son had committed the crime."

"I was surprised by Long's reaction," Courtney said. "I guess it was just a moment of huge emotional release for him." She thought about it for a moment, then added, "Edward Long obviously *believed* that Ted killed Francine Lovett. You were certainly right about that. It's hard to come up with any other explanation for his resistance to running the DNA comparison, or for his emotional meltdown the moment he heard that his son was innocent."

They were in a quiet corner, each nursing a glass of Chianti while they waited for their dinners. Pace was thinking how far the two of them had come since their first disastrous meeting, only a few days ago, in Courtney's office.

"Is Tommy Jacobs married?" he asked.

"Yes, rather recently as a matter of fact." Then, tilting her head slightly and with a barely discernable smile, she said, "Why do you ask?"

"Ask what?"

"If Tommy is married."

Did I say that out loud? "No reason," Pace said.

She was still giving him a funny look.

Pace changed the subject. "So, do you think we've got a murder on our hands?"

"Not on *our* hands, Pace. *I* don't have jurisdiction, and, just in case it's slipped your mind, *you* are a doctor."

"I know that, but what do you think?"

"I think if I wanted to murder someone and wanted to be certain the investigation was, at best, slipshod, I'd probably dump the body in a ravine off Morgan Pike in Howard County and wait for Sheriff John Wade Dash to blunder by."

"Where off Morgan Pike?" Pace asked.

"Anywhere."

"No, I mean where along Morgan Pike was Ted Long found?"

"The road's only a couple of miles long. There's just one big curve, and that's where it happened." She gave him what Pace was beginning to recognize as her "official" look. "Why?"

Pace shrugged.

"Pace, remember when I said there were two reasons it wasn't our problem? One was that I don't have jurisdiction. The other one was, and this is a big one, *you* are a doctor. If Ted Long was murdered, it was probably by the same guy who raped and murdered Francine Lovett. And that guy just might take exception to your nosing around in his tracks. You could put yourself in real danger by getting involved in this thing."

Pace didn't want to get into a big battle over the danger question, so he returned to the earlier issue.

"You might actually have jurisdiction," he said.

"How's that?"

"Like you said, it's probably the same person who murdered Francine Lovett."

Courtney shook her head. "That still doesn't get us into Howard County. No matter what, we could only act through their local law enforcement agencies. In certain cases the state could go in on their own, or the feds, but not us."

"We don't know where the murder happened," Pace said. "The crime may not have been committed in Howard County. That's just where the body was dumped. If both the suspect and the victim lived here, it's more than likely that the crime was committed here. Wouldn't that give you jurisdiction?"

"It would give us jurisdiction to prosecute, but it still wouldn't get us into Howard County without local authorization. Usually, law enforcement agencies are pretty good about cooperating with each other, but if Howard County resisted, the only recourse we'd have would be to go to court and get an order compelling their assistance."

"But for all you know," Pace said, "they'd be happy to reopen the investigation if you gave them a good reason."

"Not if the good reason is that their initial investigation was totally incompetent."

"But what about the idea that both murders were committed by the same guy?" he asked.

"What 'both murders'? It's just a wild theory of mine that Ted Long might have been murdered. I don't have anything that even comes close to being hard evidence—nothing I could take to Tommy Jacobs and say, Look, this is something we really need to move on."

205

"Well," Pace said, "I don't have any jurisdictional restrictions."

"That's right, Pace. You don't have *any* jurisdiction, *anywhere*."

They both smiled at that. Then their dinners arrived, and they moved on to other topics. Courtney reported that Keith Dobson had soared to new heights in his closing argument. He claimed he and his brother had been stalked by an obsessed Mrs. Olson for years, and he tried to introduce letters he claimed to have received from her while he was in prison. The judge informed Keith that his closing argument was not the appropriate time for the introduction of new evidence.

On hearing the judge's pronouncement, Rickie—the younger Dobson—immediately ceased work on whatever he was writing at the defense table. Courtney assumed it was yet another missive signed, "Love, Msr. Olsin." Courtney believed the spelling was a major clue to the true authorship of the letters.

After they'd eaten, Pace walked Courtney to her car. She was still uneasy about his getting too involved in any investigating.

"I meant it when I said it could be dangerous for you, Pace. There's a murderer out there somewhere. He's killed once—at least once—and he probably wouldn't hesitate to kill again."

"Don't worry. I'll be careful." He leaned down and gave Courtney a kiss on the cheek—merely, of course, a chaste expression of his appreciation for her concern.

She backed away and cocked her head, her expression suddenly very serious. "I'm trying to save your life here, Magruder. I'd think you could put a little more into it than that."

"I'd be willing to give it a try," Pace said.

—33—

In the end, absolving Ted Long of guilt in the Francine Lovett murder did not provide the peace of mind Pace had hoped for. Courtney had raised a new issue, and it wasn't the kind of thing a man like Pace could simply ignore. As relieved as he was to discover that his transplanted heart had not previously beat within the chest of a rapist and murderer, he was no less unsettled by this new possibility—that his own life had been saved only because Ted Long had been murdered. For Pace, that was a heavy burden to bear.

He could of course in no way hold himself responsible for Ted Long's murder. Pace had not caused that death. Still, he had certainly benefited from it, and in so doing he had incurred a debt beyond calculation, and he was haunted anew by the need to find a way to repay at least some small portion of what he owed. If Ted Long was murdered, Pace could no more turn his back and walk away than he could voluntarily quit breathing. If Ted Long was murdered, justice must be served.

And for the foreseeable future, Pace could envision no substantial prospect of the dispensation of justice by any hands other than his own.

Morgan Pike wasn't on Pace's GPS system, but he

did have a vague notion of where the road was located. He decided he'd just drive to the general area, then seek precise directions from the locals. It was one of those decisions in life that seems so innocuous at the time it's made but has unforeseeable—unimaginable—consequences.

When Pace pulled his car into that dismal, godforsaken, two-pump gas station on that warm spring day, he set gears in motion that could not be stopped, and more than one life would be caught in the teeth of those gears and come to a sudden and violent end.

The station attendant was sitting in one of those all-metal lawn chairs that were popular back in the forties. The chair was weather-beaten and rusted, and it was impossible to guess what color it might originally have been. He had dragged it into the shadow cast by the ramshackle old building, and he sat there, in the shade, chewing tobacco and eyeing Pace suspiciously as he climbed out of his car.

"Howdy," Pace said.

"Ain't got no tarlet," the man replied. He shifted the plug from his right cheek to the left and spat—at his feet but in Pace's general direction.

"Don't need a restroom," Pace said. "I just wanted to ask how to get to Morgan Pike."

From a distance, the man had looked elderly. Up close, Pace could see he was in his early fifties. His face was covered by several days' growth of gray stubble. On his chin and around his mouth the beard had been discolored by tobacco juice.

"Ain't nothin' *on* Morgan," the man said. "Least nothin' a city fella would be inersted in."

"There's some property I want to look at," Pace said. He had no intention of telling the man his real reason for being there.

"Ain't for sale."

"Sometimes, for the right price, that can change."

The man spat again. "You city fellas're all the same. You need any gas?"

"I guess I could top off the tank."

"You pump it yourself."

Pace figured, if he played along, the guy might eventually tell him what he wanted to know. And his only alternative was to go around knocking on farmhouse doors.

He backed his car up to the pump and put in three and a half gallons—all it would hold. He gave the man a twenty dollar bill.

"Keep the change," Pace said. Then, in his friendliest tone, "I'd really appreciate it if you could help me out with the directions."

The man eyed Pace's car like he was trying to figure a way to squeeze another dollar out of it. Then he relented.

"Down the road a mile, take a right." He nodded ever so slightly to indicate the direction.

"Thanks a lot," Pace said.

The man spat again, then closed his eyes. Nap time.

As soon as Pace was out of sight, the filling station man pulled himself reluctantly out of his chair and shambled inside to use the phone.

—34—

The man at the filling station had been right about one thing, there wasn't much to see on Morgan Pike. The land bordering the road was wooded largely by broadleaf trees. In the occasional cleared areas, cattle were pastured. Here and there, deer grazed among the cattle.

The fatal curve was easily identifiable, and Pace noted that, in the bright light of day, an approaching driver had ample warning of the impending hazard. But in the dark, the bend in the road would prove more treacherous, and an unwary—or reckless—driver might easily get himself into serious trouble.

Pace found a safe place to park his car and stepped out into the warming sun. A few of the closer deer bolted as the sound of the closing car door disrupted the peaceful morning quiet, but the cattle, unfazed by the intrusion, continued to munch apathetically.

Pace wasn't certain what he would find. In point of fact, he didn't really know what he was looking for. Nearly a year had passed since that ill-fated night claimed the life of Ted Long—a year of rains and snows and the meanderings of humans and other, less culpable animals. Nature could wreak a great deal of change in a year, and man could obliterate a treasure-trove of clues in a heartbeat. The trail had long since grown quite cold.

But when Pace traced the path a car would likely follow on missing the turn, he was amazed to discover fresh evidence of an auto accident. Black skid marks that were visible for about fifty feet on the pavement became deep ruts in the soft shoulder of the road. The car then cut a wide swath through the roadside vegetation, nicking one of two large trees the driver may have been trying to steer between. The trunk of each tree bore multiple healed scars suggesting similar incidents had occurred with a certain regularity in the past.

Pace made his way carefully forward, taking advantage of the path the car had cleared through the underbrush. The ground remained level for about fifteen feet before beginning to slope downward—the descent gradual at first, then becoming very steep. The bottom of the ravine was perhaps seventy-five feet below the grade of the road.

Pace moved cautiously to the verge of the more severe downward slope. From that vantage he could see three derelict automobiles clumped together at the bottom of the ravine. One, obviously the most recent arrival, had come to rest on top of the other two. This last car did not yet evidence the total degradation that prolonged abandonment to the ravages of the elements had inflicted on the others. Pace was debating whether to risk the climb down for a closer look when he was jolted by a harsh shout from above.

"Hey! That's private property!"

Pace turned toward the voice but could only make out a large, dark figure backlit by the bright sun.

"Sorry," Pace yelled back, "I didn't know."

He began working his way back up the slope and discovered that the voice belonged to an obese, balding, middle-aged man in a beige uniform. He squinted at Pace through narrow horizontal slits in the fat around his eyes. His car was labeled "Sheriff—Howard County."

Pace offered his hand, which the man took reluctantly. "Pace Magruder," he said.

"Sheriff John Wade Dash," the man said. "This land's not for sale."

Pace shook his head. "I'm afraid I wasn't completely straightforward with the man at the filling station. I didn't see any reason to go into it, but I'm not interested in buying any land."

"It's still private property," the sheriff said.

"About a year ago," Pace explained, "a young man was killed here, in an accident. Ted Long. After he was pronounced dead, his heart was made available for transplantation. I got the heart."

Dash appeared unmoved by this news. He continued to regard Pace in wary silence.

"For some reason," Pace said, "I felt a need to come out here and see the accident scene."

"The accident was a year ago," Dash said.

"I've had a rather tumultuous year," Pace explained, "or I would have been out sooner." He turned and gazed back toward the ravine. "It looks like you've recently had another accident."

"The other night," Dash said.

Pace looked back at the sheriff. "Is Ted Long's car still down there at the bottom?"

Dash shook his head. "Never made it to the bottom, just down to the place where the hill starts to get real steep. The senator sent a wrecker to pull it out."

"Why do you suppose it stopped?" Pace asked.

"What?"

"Ted Long's car."

"Must've got done rollin'," Dash said.

"It must not have been going very fast."

"Or," the sheriff said, "the guy hit his brakes real hard."

"But there weren't any skid marks."

At that, Dash's expression suddenly grew mean. He took a couple of steps toward Pace. "What're you tryin' to say?"

Pace could smell alcohol on Dash's breath. He shrugged and gave the sheriff what he hoped was a disarming smile. "I'm not trying to say anything. I just want to understand what happened."

Pace turned back toward the ravine. He could feel the sheriff's eyes boring into his back. After a few moments Pace turned to the sheriff once again. "Well, I've seen enough. I just needed to get this out of my system. Sorry to have troubled you."

Pace walked back to his car and opened the door. Before slipping in behind the wheel, he spoke once more to Dash. "Any idea why Ted Long had a gun in his car that night?"

"Lots of people have guns," the sheriff said.

Pace nodded. "There was a rumor Long had a lot of cash on him that night."

Now Dash walked directly up to Pace, the two men standing face to face with only the open car door between them.

"The rumor was wrong," Dash said.

Pace knew he'd hit pay dirt. Dash had just pegged the meter on Pace's internal lie detector.

Pace smiled and affected not to notice the sheriff's agitation. "These stories always seem to develop a life of their own when somebody famous is involved," he said. "Thanks for straightening me out, Sheriff. You've been a big help. I won't take any more of your time."

With that, Pace climbed in behind the wheel and quickly had John Wade Dash in his rearview mirror.

—35—

Her dad still lived in the fine old Dutch colonial that was the only real home Courtney had ever known. She'd lived other places—at school, in various apartments—but none of those places had ever been home.

As soon as she pulled into the drive, he popped out the front door and waved. He was in casual mode today—blue jeans, polo shirt, and boat moccasins.

Her dad hadn't seen her car since the repairs were completed, and he gave it a critical once-over while she was getting out.

"I'll say this," he said, "they did a pretty good job once they decided to get on with it."

"Hi, Dad," she said, giving him a hug.

He turned his critical eye on her. "You didn't forget the pizza, did you?"

"It's on the other side."

He headed around to open the passenger-side door. "Did you get *everything* on it?"

"Everything but anchovies."

He stopped and turned to look back at her.

"Just kidding, Dad. I told them to put *extra* anchovies on three quarters of it."

"Good girl."

"I don't know how you can eat those things."

Her dad had wanted to meet downtown and go someplace nice for dinner, but Courtney had warned him that her schedule was too uncertain to make any plans that definite. She said, why didn't she just come by with a pizza whenever she was able to shake free, and that had sealed the deal. Her dad had always been a pizza fanatic.

Inside, he had set places in the dining room. He put the box right on the table. Courtney felt a twinge of guilt. Her mother would never have let them put a pizza box on the dining room table. Courtney still expected her mom to burst out of the kitchen at any moment. The first couple of years after her mother's death Courtney couldn't enter the house without growing tearful.

"So, how's business, sweetheart?" her dad asked when they'd settled in and started eating.

"Frantic as ever."

"I saw that the Dobsons got twenty years," he said.

"Couldn't have happened to a more deserving pair."

"Well, at least their life of crime is over."

"No, it just means we have twenty years to wait for their next felony—at least the next one perpetrated on the public at large. God knows what they'll get up to in prison."

"What's new in the Lovett-Long murders?" he asked. It was her dad's favorite case. He fully endorsed her theory that Ted Long had been murdered.

"Not much has happened since the DNA test. The only thing going on is Pace Magruder, the cardiologist who received the transplant from Long. He's been doing some investigating on his own. That bothers me. It could be dangerous."

"A man's gotta do what a man's gotta do," her dad said. "Actually, he sounds like a man after my own heart."

Courtney smiled. "Actually, he may be a man after *my* heart. Or it may only be that I'm after his."

Her dad's eyes grew wide.

"He's a pretty terrific guy, Dad." She couldn't have kept the emotion out of her voice if she tried.

"I always knew that someone would come along, sweetheart."

They ate in silence for a few moments.

"How's he doing with the transplant thing?" her dad asked.

"Fine," Courtney said. "He's strong as an ox, runs several miles a week. He doesn't seem to have any limitations or anything."

"How come you're wasting time eating pizza with your old man instead of being someplace exciting with the boyfriend?"

"Actually, I'll see Pace later tonight. He's off doing more investigating. I told him I'd pick him up at the airport when he gets in."

"Where'd he go?"

"Miami."

"Miami?"

Courtney hadn't been all that pleased when she heard about Pace's run-in with Sheriff Dash, and she hadn't been overly eager to provide Melissa Gardner's name. At first she would only tell him that the woman had moved out of state, to Miami. But Pace persisted, and Courtney finally relented.

Pace decided not to give Melissa Gardner any warning he was coming—which meant his trip to Miami stood a good chance of becoming a complete wild-goose chase. She might refuse to talk to him. She might simply not be home.

He took a late morning flight, then rented a car. The afternoon shadows were lengthening by the time he located her upscale, South Beach address. Melissa Gardner's apartment wasn't directly on the beach, but it was in one of those fashionably retro art-deco buildings, and Pace suspected it was probably a very pricey place to live.

When she opened the door, the first thing that struck him was how tiny she was. And young. Somehow it hadn't occurred to Pace that she would be so very young. She was slender, with long blond hair and wide brown eyes, and she stood there, waiting patiently, the door half open, her expression exhibiting neither interest nor fear.

"I'm Pace Magruder," he said, knowing the name would mean nothing to her. "Are you Melissa Gardner?"

She nodded hesitantly.

"I understand you were a friend of Ted Long," he said, "and that you were with him in the car the night he was killed. If it wouldn't be too difficult for you, I have a couple of questions I'd like to ask—about that night."

"Are you with the police?"

Pace shook his head. "No, this is personal. I'm a heart transplant patient. When Ted died, his heart was donated, and I was in desperate need of a new heart. His heart was transplanted into my chest. I owe him my life."

She seemed dumbstruck. Her expression remained flat. There was not a hint of comprehension in those large brown eyes. There was no sign she had even heard him.

"You're right to be wary, Ms. Gardner. You don't know me from Adam. I could be a con artist—or worse. If you like, I'd be happy to wait while you check out who I am. You could call Courtney Bond, who I think you'll remember from the district attorney's office. She'll vouch for me."

Melissa shook her head, then spoke haltingly. "I didn't know his heart was transplanted." Her voice trailed off at the end as she became immersed once more in her own thoughts. Then she turned and walked back into the apartment, leaving the door open behind her. Pace followed. He started to close the door behind him, then thought better of it. The young woman might be more comfortable with it open.

He had guessed she was living pretty high, and his suspicions were confirmed as he followed her in. The apartment was crammed with new, expensive-looking furniture—big heavy pieces—not exactly Pace's taste and not exactly in keeping with the atmosphere of the neighborhood, but pretty fancy stuff all the same.

Melissa Gardner slumped heavily into a large, over-stuffed chair. When at last she spoke, it was to no one in particular. "I could really use a drink," she said.

"Go ahead, if you want," Pace said. "Don't worry about me."

She shook her head. "I've been sober for six months now. This is the first time I can say that since I was thirteen years old." She stole a glance at her watch. "But I can tell you one thing, I'll need to go to a meeting tonight. I usually go to a church right around the corner. You practically have to get there an hour early just to get a seat. You wouldn't believe how many drunks there are in Miami."

Her strawberry blond hair hung straight down her back, nearly to the waist. She wore a light-blue tennis shirt and white shorts. Her feet were bare. She looked even more diminutive in that oversize chair.

Pace took a seat on a couch several feet away. "I'm sorry to bother you," he said. "It's just that, for my own peace of mind, I'm trying to sort out what happened that night—the night Ted was killed."

"Well, to find out anything about that, you're talking to the wrong person," she said. "The only thing I know for certain about that night is that it was no different from any other night back then—meaning I was drunk. All I remember is waking up in a hospital and wanting to get the hell out of there. Mostly I just wanted to go somewhere and get a drink."

"How about earlier that day, or the day before? Is there anything you remember?"

She shook her head. "I went over all of this with the lady prosecutor. Everything was a haze in those days. I have this vague memory that Ted was angry about something, but he was always angry about *something*."

"Is that why he had the gun? Could he have been angry enough to want to kill somebody—or could someone have been after him?"

"Yes and yes," she said. "Ted was always angry, and people were always mad at him. But I don't know anything about a gun. Ted was more of an up-close-and-personal kind of guy. He kept a baseball bat under the driver's seat in case he ever needed a weapon."

"Did he ever use it?"

"Not that I know of. I saw him wave it in the air a few times, pound it into the palm of his hand—usually when he was telling everybody what he could have done to someone—if he'd wanted to. It might have been terrifying if I hadn't been drunk."

"When was that?" he asked.

"When was what?"

221

"When was he waving the bat when you were drunk?"

She shook her head. "How would I know? I was *always* drunk."

Pace could see that this line of questioning wasn't likely to bear much fruit. He shifted to another area he'd been wondering about. "Any idea why Ted would have been carrying a lot of money that night?"

"What's a lot of money?"

Pace shrugged. "A few thousand dollars."

"Ted could always get his hands on money when he needed it."

"From his father?"

"I don't know. I doubt it. I think it was probably something illegal, but I never knew what it was."

"Drugs?"

"I doubt it." She tilted her head and narrowed her eyes. "Are you sure you're not a cop?"

"Actually, I'm a doctor, but I've been off the job for a while, getting used to my new heart. So I have lots of time to worry about things."

They sat in silence while Pace considered how best to get at the last remaining issue. Finally he just asked, "Did you know Ted's name had been mentioned in connection with a rape and murder?"

"Now *that* made him mad," she said. "That guy always had it in for Ted. His name was Arnold something. He was the one who went to the police."

"And now," Pace said, "the police have clear evidence that Ted wasn't the rapist."

Pace still wasn't certain what Dean Arnold's game had been. "It's my understanding that all he did was place Ted in the park at the time of the crime. Arnold never said he saw Ted do anything. Then Senator Long's chief of staff provided an alibi for Ted. He said the two of them had spent the evening together. Does that seem plausible to you? Did Ted and Charles Styles spend a lot of time together?"

"Ted and Chuck had a very weird relationship, but basically they hated each other. Ted was always picking on Styles and ordering him around, making him do really menial stuff. I guess Ted figured since Styles worked for his father, Styles had to do whatever Ted told him to do. I guess Styles figured the same thing, because he pretty much did whatever Ted demanded. But Styles would do things to get back at Ted—passive-aggressive stuff.

"I remember one time Styles was supposed to pick up Ted's dry cleaning, and he left it hanging on the front door in the rain. And another time Styles tried to get out of doing something by saying his car was acting up, so Ted said to take his. Styles didn't bring Ted's car back for three days."

"So if Styles hated Ted so much," Pace said, "why was he so willing to provide an alibi?"

"That's easy," she said. "The good senator *told* him to provide an alibi."

Pace was about to ask another question when the look on Melissa's face caused him to lose his train of thought. Her eyes opened wide. She was suddenly slack-jawed. It was, for all the world, a look of mortal terror.

"Don't get crazy," she said.

A second or two elapsed before Pace understood that Melissa was not talking to him, but rather *through* him. He turned to see a tall, long-haired young man in his early twenties.

"Who's he?" the man said in a there's-gonna-be-hell-to-pay tone.

"Just a guy with some questions," Melissa said.

Pace rose to his feet and started to offer his hand and introduce himself. The intruder, who Pace assumed was The Boyfriend, took this as a threat and lunged at Pace. The wrestling match that ensued reminded Pace of his grade school days. The kid was big, but soft. He seemed content to just hang on to Pace and gradually work his way toward the wrestling hold that defined grade school, The Headlock.

Melissa was screaming for the boyfriend to stop, warning him that Pace had a heart problem. Pace was trying his best to reason with the guy, telling him he had just come by to ask Melissa some questions. Pace felt more silly than anything else.

But when it began to look like the kid might settle for a choke hold instead of a headlock, Pace decided he'd had enough. With a single concentrated effort he managed to twist free. Then, standing upright, face-to-face, Pace was ready for whatever the guy wanted to try next.

"We wouldn't want lover-boy to have a heart attack," the kid said. He started to turn as though he was quitting the field. But really he was just loading up a big, roundhouse right hook.

Pace saw the punch coming about a half hour before it was delivered. He parried the blow with his left forearm, then countered with two quick right-handed jabs to the kid's nose—hard enough to stun him and draw blood, but not nearly enough to knock him out or even break his nose.

"It's not that kind of heart condition," Pace said.

The jabs took all the fight out of The Boyfriend.

Pace turned to Melissa. "Thanks for answering my questions. I'm sorry if I caused you any trouble."

He turned one last time just before walking out the door and spoke directly to Melissa, "Congratulations for staying on the wagon the last six months. I know how hard that must have been."

"Thanks," she said.

He managed to get on an early evening flight home. Courtney picked him up at the airport.

"What happened to you!" she said.

He rubbed the small mouse under his left eye caused by the boyfriend's attempted headlock. "It's nothing," he said. "It turns out Melissa Gardner has an extremely jealous boyfriend."

He related the entire episode to Courtney. By the time he'd finished, she was smiling slyly and studying him under raised eyebrows.

"What's so funny?" he said.

"Well, on the one hand," she said, "I'm not too crazy about your running all around the country playing detective. On the other hand, though, I'm kind of pleased to hear that you're feeling up to a little vigorous, physical activity."

Pace regarded her with a sideways glance. When were these people ever going to learn?

"It's not that kind of heart condition," he said.

—36—

As soon as Anne Curtis got wind of Pace's budding relationship with Courtney, she was on the phone to Pace. "I do believe I hear wedding bells," she said.

For the first time in memory, Pace did not object.

"This doesn't sound like Danica redux," Anne said.

"No, it's not."

"So, what are you guys doing for dinner tonight?" she asked.

Brian and Anne Curtis lived quite modestly for people who had more money than God. Their little house was snuggled into the end of a small cul-de-sac and always felt warm and cozy. It was obvious from the start that they liked Courtney, and she quickly felt very comfortable with Pace's old friends.

"So, Pace," Brian asked, "when are you coming back to work?"

"Soon," Pace said. "I got a call from Boyd Edington. He said they're looking forward to my return, and that, coincidentally, it looks like the Wolfe family is going to drop their suit."

Brian shook his head. "The same suit that just a few weeks ago the medical school thought it would have to settle?"

Pace nodded. "It seems those DNA results solved

quite a few problems at the school."

"Okay," Anne said, "no more shoptalk. What are you doing with all your spare time, Pace?"

"He's playing detective," Courtney said, "and getting into fights."

"So that's what's going on with the eye," Brian said. "I'm not going to have to check your platelet count after all."

"It was just the same old problem I've been plagued by all my life," Pace said. "The jealous husband comes home unexpectedly. You'd think I'd learn."

"He's sticking his nose in where he shouldn't," Courtney said with considerable emotion. "He doesn't seem to understand how dangerous that could be."

Pace realized he hadn't fully appreciated the extent of Courtney's concern. It was something they needed to discuss.

Brian quickly changed the subject. "Are you keeping up with the exercise program?"

Pace smiled. "Max won't let me miss a session."

And then, with a very concerned expression on his face, Brian asked, "And sexually, is that working out all right?"

Pace nodded solemnly. "We've been having wild monkey sex."

In the car on the way back to Pace's house, Courtney was unusually quiet.

"I know you're worried about what I'm doing, Courtney. But I'm being careful. That little wrestling match was nothing."

"I know you have to do what you have to do, Pace, but if Ted Long *was* murdered, there's someone out there who's going to take serious exception to your snooping around."

"Anyway, I'm almost done."

"Almost?"

"I want to talk with Dean Arnold's family."

Courtney let out a deep breath. "Whatever for?"

"I'm not sure. I'm just turning over rocks, Courtney. Unless I do that, I'll never know if there's anything important under them."

"I wouldn't want anything to happen to you, Pace."

Pace smiled and reached for Courtney's hand. "This may come as a shocker, but I wouldn't either."

Later, settled on the couch in Pace's living room, Courtney remained unusually quiet.

"There's something else, isn't there?" Pace said.

"I'm afraid so."

"What?"

"We have *not* had wild monkey sex."

"I believe we have," Pace said.

Courtney pulled herself off the couch and started to walk out of the room.

"Where are you going?"

"Upstairs," she said, tugging the tail of her blouse out of her skirt. "Someone has to teach you the difference, and I guess I'm stuck with the job."

Halfway up the stairs she turned and looked back down at him. "You better take your pills before you come upstairs, monkey boy. You're in for a long night."

"It's not *that* kind of heart condition," Pace said.

—37—

George Arnold's tiny print shop was located in a part of town that was no longer fashionable or even remotely prosperous. It was a neighborhood still unswept by the broom of urban renewal and unable, by its own bootstraps, to pull itself out of the state of decomposition into which it had fallen.

But the Arnold shop stood out from the others. It was neatly painted and fastidiously maintained. Pace suspected that was more a reflection of the pride the owner took in his business than any profit he might be taking out of it. A sign in the window offered "Elegant Engraving."

The loud door buzzer that announced Pace's entrance into the shop bespoke a happier, busier time—a time when the presses in the back would have been noisily cranking out print jobs, a time when the proprietor would have been hard at work in the pressroom, not sitting out front, reading his morning newspaper.

On seeing Pace, the man was instantly on his feet, his face suddenly brightened by the prospect that this unheralded newcomer might actually be a customer.

"Good morning, sir," he said. "What can I do for you?"

Pace felt an immediate pang of guilt. The man was

hoping for new business. Pace was bringing him something very different.

Pace offered his hand. "I'm Pace Magruder."

"George Arnold, Mr. Magruder. How can I help you? I can meet just about any printing need you might have. No job is too large or too small."

Pace intended to tell the truth and see how far it got him. He had no more desire to cause this man pain than he had Senator Long.

"I've come on a personal matter, Mr. Arnold. I'd like to speak with you for just a few minutes, but if this is a bad time, I'd be happy to come back when it would be more convenient."

Pace could see the air go right out of the man. The bright light of expectation dimmed in his eyes and was quickly replaced by a look of wary uncertainty.

Arnold was wiry and several inches shorter than Pace. His full head of hair was gray going to silver. He had bright, knowing eyes. He looked much too old to have a son the age of Dean.

George Arnold shrugged his shoulders and smiled in a vain effort to mask his disappointment. "Now's just as good a time as any, Mr. Magruder."

"I'm a heart transplant patient, Mr. Arnold," Pace said. "I've had my new heart for about a year now."

The uncertainty only intensified in Arnold's face. His expression asked, How could this possibly have anything to do with me?

"My transplanted heart came from a young man who was killed in an automobile accident," Pace continued. "His name was Ted Long."

With this, the first spark of understanding appeared in Arnold's eyes.

"The reason I'm bothering you, Mr. Arnold, is that I've discovered that, since my transplant, I've developed this deep-seated need to learn as much as I can about Ted Long's life—how he lived, and how he died.

"I'm a cardiologist, and I've had many heart transplant recipients as patients over the years. They'd talk to me about their feelings, and I'd try my best to be sympathetic, but I realize now that I never really understood what they were going through—not till I went through it all myself. So when I discovered I had this need to learn about Ted Long, it really took me by surprise. I tried to ignore it, but in the end there was just no escaping the fact that Ted's death made it possible for me to go on living, and that's had a greater emotional impact on me than I could ever have imagined—or sometimes even like to admit."

Pace couldn't be certain how his words were being received, but Arnold appeared willing to listen—at least he hadn't ordered him out of the shop. So Pace pressed on.

"I know that your son was an acquaintance of Ted Long -"

That was as much as Arnold would let him say. "I was afraid that was where this was going, Mr.—Dr. Magruder." Arnold's tone was more sympathetic than angry. "I never knew Ted Long myself. I only knew about the problems my boy Dean had with him. All that's over and done with now. Ted Long is dead, and I bear him no grudge. I don't like to speak ill of the dead, Doctor, and besides, I don't see what good it does you to hear a bunch of negative stuff about the kid who gave you his heart. He's dead. You have his heart—that's a good thing. Why not let it go at that?"

"You sound a lot like me—before I had my transplant," Pace said. "And, intellectually, I'm still inclined to agree with you. But I'm trying to deal with something that's more emotional than rational. I don't completely understand it myself, so I have a lot of difficulty trying to explain it to others."

There was a moment of silence before Pace tried another tack. "I know your son went to the police about something he saw. He thought Ted Long might have somehow been involved in the Lovett murder. Do you know anything about that?"

Arnold shook his head. "The first I heard about it was when the police came around. That was after the auto accident. Dean never mentioned it to me. But, I'll tell you one thing, if Dean said it, it's true."

"I'm sure he thought it was true, Mr. Arnold, but he could have been mistaken."

Again Arnold shook his head. "Not with that fancy car the Long boy drove. There would be no mistaking that."

Pace had only one place left to go. "Mr. Arnold, is there any chance I could talk with Dean about this?"

George Arnold was suddenly ten years older and had the weight of the entire world pressing down on him. He shuffled a few feet backward and collapsed into a chair. His gaze was fixed at his feet.

"I wish you *could* speak to Dean, Doctor. I wish *I* could speak to Dean. His mother cries herself to sleep every night, wondering where he's got to."

Pace rested his hand on the man's shoulder. "You have no idea where he is." It was more a statement than a question.

"There was this girl," Arnold said, "that Dean knew at school. They had a couple of dates, that was all, then Dean tried to break it off, but she wouldn't leave him alone. She was one of those stalkers. She'd follow him around, then he started to get these threatening letters. She accused him of things. Dean—he'd always been a good student, not A's or anything but good solid B's—well he couldn't keep his mind on his studies. He was flunking everything. Finally the school said he could just start over the next semester. None of this would count against him. Meanwhile, they'd try to get this girl some help.

"Then when Dean took off—that's just not like Dean, running off without a word to anyone—I figured maybe this girl had done something. So I went down to the school, but all they knew was that the girl was gone—could have disappeared along with Dean for all they knew. The police weren't any help at all . . ." His voice just trailed off into the yawning chasm of his grief.

Pace felt like he was spreading misery everywhere he went. "I'm sorry, Mr. Arnold. I didn't mean to cause you pain. I'll go now, and let you get back to work."

That brought a snicker from Arnold. "Work," he said, "that's a joke. Not much work for an old-fashioned print shop like mine. It's all these franchises now—Speedy-Quick Printing—'We'll have your job done by tomorrow if we're in business that long'." He gave his head a shake. "Dean had got it into his head to modernize me. He said I could get a small business loan, and he'd get me into computers. That's what all the printers use now, computers. Dean knew all about that stuff."

Pace found a piece of paper and wrote his name and phone number on it. "If I find out anything, Mr. Arnold, I'll let you know. And if there's anything I can do for you, please don't hesitate to give me a call."

He shook the man's hand once more before he left. Arnold's grip felt drained of life.

Outside, Pace decided he'd had just about as much of this as he could stand, spreading heartbreak everywhere he went. He decided it was time to stop pursuing whatever it was he was pursuing and begin to focus on the future—his own future, and Courtney's. He needed to simply put this all behind him and get on with his life.

—38—

Courtney suggested they dress up and go out for dinner. She hoped to draw Pace out of his funk and get him talking about something other than those muddled events of a year ago. It didn't work.

"Why the gun and the money?" he asked over dessert.

"What?"

"Why did Ted Long have a gun? Why was he carrying all that cash?"

"I see," Courtney said, "we're back at the beginning."

"There was something going on that we haven't figured out. Where did the money come from?"

"We don't know for certain there was any money, Pace."

"We know there was a gun."

Courtney leaned across the table and said, sotto voce, "For the last twenty minutes I've been trying to figure out who this woman is, sitting a couple of tables behind you. I thought she was a movie star, but she just stood up and I can see how tall she is."

Pace felt a big "uh-oh" coming on.

"She's that model," Courtney said. "What's her name?" Then, "Here she comes."

"Pace! I thought that was you!"

Pace stood and gave Danica a brief hug, then introduced the women to each other. Danica's date had wandered on ahead. Danica hardly glanced at Courtney.

"So, Pace, you look terrific!"

"Are you doing a shoot in town?" Pace asked.

Danica must not have heard him. "I mean, you really look *terrific!*"

"Doesn't he?" Courtney said.

Now Danica glanced down at Courtney. "Do you work at the hospital?" she asked. "That must give you so much to talk about—all those diseases and everything."

"Mostly we just have wild monkey sex," Courtney said.

Danica didn't appear certain she had heard that quite right. "I'm sorry?"

"I'm not," Courtney said.

"It was good to see you, Danica," Pace told her.

"So nice to meet you," Courtney said. "If you're ever near the hospital, give me a call and we can have lunch in the cafeteria—my treat."

Later, at home, Pace was wrestling on the floor with Max while Courtney regarded them from a comfortable chair. She had her shoes off and her legs curled up under her.

"So what's the story on the beanpole?" she asked.

"Excuse me?" Pace said.

"Just think how skinny she'd be without all that makeup."

"I can't imagine," Pace said.

"She was really on the make."

"You think?"

"She wasn't too subtle."

"I didn't realize you noticed."

"So what's her story, Pace?"

"I had a couple of dates with her, back in my 'celebrity' period."

"Your 'celebrity' period?"

"Back when I only dated internationally prominent celebrities."

"What period are you in now?"

"This is my 'lawyers who are sex addicts period,'" Pace said.

"You wish," Courtney said.

Max suddenly tensed and let out a low, rumbling growl.

"Even Max has an opinion," Pace said.

It took Pace several seconds to fully comprehend what happened next.

Max was suddenly on his feet, snarling. Then he lunged at the large picture window at the front of the living room. The glass shattered, and Max fell, whimpering, to the floor. Seconds later, Pace heard the roar of a car engine and the screech of tires.

There was blood on the floor, and in those first moments he thought Max had been injured by the glass. But Pace knew a bullet hole when he saw one, and that's what he found when he examined Max.

Pace looked at Courtney, still in the chair. "He's been shot," he said. "Somebody shot Max."

At that moment there was only one question on Pace's mind, Why would anyone want to shoot Max?

Pace knelt over Max, trying to make a rapid assessment of the dog's injuries. Almost as an afterthought, he said, "Whoever fired the shot is long gone. I heard the car."

He put pressure on Max's bullet wound and was easily able to stop the bleeding. "It's his shoulder," he told Courtney. "He seems to be breathing okay, so it's probably going to be a question of what's broken, or whether the joint itself is damaged."

"I'm calling the police," Courtney said.

"Let's use your cell phone," Pace said, "so you can talk to them from the car while we get Max to a vet."

"But they'll need to come here."

"We can leave the front door unlocked for the police and then come back and talk to them as soon as we get Max taken care of—but we have to get Max to a vet, and you certainly can't stay here by yourself."

"No one was trying to shoot me, Pace. If they wanted to do that, they had a clear shot—Max or no Max. They were trying to shoot you."

"Maybe," Pace said, "but I still wouldn't consider leaving you here alone."

Courtney didn't argue the point any further.

Max let out only one long, pathetic whine as Pace lifted him off the floor. Trusting Pace, he didn't resist.

Once they got to the car, Pace decided it would be easier if he just climbed into the backseat and continued to hold Max. Courtney could drive.

"So much for calling the police," Courtney said.

"There's no hurry," Pace assured her. "The bad guys are long gone, and the only evidence the police are likely to recover is the bullet buried in Max's shoulder."

He directed Courtney to a twenty-four hour veterinary hospital that wasn't too far away. The drive took less than ten minutes. Courtney held the door as Pace carried Max inside. Two women looked up as they entered. Both were strikingly attractive. Courtney guessed that the taller blonde was the veterinarian. The redhead was probably an assistant.

The two spoke almost in unison.

"Pace!"

That brought a major-league eye roll from Courtney.

"What's wrong with Max?" the blonde asked.

"He's been shot," Pace said.

"Shot?"

"It's a long story, but I'm sure the police will be wanting the bullet—if you get it."

Within seconds Max was in a treatment room being examined. Pace made hurried introductions. The veterinarian was named Barbara Donaldson. Her assistant was Kathy Lewis.

Donaldson made a rapid, thorough examination of Max. "Other than the pain he feels every time he moves, Max doesn't seem to be in any great distress right now," she said. "He's moving air in both lungs, and his heart rate isn't too fast, so it doesn't look like he's collapsed a lung or lost a lot of blood. I'll start an IV and draw some blood work, then we'll need to get x-rays to help sort out the bone damage and see how much surgery is going to be required."

It looked like Max would be tied up for a while, so Pace and Courtney called the police and made arrangements to meet them back at the house. Pace went back into the examining room to say good-bye to Max. Max gave him a look that almost broke his heart.

"Don't worry, boy," Pace told him. "I'm not abandoning you, and you're in good hands. I'll be back later to check on you." He gave Max a gentle farewell pat on the head.

On the way home, Pace said, "Here's the thing that's been driving me crazy—why now? I could understand why somebody might have wanted to take a shot at me *before* the biopsy, but why now? What are they afraid of?"

"Maybe it's retribution," Courtney said, "payback for what you've already done. Or maybe it's a warning, telling you not to stick your nose in any further."

"Well, it's not going to work," Pace said.

Courtney gave him a look. "I figured you'd say that."

Two uniformed police officers were just climbing out of their patrol car as Pace and Courtney arrived home. Within a minute a second car pulled up, and a couple of detectives got out. A guy named Marks appeared to be in charge. Courtney seemed to know him.

Pace told his story while Marks took notes.

When Pace finished, Marks asked a simple question. "So who do you think the shooter was?"

Pace shook his head. "I don't have a clue."

"How about Melissa Gardner's boyfriend?" Courtney asked.

"I seriously doubt it," Pace said.

Marks scratched the back of his head, right at the bald spot. "That name's familiar. What's her story?"

"She was the girl who was with Ted Long the night of his fatal accident," Courtney said. "When the Long kid died, his heart was donated. Pace was the recipient."

Marks gave them a blank look.

"Pace has been sniffing around," Courtney explained, "trying to sort out the events of that night. It's possible someone doesn't like what he's doing. Remember, there's kind of a tenuous link between the Long accident and the Lovett case. Anyway, apparently the Gardner girl has a new boyfriend who didn't like the idea of Pace talking to Melissa—for whatever reasons."

"You should know better," Marks said, shaking his head, "than letting him snoop around like that."

"For the record," Pace said, "she's advised me not to, but I'm an adult and therefore free to exercise my own judgment."

"And get shot," Marks said. Then he changed the subject. "What did the shot sound like?"

"I didn't hear it," Courtney said.

"Me either," Pace said. "Just the glass breaking, then the sound of the car roaring off."

"Show me again where you and the dog were lying on the floor," Marks said.

Pace lay back down on the floor and looked up at Courtney. She nodded.

"That low and that close to the window," Marks said, "means the shooter had to be within a few feet of the window—to get the angle he needed."

"I suppose," Pace said.

"So why didn't you hear the shot?"

Pace shrugged. Marks was beginning to make him

feel guilty.

"The guy must have been using a suppressor—a silencer," Marks said. "Which generally means . . ." He left it hanging there for Courtney.

"Which generally means that he's a pretty serious shooter," Courtney said.

Marks nodded. "But on the other hand, if he's such a red-hot gunslinger, how did he miss?"

—40—

When they had finally finished with the police, Pace and Courtney checked back on Max. The news was good. His humerus, the large bone in the upper leg, had been chipped by the bullet but not broken. There had been muscle injury that would take time to heal, but there should be no long-term sequelae. Dr. Donaldson would need to explore the wound and remove the bullet and perhaps repair some of the tissue damage, but Max was in good general condition and was expected to tolerate the procedure well. Bottom line—Max should be fine.

Courtney suggested they go to her apartment for what was left of the night, but Pace wasn't certain that was such a good idea. Whoever had taken a shot at them might well know where Courtney lived and might look for them there. For now, a hotel would probably be less risky.

Pace decided that downtown would be safest, and they ended up at the Ritz Carlton. Pace hadn't been there since the night of the hospital guild auction. He registered while Courtney fidgeted uncomfortably in the lobby.

"We should have gone to a motel," she told Pace when he returned with the key. "Then it wouldn't have been so obvious that we don't have any luggage."

"This time of night," Pace said with a smile, "they know we could only be here for one thing."

"A little danger make you feel amorous, Pace?"

"Define 'amorous,'" he said.

She gave him a shot in the ribs with her elbow.

Later, when they actually did try to get some sleep, Courtney managed to drift off, but Pace's mind refused to rest. A possibility had been gnawing at his brain, and it refused to go away.

When Courtney awoke the next morning, she found Pace sitting in a chair, staring off into space.

"Are you okay, Pace?"

He nodded, not wanting to worry her with his thoughts. "Just a little too much excitement, I guess. I couldn't seem to get to sleep."

She glanced at the bedside clock. "Look at the time! I guess I didn't have any trouble sleeping."

"That's because you were sated beyond mortal woman's wildest dreams."

"Are you saying that you weren't?"

"I'm not a mortal woman," Pace reminded her.

"Meaning?"

"A man has needs a mere woman can never even hope to understand."

"Pace."

"What?"

"Come here."

And for a short while Pace was able to set aside the question that had plagued him all night—What real evidence was there that Ted Long was actually dead?

When the idea first occurred to him, Pace's initial instinct was to discard it out of hand. It was simply too ridiculous to even consider. How could Ted Long possibly be alive? But the notion continued to haunt him, and each time his mind returned to it, new questions arose.

It was his visit to Melissa Gardner that had planted the first subliminal seeds of this new idea—the inexplicably hostile boyfriend who had suddenly appeared out of nowhere. Then the shot through the window that hit poor Max had raised new issues. Who was the shooter? Why now, all of a sudden, did someone want to kill Pace? It would have made a lot more sense, before the biopsy, that someone wanted him dead.

But what if Melissa's new boyfriend was really her *old* boyfriend? What if he was Ted Long? If Ted Long was alive and—knew that Pace had seen him—he might believe it was only a matter of time before Pace figured out what was going on.

Pace tried to remember if he had ever seen a picture of Senator Long's son. He didn't think so. There might have been one on display at the senator's house, but Pace had no memory of it.

Finding a picture of Ted Long probably wouldn't be much of a problem. The trick was not to get killed in the process.

For the time being, he didn't share his thoughts with Courtney. He took her by her apartment so she could get fresh clothes for work, then dropped her downtown. They'd decide later what they'd do that night.

Pace had a busy day ahead of him. It started with a visit to Jefferson High School—Ted Long's alma mater.

The public library Pace had recently visited had seemed fresh and modern and very different from the ancient libraries of his childhood. Jefferson High, on the other hand, was a trip down memory lane. Even the musty odor that greeted him when he first stepped inside was familiar, although at first he couldn't quite place it. The screech of tennis shoes on a gym floor and the shrill blast of a teacher's whistle provided the necessary clues. He was downwind from a locker room and its hundreds of damp towels, sweaty sneakers, and other phys ed paraphernalia molding away in rows of cramped, airless lockers. Pace felt a wave of guilt pass through his body and realized it was a reaction to the prospect of being late for gym class—again. When he sought directions to the library from a student hall monitor, he almost expected her to ask to see his pass.

Pace had worried how best to go about getting the information he wanted. In the end he once again decided that honesty was the best policy. He would tell the truth. Well, some of the truth.

The young woman working the main desk at the library didn't look much older than the students. Pace gave her a bright smile and introduced himself.

"Hi, my name is Pace Magruder," he told her. "I'm a cardiologist and I'm also a heart transplant patient."

The librarian had initially returned his smile but now had a why-are-you-telling-*me*-all-of-this look on her face.

Pace continued to smile—reassuringly—he hoped. "I received my transplant about a year ago. The donor was a graduate of this school who was killed in an auto accident. His name was Ted Long."

She began to nod now, perhaps indicating nothing more than that she had heard of Ted Long's tragic accident.

"Since the transplant," Pace continued, "I've discovered I have this real psychological need to learn about the young man whose death made my life possible. I thought the school might have something, maybe just some old yearbooks, that I might be able to look at and get some feeling for who Ted Long was when he was here."

She stood there, just staring, not responding.

"Do you have yearbooks from when Ted Long was a student?"

"Oh, we have *all* the yearbooks," she said.

Pace waited for something more, then decided he was waiting for Godot. "Would it be possible for me to see the yearbooks?"

"Sure," she said. "I'll have to get them. If we leave them on the shelves—the recent ones anyway—they do a vanishing act."

She disappeared and returned quickly with the relevant volumes, then left Pace to study them in private. Pace took a deep breath before starting in. He wasn't at all certain what he'd find, but he understood it might well change his life forever. He wasn't wrong.

He started with Ted Long's senior year and looked in the back where the seniors' pictures were displayed along with a listing of the various activities they'd participated in. Ted Long's photo, like most of the others, was a professionally done head-and-shoulder shot. In the picture at least, he didn't look a thing like his father. He also didn't look a thing like Melissa Gardner's boyfriend, so scratch that idea.

Long was listed as having participated in student council, wrestling, and junior varsity track, so Pace looked in the sections dealing with sports teams and other student activities. What he found almost made his heart stop.

He checked the older yearbooks for confirmation, to make certain a picture hadn't been mislabeled, but all the photos that were said to be of Ted Long were clearly of the same guy. There was no mistaking that.

Pace was beginning to think that this investigative work was a lot like practicing medicine—sometimes successful outcomes weren't so much a result of being smart as they were a reward for being thorough. Pace had come to the high school to determine whether or not Melissa Gardner's "new" boyfriend was, in fact, Ted Long. Well, he wasn't. Pace was now certain of that.

But Pace was now also certain of one other thing. Melissa's new boyfriend wasn't Ted Long, but neither was the guy who died that night in Ted Long's car.

—41—

Pace now knew that Ted Long had not died in that crash. The big question, who else knew? Obviously Ted Long, for one, but Pace had no idea where he was or how to find him. Pace needed a more accessible suspect. For that, he needed to talk to Joan Bennett—which meant another foray into Howard County.

Pace understood there was a strong possibility that Courtney's suspicion would prove correct—that a murder had been committed that night. Which meant that her other concern was also probably valid—that there was probably at least one bad guy out there who might take violent exception to anyone's sticking his nose into his business, especially an amateur like Pace. But Pace had no intention of playing the hero. He just needed a little more information before he turned the whole thing over to Courtney and the police. They could sort out who all was involved in the murder, and, for that matter, who the victim had been. Pace had pretty clear thoughts about that as well.

It was one of those sullen, muggy days when you wished the thunder clouds would just open up and get it over with. And it was the kind of day when it paid to keep a watchful eye on the heavens. These were the black swirling skies that spawned funnel clouds, and this was the season.

As he drove, Pace's mind was elsewhere, and it was only by chance he happened to notice the police car. He instinctively took his foot off the accelerator and touched the brake pedal. By the time he checked the speedometer, he was well under the speed limit. He wasn't certain he'd ever been above it.

The cruiser was pulled off the highway on the opposite side. Pace was past it in an instant, but in that instant he recognized Sheriff John Wade Dash, and he was pretty certain Dash recognized him.

Watching in his rearview mirror, Pace saw the cruiser's flashing lights come on, then saw the car make a wide U-turn to follow him. When he was closer, Dash flipped on the siren. Pace figured he'd better pull over before Dash escalated to a warning shot.

Dash parked at an angle, the front end of his cruiser pointing out toward the highway. He left his flashers on when he got out of the car. He was drenched in sweat. The police car either didn't have air conditioning, or it was on the fritz.

Pace suppressed a smile as he rolled down his window. He also resisted any number of wisecracks that occurred to him. "Morning, sheriff," he said.

"Get out of the car."

Pace shut off the engine and joined Dash in the sweltering heat.

"Step to the front of the car. Put your hands on the hood." Dash yelled the command like he was twenty feet away.

"Mind telling me what this is about, sheriff?"

"Do as you're told, or I'll put you under arrest."

Pace assumed the position. Dash frisked him— roughly and thoroughly. Pace once again resisted the standard wisecracks.

"Put your right hand behind your back."

Pace felt the slap of a handcuff against his wrist.

"Now the other hand."

Pace was tiring of this game pretty quickly. "What am I being arrested for?"

"You're not under arrest—yet. I'm just placing you in custody while I perform my investigation."

"Investigation of what?"

"That depends on what I find."

So Dash wasn't going to pretend this was anything other than harassment.

Pace could do nothing but watch as the sheriff searched his car. Dash did his best to make a mess, pulling out floor mats and throwing them onto the highway, taking the backseat apart, emptying everything—including the spare tire—out of the trunk and chucking it all into a nearby, water-filled ditch.

When Dash came back to confront Pace, he was carrying the envelope that contained the next couple of doses of Pace's medication.

"*This*," Dash said, "is what I was looking for."

"That's just my heart medication," Pace told him.

"That's what they all say," Dash said. "Why don't I just take you in on suspicion and see where it leads us?"

"Because," Pace told him, "you can probably get away with what you've done so far. It's harassment, but it's so petty it's not worth doing anything about. But, if you take me in, I'm going to call a lawyer. He's going to ask questions, and you're going to have to provide answers."

Dash didn't say anything. He just spun Pace around and grabbed Pace's wallet out of his back pocket, then took his time rummaging through it.

"What're you doing with all this money?" Dash

asked.

Pace just shrugged. He knew he couldn't have much more than a hundred dollars in the wallet. Any less and Dash probably could have held him on a vagrancy charge.

"I asked you a question, boy!"

Dash had been watching too many movies. Pace fought to control his temper. There was no point provoking a man like Dash—especially while you were in handcuffs.

"I made a withdrawal at the bank," Pace said, "and took out extra money for the weekend."

"How do I know this isn't drug money?"

Pace gave him a tired look.

Dash had carried things about as far as he could. He grabbed Pace's arm and began to roughly remove the handcuffs.

"I'm gonna let you go this time," he said. "Next time, you won't be so lucky. My advice to you, stay out of Howard County."

Pace held his tongue. He just watched as Dash once again wedged himself behind the wheel of his cruiser, then slowly pulled away.

—42—

If Sheriff John Wade Dash had understood the first thing about Pace Magruder, he would have known that threats and intimidation were likely to have an effect exactly opposite to the one Dash desired. To keep Pace out of Howard County, what the sheriff really should have done was offer him a bribe to come and work there. Dash's ham-fisted attempt to discourage Pace through petty harassment had accomplished nothing more than a further stiffening of Pace's resolve.

Ten minutes after Dash pulled away, Pace had finished loading his scattered belongings back into his car and was headed for the hospital. He arrived to find the emergency room enveloped in the kind of frenetic whirl that to an outsider gives an impression of absolute chaos, but to the seasoned ER infighter reflects only a typically hectic day.

"My name is Pace Magruder," he told the ward clerk. "Dr. Bennett is expecting me, but I can see that things are a little frantic right now. If you'll let her know I'm here, I'll just have a seat in the waiting area."

"Are you a patient of Dr. Bennett's?"

Pace shook his head. "No, just a friend."

"It may be a while," the clerk warned.

"That's fine. I'll find something to read." Then, worried that Joan might feel even more pressed with

253

him hovering in the waiting room, Pace asked for directions to the medical library. "Tell Joan not to worry. I have lots of reading I need to catch up on. When she's available, just give me a call and I'll come back to the ER."

It was an hour and a half later when Pace, lost in a cardiology journal, felt a gentle hand on his shoulder.

"Sorry, Pace," Joan said. "It's just one of those days."

Pace stood and gave her a hug. "It's my fault for bothering you in the middle of a workday. I won't take much of your time. There're just a couple of questions I had. Do you want to sit here, or should I walk you back to the ER?"

Joan didn't need a second invitation to take a seat. "I'd like to sit for a couple of hours if I could, but I'll settle for a couple of minutes."

Pace sat back down. They had the small library to themselves.

"It's about the night Ted Long was brought in," Pace said. "Do you remember who visited his bedside? Any family?"

"No," she said. "I mean, I remember, but there was no family. Just that one guy, the chief of staff."

"What about the girlfriend?"

"She was here, but she was in no condition to visit anyone. I was in and around the ICU most of the night. She was never there as far as I know."

"And no family?" Pace asked again.

"The only family I ever heard about was the father, and he supposedly was on Air Force One headed for Europe. No one else was here."

"And you're sure that Styles, the chief of staff, actually went to the bedside?"

Joan didn't hesitate. "Absolutely. He and the sheriff

came in together. The sheriff was following him around like a puppy dog."

Pace knew he was about to enter a potentially touchy area. He wanted to be careful. "Who identified Ted Long, Joan? How was that done?"

Joan gave him a long look before answering. "It was never an issue. The sheriff brought him in with his identification. He was signed in under his own name." She stopped herself, clearly trying to sort things out in her own mind. "Are you saying that the victim might not have been Ted Long? I mean, it's not like the senator's son turned up the next day and said, Wait a minute, I'm not dead."

"No, of course he didn't," Pace said. "I'm just trying to understand some things." He hesitated a moment, gathering his thoughts. "What did Ted Long look like that night?"

"What do you mean?"

Pace didn't want to lead her. "Physically, what did he look like?"

"He was a mess, Pace. What do you think he looked like?" She was clearly upset by the thinly veiled suggestion that the identification might have been mishandled. "If you're still talking about ID-ing the victim, I can assure you there was no way to do that by looking at his face. What wasn't covered with bandages was totally unrecognizable."

Pace nodded. "What did he look like in his bed in the ICU? Was he covered?"

She shook her head. "You know how that goes, Pace. He was practically naked. Most of the night he was in thermoregulatory crisis, and we were doing everything we could to keep his temperature down. We had a cooling blanket under him and a towel over his pelvic area. Modesty wasn't high on our list of priorities."

"So, what did he look like, lying there?"

Joan knitted her eyebrow together. "I'm not sure what you want from me, Pace. He was just this great big, muscular young kid lying in a hospital bed."

"How big?"

"I don't know, Pace. Huge. Like you. I'd have to look at his chart, but he certainly weighed well over two hundred pounds and must have been six foot six or so. I remember that his feet stuck out beyond the end of the mattress. It's one of those bizarre little details that impress themselves on your memory forever."

Pace smiled. "I know," he said. "Things like that stick in your mind." Then he glanced at his watch. "I've taken too much of your time, Joan. I really appreciate your talking with me. Let me walk you back to the ER."

Again Joan shook her head. "Not so fast, Pace. What's going on?"

"I'm not sure yet. Maybe nothing."

"But it's possible the victim that night wasn't Ted Long?"

"It's possible, Joan—*likely*, even. I'll let you know as soon as I know for certain. In the meantime, please don't say anything to anyone."

"I'm sure the hospital's attorneys would want a heads-up. The hospital could have some significant exposure here. Hell, *I* could have some pretty significant exposure here."

"I don't think so," Pace told her. "If there was a misidentification, it happened because someone deliberately misled the hospital. Think about it. People are brought into hospitals all the time—after accidents and so forth. The family comes in. They visit the patient. They see who it is. No one ever double checks to make sure the family isn't lying—that the kid they're visiting and paying the bills for isn't really their son."

"What are you going to do, Pace?"

"Well," he said, "if you'll tell me where his office is, I'm going to pay a little visit to Sheriff John Wade Dash."

"Pace, be careful. If Dash is involved in this, there's nothing he wouldn't do to keep himself out of trouble."

She was probably right, but Dash knew things that no one else could tell him. Pace couldn't resist giving the sheriff's chain a little tug, just to see what happened.

—43—

The Howard County jail was not an uplifting sight. The red brick building was old and dilapidated and grim. It looked like something out of the 19th century, which it probably was. The architectural themes of disrepair and disorder were carried through to the interior where the addition of a pervasive foul aroma did nothing to enhance the ambience. Pace suspected the odor wafted up from detention cells below, but his mind shied away from any attempt to further identify the precise etiology of the stench.

An obese, middle-aged woman with bright orange hair sat behind an ancient wooden desk in the middle of the room and studiously ignored Pace as he approached. A handmade sign Scotch-taped to the front of her desk said, "I'm not a cop. I just answer the phone."

"I'd like to speak with Sheriff Dash," Pace told her.

For an answer, the woman lowered her gaze and nodded ever-so-slightly in the direction of the sign.

"I'm sorry," Pace said, "but how do I contact the sheriff?"

"Not my problem," she said.

Pace considered a number of responses, none of which was likely to get him anywhere, and some of which would probably insure his ending up in a cell downstairs. He eyed the closed door not ten feet away and assumed that it must lead to Dash's office, then he noticed the pay phone in a distant corner of the room.

He availed himself of the tattered phonebook and dialed the number. When the phone on the desk rang, Pace couldn't resist a peek. The orange-haired woman had him fixed in a glacial stare that warned, *This better not be you,* as she reached for the phone. Pace rendered his most beguiling smile.

"Howard County jail," she told the phone.

"Hello, this is Pace Magruder," Pace said. "I'd like to set up an appointment to meet with Sheriff Dash."

About halfway through his spiel she slammed the receiver down on its cradle. Pace thought it would surely break. Then the door behind her opened and none other than John Wade Dash himself appeared.

"You come to turn yourself in?" Dash asked.

"I came to turn *someone* in," Pace told him.

Dash gave him his much-practiced long hard look, then turned his back and started down the hallway behind the door. But he left the door open behind him.

Pace gave the woman behind the desk one last adoring smile, then followed Dash down the corridor and into his office. The place smelled like a brewery—a welcome reprieve from the odor that pervaded the rest of the building. In the window behind the sheriff's desk, an air conditioner railed loudly against the perversity of Nature.

Dash fell heavily into the cracking leather chair behind his desk, then cast a furtive eye in the direction of a lower right-hand drawer. Since he was wearing his pistol on his hip, Pace assumed the drawer must contain his bottle.

"So what the hell do you want?" Dash said.

"Answers."

Dash didn't care for his attitude. "Don't get cute with me, boy. Not in *my* county."

Pace didn't figure there was any point in being coy. "I want to know who died that night in Ted Long's car," he said. "I know it wasn't Ted Long."

He could see that Dash was off balance. Pace had taken him by surprise. Whatever Dash was worried about, this wasn't it.

But Dash was taking his time. He was a wary old bear.

"I know that some money disappeared that night," Pace said. "I don't care about that. It's none of my business. But I want to know whose heart this is." He gave his chest a tap with the first two fingers of his right hand.

"I don't know anything about any money," Dash said.

"Like I said, I don't care about that," Pace said. Then he shifted to the attack. "How was the body identified that night?"

He got nothing but a sullen glare from Dash. Bingo.

Pace pressed ahead. "Did you get a good look at the victim? What did he look like?"

Dash shook his head. "You couldn't tell nothin'. His face was a mess. His own mother couldn't have recognized him."

"But you saw him in the hospital. What do you remember?"

Again, Dash shook his head. "They cleaned him up some, but then they wrapped his head in bandages. You still couldn't see anything."

"But what *do* you remember? What about his size?"

Dash was briefly wary, then plunged forward. "He was a big kid—bigger than his daddy—what I can tell from pictures and on television."

"How big?"

Dash shrugged. "Big. Well over six feet, I'd say. Maybe six and a half."

"How much did he weigh?"

"A ton. I had to help the medics haul the stretcher out of the ravine. One of 'em said he probably weighed more than me. Incidentally, that medic later paid for his remark." Dash threw in his hard look again, at the end—to remind Pace what a tough guy he was.

Pace ignored the look. It was time for the *coup de grâce*. "Ted Long was five feet six inches tall. His senior year in high school, he wrestled in the 125 pound weight class."

You could almost see the wheels turning in the sheriff's head as he digested this last piece of news. Even with the wheels turning at what was, for Dash, full speed, it took a while for him to sort it out. Finally, he had it.

"If that wasn't Ted Long, the one who was killed, how come the senator and none of the rest of them never said nothin'? How come the Long kid didn't just turn up?"

"Good question," Pace said.

"What do you expect me to do?"

"Call the cops," Pace told him.

Pace was in his car, heading back toward home, trying to decide what to do next. It was time to tell Courtney everything he knew and let her take it to the police. Pace wouldn't be holding his breath waiting for Sheriff John Wade Dash to begin his investigation.

But no sooner was the thought in his head than Pace heard the distant wail of a police siren. With every passing second the siren grew louder. Then he saw the flashing lights in his rearview mirror.

What would Dash do? That was anybody's guess. Pace had figured Dash as a corrupt cop—a thief, but not a murderer—at least not on the night of the accident. But did Dash have murder on his mind now?

Pace briefly wondered if he was still in Howard County. Should he try to make a run for it? Did the county line offer any kind of protection? But Dash was gaining on him too quickly. There was no way to outrun him. Better to make certain he was well under the speed limit when Dash caught up.

Then, in the blink of an eye, it was over. Dash blew by Pace's car like it was standing still. The sheriff must have had his cruiser doing well over a hundred.

Within seconds he was out of sight, the flashing red lights no more than faint green afterimages. Dash was headed like a bat out of hell for someplace.

—44—

Courtney was scheduled to be tied up before a judge all afternoon, presenting pretrial motions, and Pace wasn't about to go to anyone else with what he'd discovered until he had a chance to bring Courtney up to speed and see how she wanted to proceed. So that gave him time to check on Max, and he learned something about the dog he never would have suspected.

Max, it turned out, was a great big baby. That was the overwhelming consensus at the veterinary hospital.

"We can't get him up," Barbara Donaldson told Pace. "He hurts, and instinct tells him not to use the leg. But if he doesn't mobilize that shoulder it's going to freeze up, and he'll be badly crippled for the rest of his life."

"It's a problem with human patients, too," Pace assured her.

"We see it all the time in dogs, it's just that with a dog as big as Max, it's pretty tough to get him to do something he doesn't want to do."

Max was lying on his side, staring up at them.

"He hasn't snapped at anyone or anything like that, has he?" Pace asked.

Dr. Donaldson shook her head and smiled. "Max? You've got to be kidding. No, Max has mastered the art of passive resistance. He just lies there in a great big lump. We're thinking about changing his name to Mahatma."

"Well," Pace said, massaging the dog fondly behind an ear, "let me give it a try. Old Max nursed me back to health not too long ago. Now I guess it's my turn."

Pace tried to coax Max out of the kennel. When that failed, he reached in and got his arms around the dog, then gently pulled him out. Max was one hundred and twenty pounds of dead weight in his arms.

"See what I mean?" Donaldson said. "You can take him out back, if you want, or feel free to just carry him around inside."

"Thanks for the vote of confidence," Pace said. "I believe we'll try it outside."

It was slow going. Max had very strong feelings about what he should—or rather should *not*—be doing.

"Come on, Max," Pace told him, "you wouldn't let me lie around when I wanted to."

Pace set Max down gently on his feet. Max slowly lowered himself until he was lying on the ground.

Pace raised Max back up. Max lay back down.

Pace picked Max up once again. This time, Max hovered, trembling, about halfway down. It was painful to watch.

Pace picked him up one more time. "Come on, Max. It'll be easier if you just stand all the way up."

And Max did it. He wasn't happy about it, but he did it. But try what he might, Pace couldn't get Max to take a step.

"I got him to stand," Pace reported to Barbara Donaldson, "but he wouldn't walk."

"That's a start," she said approvingly. "We'll keep working on him."

"And I'll come back tomorrow and spend some time

with him," Pace said.

When he saw that Pace was leaving, Max started to struggle to his feet. He looked desperately unhappy.

Pace knelt down and gave Max another affectionate rub behind the ear. "Sorry, Max. I can't take you to the hotel with me, but I'll be back to see you bright and early tomorrow—I promise."

—45—

It was only their second night, but staying at the hotel was already becoming a pain. And Courtney was tired and perhaps just a slight bit irritable after a long day in front of a judge who seemed less than sympathetic to the "people's" point of view.

"She's one of those judges," Courtney said, "who's a lot more interested in social engineering than in seeing justice done. She thinks it's society's fault that the defendant shot his wife to death because his dinner was late getting to the table for the second night in a row. Judge Watson thinks society should never have made it possible for the man to own a gun. I asked her if she would be any happier if the defendant had decapitated his wife with a butter knife because he was sure as hell going to kill her one way or another.

"So Judge Watson has asked me to go home and consider why I shouldn't be held in contempt of court, which means I have to go back into her court on Friday and apologize for my outrageous behavior—instead of asking her to sign a petition to ban butter knives, which is what I'd rather do."

Pace decided Courtney needed a little time to decompress before he hit her with his news. She took a long shower, and then they went downstairs for dinner in the main dining room. Pace told her about Max.

"Basically, he's going to be fine. He just needs to begin using that shoulder before it freezes up on him. I'll bring him home in a day or two and start giving him regular workouts."

Pace waited until they were back in their room before he broached the other subject. Courtney had slipped into a nightgown and crawled into bed. Pace was still dressed and was momentarily tempted to join her, maybe put his news on a back burner for just a little while longer, but he managed to get his more primitive instincts under control and sat down on the side of the bed.

"I've learned something important," he said.

His tone instantly captured Courtney's attention.

"I found out that Ted Long was five and a half feet tall and weighed about a hundred and twenty-five pounds."

Courtney stared at him, frowning. "I know that's important, Pace. I'm just trying to remember . . . " And then, "Oh my God, Pace! Your heart! Ted Long's heart is too small. What does that mean?"

Pace smiled affectionately. Courtney's first thought had been that he was going to tell her about a medical problem—this big mistake had been made. Pace had received a heart that was too small, and medical complications were imminent.

"Not to worry," he told her. "Fortunately for me, even though Ted Long was of smaller stature, the victim that night was at least as big as me."

Now Courtney understood. "So the guy who died wasn't Ted Long." She was nodding and thinking. "And it wasn't just some simple mistake in identification. I mean, that could have happened in the short run, but in a matter of hours—if nothing else—Ted Long would have turned up somewhere. So this was deliberate—which means that Ted Long had a hand in it and is hiding out somewhere."

Then a new idea crossed her mind. "Pace! Melissa Gardner's new boyfriend!"

"I had the same idea—before I knew how small Ted Long was. The new guy is too big, and, besides, he doesn't look a thing like Ted Long."

"But why didn't anyone put this together a long time ago—if the size discrepancy is such a big deal? It should have been obvious that Ted Long couldn't have donated your heart."

"It would have been apparent to some people," Pace said. "Joan Bennett would have known. Brian Curtis would have known. But neither of them knew about Ted Long's size. Senator Long is tall. Anyone might have assumed that his son would be tall as well. And there was no general knowledge that Ted's heart had been transplanted, much less that I was the recipient. People who knew Ted probably weren't even aware he had been a donor. And, if they *were* aware, they wouldn't have known that I was the recipient. And even if they knew *both* of those things, the general public couldn't be expected to know anything about matching heart transplant donors and recipients. It just worked out that the handful of people who actually knew that Ted was the donor and that I was the recipient had no idea of Ted's actual size. When you think about it, the really remarkable thing is not that it wasn't discovered sooner, but that I happened to tumble to it at all—and that was only an accident. I had the same thought you did. I was just looking for a picture of Ted to see if he was the guy I ran into at Melissa Gardner's apartment."

"What about at the hospital?" Courtney asked.

"How was he misidentified there?"

"Incompetence on the sheriff's part certainly played a major role."

Pace told her about his Howard County experiences earlier in the day. When he finished, Courtney cut through all the details with a single, incisive question.

"Why did you have to see Joan Bennett in person?"

Pace leaned over and gave her a kiss. "A crack investigator has to go wherever the clues lead him."

Courtney didn't appear totally convinced. "Leaving that aside, just for the moment," she said, "what about Styles? Is there any way Styles could have failed to realize Ted Long *wasn't* the victim that night? Could it have been just a simple mistake?"

"I don't see how," Pace said. "Joan said the patient looked huge. He was too big for his ICU bed."

"So Styles knew, and he also knew there was a good reason to let the world think Ted Long was dead— most likely to keep Ted from being implicated in the rape and murder of Francine Lovett."

"That would be my guess," Pace said.

Courtney had another thought. "I was thinking, wait, we know Ted Long didn't rape Francine Lovett, we did the DNA tests. But of course all they proved was that the heart donor didn't commit the rape. If Ted Long wasn't the donor, he's still a suspect."

Courtney considered this silently for a few moments, then asked, "What about the senator? What does he know?"

"No way to be certain. Sometimes, I can think it through and reason that he had nothing to do with it— at least not *before* the accident. Other times, I see him orchestrating the whole thing."

"He seemed genuinely relieved," Courtney said, "when he heard that the DNA testing had exonerated his son."

"He's a politician," Pace said. "They can be awfully good actors."

"Tell me about it," Courtney said. "But Styles is definitely dirty."

"I don't see any way around that."

"And Ted Long is out there somewhere, sipping margaritas on some warm, tropical beach and laughing at us."

"Seems likely," Pace said.

"That makes me mad."

"Me, too."

"Do you think the accident victim wasn't really an accident victim at all—that he was murdered and it was made to look like an accident?"

Pace nodded. "That was your original idea, and it certainly looks dead-on to me."

"Murdered by Styles and Ted Long," Courtney said, "which still leaves us with one question—who was the victim?"

"I think I could make a pretty good guess," Pace said.

Courtney nodded.

They talked for a while longer, then Pace crawled into bed and snuggled up next to her.

"There's one thing I'm still unclear about," she said.

"What's that?"

"Why you had to see Joan Bennett in person."

Jealousy, thy name is woman.

They were awakened early the next morning by the sound of Courtney's pager going off on the bedside table. She answered and had a brief conversation with whoever had paged her. When she hung up the phone, she turned to Pace.

"That was about Sheriff John Wade Dash," she said. "He's dead."

—46—

The area was mostly wooded, but here and there Pace could see evidence that someone had gone through, years earlier, with a bulldozer.

They were at the very outskirts of the city, and the large tract of land had obviously been purchased with development in mind, but the developers didn't get very far before the money ran out—or the market turned down—or both. There were a few vestigial streets—the only improvements that remained. The tangled brush that took over after the dozers left was already being replaced, in many areas, by small trees. Older growth trees were prominent in portions the bulldozers had never reached.

This half-paved, half-overgrown warren of blind streets and isolated cul-de-sacs was just the kind of place kids loved for various types of mischief. But sometime in the last twelve hours or so someone had used it for a far more sinister purpose.

The crime scene was an anthill of activity. There were police in uniform and detectives in shirt sleeves. Evidence technicians were everywhere. More than a dozen vehicles were parked around the perimeter, including a coroner's wagon awaiting the signal that the body could finally be removed.

They took two cars, Courtney not being certain

what the day would hold for her. Pace pulled in behind her and surveyed the scene. From this distance, well behind the yellow crime-scene tape, Pace could see Dash's cruiser and perhaps a dark form slumped behind the wheel—or maybe that was only his imagination. Courtney climbed out of her car and headed directly for Dash's cruiser. She ducked under the yellow tape without breaking stride. Pace had only a brief flicker of hesitation before following.

Seconds later they were intercepted by the ubiquitous Detective Marks.

"You official?" he asked Courtney.

She shook her head. "Not yet. The case hasn't been assigned."

"You can stay," he said, "but the doc has to get back behind the tape."

"Anybody formally identify the body yet?" Courtney asked.

"Not yet."

"I thought maybe Dr. Magruder could help us with that," Courtney said. This wasn't an idea she had discussed with Pace.

"You can identify him?" Marks asked Pace.

"*If* it's Dash," he said, "and *if* he's identifiable."

"How do you happen to know Dash?" This was turning into too big a coincidence for Marks to just passively swallow.

"I've spent some time in Howard County," Pace told him.

"When did you see him last?"

"Yesterday afternoon," Pace said.

Marks gave Courtney a long look.

"Dr. Magruder might have some relevant information," she said. "I'm sure he'll be happy to give you a statement when it's appropriate."

"How about right now?" Marks said.

"First," Courtney said, "let's see if it's really Dash. No point wasting Dr. Magruder's time—or yours—if it's not."

"All right," Marks said. "Just don't touch anything."

It wasn't an order that Pace particularly resented. He didn't pretend to have much knowledge of crime scene procedures. But he noticed Marks made no effort to indicate his order was directed only at Pace, and Pace couldn't help but wonder if that was a deliberate shot at Courtney.

For her part, Courtney appeared not to notice. She just set off toward Dash's car, leaving the two men to follow—or not.

Death, the physician's perpetual enemy, was no stranger to Pace, but he found himself strangely moved by the sight of Dash's lifeless body. This violent, unnatural death—even of a man for whom he had no respect, much less affection—left Pace disgusted by its wastefulness and senselessness. Life was far too precious a commodity to be extinguished so carelessly.

Marks was less philosophical. "Is it Dash?" he asked.

It was not a tidy picture. Death had been caused by a bullet wound to the temple. Damage to the cranium had been considerable. But the face was recognizable.

"It's Dash," Pace said.

Courtney had worked her way around to the other side of the car, exploring the scene. When she returned she said, "His gun's still holstered."

"I figure he was meeting someone," Marks said. "Whoever it was came up to the car to talk. Dash didn't see it coming. He just got popped." Marks made a shooting motion with his thumb and first finger.

Pace tried to sort out what must have happened, the series of events the day before that culminated in the sheriff's death. He had some ideas, but there were still some pretty big pieces missing.

Marks had pieces of his own to fill in. "Okay, Doc," he said, "now I need to hear what you know. Let's go back to my car so we can sit down."

"Go ahead," Courtney said. "I'm going to poke around here a little while longer."

Pace had taken only a couple of steps when an evidence technician stepped out of a wooded area forty or fifty feet away. He waved at Marks to get his attention.

"Detective! We've got another body over here."

The discovery of the second body meant that Courtney and everyone else would be tied up for additional long hours at the murder scene. Pace wanted some peace and quiet to think things through on his own, so he climbed back into his car and headed for a small park not far away where he could sit and think.

He spent most of that afternoon going over everything he knew, again and again. By the time he returned to look for Courtney, he figured he had a pretty good handle on what might have happened— beginning with the night of the transplant.

The crime scene was much-changed from when he left it, primarily due to all the media crews now milling around outside the yellow-tape perimeter. Another difference was the unexpected presence Senator Edward Long.

Courtney was sitting in the passenger's seat of her car, making notes. Pace slid in behind the wheel.

"What's the story on Long?" he asked.

"Turns out he owns this property," Courtney said. "Lost a ton of money trying to develop it."

"Now, there's a coincidence," Pace said.

"Isn't it?"

"What's the story on the second body?"

"Probably unrelated," Courtney said. "It's been there a long time—at least months."

"What kind of a description do you have?"

"Male, medium to small stature. Probably fairly young, based on the teeth. Either a murder or a suicide—there's a bullet hole in the skull."

Pace nodded. "The bullet they take out of Dash," he said, "be sure they check it against the one that was taken out of Max's shoulder."

Courtney gave him a searching look. "Anything else?"

"I don't think the other body's unrelated," Pace said.

—47—

For Joan Bennett it had been another of those long, difficult days. She had stayed on in the ER until nearly seven o'clock that evening—well past the end of her shift—and she was tired and hungry and not in a very good mood. It was the kind of night when David really shined. He'd have a bottle of wine open and dinner on the stove when she got home. He'd listen attentively to the story of her day. What had begun as a very difficult day would end in a warm, romantic evening.

But David was out of town—a visit to New York to lay the groundwork for his upcoming one-man show—and she didn't think she could face that big empty house and its equally empty refrigerator. Not tonight. So she was driving around, trying to decide what she felt like eating and where she wouldn't mind being seen, slightly disheveled, after a long day at work.

She had a kind of subliminal awareness of the car behind her—the same car, at least twice, despite her directionless wandering. But no alarm bells rang. In her preoccupied state, it did not occur to her she was being followed.

Joan finally decided on a little soup and sandwich place in a nearby mall. She toyed briefly with the idea of getting something to take home, then decided she still wasn't ready for that. She was sitting at a table waiting for her food when she noticed the man staring at her.

He had walked by, then turned, and now he was just standing there, staring.

He was well-dressed, probably in his late thirties—his beard made it difficult to guess how old he was. And the beard seemed somehow wrong, but she couldn't quite put her finger on the problem. He just kept staring and staring.

And then he walked toward her. Directly to her table. He kept staring at her. Then he was at her side.

"You're Dr. Bennett, aren't you?"

Joan didn't know what to do. She gave him a half nod. He was terrifying her.

"I'm Charles Styles," he said, "Senator Long's chief of staff. We met at the hospital, the night of the accident."

Joan wanted to say, No you're not! He was vaguely familiar, but surely this wasn't the same man. She was speechless.

"It's the beard," he said. "It's new. Nobody recognizes me anymore."

Maybe, she thought.

"I don't want to impose," he said, "but there's something I'd like to ask you about. It concerns that night at the hospital. I have this haunting fear that a terrible mistake may have been made."

Joan felt a sinking feeling in the pit of her stomach. Now she knew what this was about—the same question Pace had raised. Who really died that night?

"Mind if I sit down?"

"Please," Joan said, but without much enthusiasm. Based on her interactions with Styles at the hospital, he wasn't a man she really wanted to get to know. But the fear was gone. This was the chief of staff of a

United States senator. He wasn't some pervert stalking women in a shopping mall.

When he sat down, Styles started right in. "That was such a terrible night. I was devastated when they told me Ted had been killed. I was so distraught, I just went through the motions. I didn't think. I couldn't think. I only felt."

Joan could see how upset he was, even after all this time. "I think that's pretty normal," she assured him, "under those kinds of circumstances."

"But dealing with things under pressure is my job. It's what I do. There's no excuse for messing up. Senator Long was unavailable. He counted on me to do the right thing, and I let him down."

"In what way?" Joan asked—knowing full well what was coming.

"I have nightmares," Styles said, "almost every night. And it's always the same. I'm in the ICU. It's the night of the accident. The victim is lying in the bed with all those tubes and machines around. His head is bandaged so I can't see his face. I remove the bandages. I see the face. And it's *not* Ted."

"I'm sure it's terrifying," Joan said, "but it's only a dream."

Styles shook his head. "It's more than that. I also have very real memories of that night. I can close my eyes and see the ICU, like I was still standing right there. And when I look at that bed, I don't see Ted. I mean, I can't see his face, but I see this huge form lying in the bed. That couldn't have been Ted. He was a guy of average size—less than average even. He was *small*."

Joan tried not to let her expression give anything away.

"Do you remember the patient?" Styles asked. "Do

you remember how big he was?"

"That was quite a long time ago," Joan said, noncommittally. "I've seen a lot of patients since then. It's hard to remember each one."

The waitress came with Joan's food. Styles ordered coffee, then pressed her again.

"But what about the size of the guy who received the heart that was removed that night?" he asked. "How big was he? Wouldn't that tell us something about the size of the donor? I mean, if the donor was someone Ted's size, the recipient would also have to be a person of small stature."

"Sure," Joan said. "But people like me who work on the donor end don't usually know much about the recipient. There's kind of a firewall that's maintained to protect identities."

While they talked, Joan picked at her food, but she no longer had any appetite.

Styles appeared to lose interest in pursuing the issue any further. He tried to lead the conversation in other directions, but Joan wasn't feeling much like casual conversation.

Finally she said, "I've had kind of a long day, Mr. Styles. I need to go on home and rest up for another long day tomorrow."

"Of course," Styles said. He looked at his watch. "My goodness, I had no idea how late it had gotten. Let me walk you to your car."

Joan tried to dissuade him, but he wouldn't be put off. In fact, she knew it was a good idea. Shopping mall parking lots could be pretty dangerous places for a woman alone after dark.

She found her car and unlocked the door, then slid in behind the wheel. Styles, ever the gentleman, closed the door behind her, then waved and walked off to find his own car. He was gone.

Joan sat there for several seconds trying to sort things out. It was now much more clear to her what Pace had been after. He had somehow tumbled to the size issue as well.

Joan remembered that night vividly. The ER was swamped. Did she miss something she should have seen? Could she have done something that night to prevent the misidentification? Joan had every confidence that *somebody's* lawyer would claim she could have.

Then, the sinking feeling returned to the pit of her stomach. She had held a driver's license in her hands, if only briefly, that night. She'd paid no attention to anything other than the consent to donate organs. Who's license was it? Long's, she imagined.

But another thought immediately entered her mind, totally replacing the driver's license issue—if the identification problem had been discovered that night, no transplant would have been performed. Unless some other heart had magically come along, Pace Magruder would long since have died.

There was nothing she could do about any of that tonight. She'd give Pace a call in the morning and tell him about her meeting with Styles.

She reached for the ignition key. When she turned it, nothing happened.

She tried again.

Nothing.

She pumped the accelerator, then tried again.

Still nothing. Not a whine. Not a whimper. Damn!

She looked around. She was alone. There was no chance of her getting her car going, and no way she was going to spend the rest of the night dealing with a garage. She'd call a cab and go straight home. She could deal with the car in the morning.

She was just getting out from behind the wheel when another car drove up. It was Styles. He leaned over and lowered the passenger side window of his car.

"Everything okay?" he asked.

"My car won't start."

"What me to have a look?"

"I'd appreciate it."

Styles got in behind the wheel, but didn't have any more luck than Joan had.

"There should be plenty of gas in the tank," Joan said.

"I'm sure there is," Styles said. "Gas isn't the problem. It's something electrical. When you turn the key, you don't even hear the starter. I'm afraid it's a little beyond my abilities as a mechanic. You're going to need to call a garage."

"I don't think I could face that tonight," Joan said. "It's been one of those days. All I want to do is go home and crawl into bed. I was about to call a cab when you came by."

"I'd be more than happy to drive you home," Styles said.

"Oh, no. I couldn't let you do that. I've delayed you enough already."

"Don't be silly," Styles said. "It would be my pleasure."

Pace and Courtney also ended up at a restaurant—theirs not far from where Dash's body had been found. By the time Pace had arrived back at the crime scene that afternoon, Detective Marks had disappeared. Pace hadn't seen any point in waiting around for him.

Pace and Courtney still had their separate cars. After a quick bite to eat, Courtney needed to go back downtown and deal with all the issues that had accumulated while she was at the murder scene. But first, Pace had a few things he needed to tell her. They found a corner booth where they could talk in private.

"I think I've pretty much got all the pieces put together," Pace said. "I think I know most of what happened, and why."

"Do you still think the second body they found today is related?"

Pace nodded. "But let's start at the beginning. Let's start with Styles. That's the biggest clue in this whole thing—Styles' not recognizing that the victim was far too large to be Ted Long."

"And that couldn't have been an accident?" Courtney said.

"No way," Pace said. "The size discrepancy was just too great. Styles *knew* Ted wasn't the victim, but he didn't say anything. Why?"

"Because Long was a suspect in the Lovett case—presumably a *guilty* suspect—and Styles thought it would be helpful if everybody thought Long was dead."

"That's what I thought, too," Pace said, "but not anymore. And there's one other thing to understand about the beginning—Styles knew, before he ever came to the hospital that night, that Ted Long wasn't the victim, and he also knew that Ted wasn't out partying somewhere with a hundred other people who could later say, Wait a minute, Ted was with *us* that night. He wasn't killed in any car accident."

"So Styles needed to have Ted safely tucked away someplace," Courtney said, "and Ted had to be involved."

"One way or another," Pace said, "Ted Long had to be involved before Styles got to the hospital."

"So you think they planned for the victim to be misidentified, to get Ted off the hook on the murder rap?"

Pace smiled. "That's the most interesting part. The misidentification was totally unintentional. It had to be a complete accident."

Courtney shook her head. "Now you've lost me."

Pace was still smiling. "As soon as you think about it this way, nothing else makes sense. No one, I mean no one, could possibly have anticipated that the victim that night would be misidentified as Ted Long. That is simply not possible. Long was a foot shorter and weighed maybe a hundred pounds less than the accident victim. Not even a complete idiot would have embarked on a plan dependent on such an improbable mistake being made."

"So how did it happen?"

"Primarily ace police work on the part of Sheriff

John Wade Dash. But once the initial mistake was made, the fact that Ted Long was handled like a VIP meant a lot of corners were cut. It happens all the time. Add to that the time pressure of the transplant. Styles saw all of this coming together and just let it ride."

"So what was *supposed* to happen when Long's car was found?" Courtney asked.

"Nothing but the truth. Here was a guy driving Ted Long's presumably stolen car, carrying a gun and a lot of money—in Ted's presumably stolen wallet—and transporting Long's girlfriend."

Courtney smiled. "Transporting?"

"Give me a break here. I'm working without a script."

"So you're saying it was supposed to look like a carjacking or something. He grabbed the car and the girlfriend and was heading for parts unknown when he lost control and had the accident?"

"Almost," Pace said.

"What am I missing?"

"The gun."

"For the abduction," Courtney said.

"It had been fired."

"So there was another victim to be found?"

"Bingo," Pace said. "Anyway, that was Plan A. When the misidentification occurred, Styles went to Plan B."

"And we found the victim today in the woods near Dash's car."

"That's another bingo."

"Styles would have been counting on a lot, expecting the second body to be found at the time of the accident. The techs said the only reason they found it today was that some animal had uncovered it."

"After the identification mix up," Pace said, "Styles

no longer *wanted* the body to be found. Under Plan A, it would have been left lying somewhere in plain view. When he went to Plan B, he had to hide it somewhere—so he moved it into the woods."

"And the body we found today," Courtney said, "constitutes the mortal remains of Ted Long."

"I'd bet a lot on that."

"And the gun he was shot with is the gun that was found in Long's car the night of the accident."

"I'd give you real good odds on that one, too."

"And Charles Styles, the chief of staff of a United States senator, was the shooter."

"It sure looks like it."

"Just one question then, Pace."

"What's that?"

"Why?"

"Why did Styles want Ted Long dead?"

"Yep."

Pace shook his head. "This is where things start to get a little fuzzy."

"Try me," she said.

"I think Styles raped and murdered Francine Lovett, and I think Ted Long knew it."

"And Styles killed Long to make certain he didn't share the dirty little secret with anyone?" Courtney didn't sound completely convinced. "How did Ted find out about Styles?"

Pace shrugged. "No way to know for certain, of course, but I've wondered if maybe Dean Arnold didn't tell him, indirectly. Maybe Arnold didn't really see Ted Long that night. What he really saw was Ted Long's car. When Long heard about Arnold's claim, he knew the truth—because he knew that Styles had been driving *his* car." Pace thought for a moment. "Actually, it was Melissa Gardner, Ted's old girlfriend, who told me Styles sometimes drove Ted's car."

"The one thing we're both thinking, but not saying," Courtney said, "is who the victim was—Dean Arnold."

"If Arnold's a big guy," Pace said, "I'd bet on it."

"Oh, he's a big guy, all right," Courtney said. "I met him back at the beginning of all of this."

"I met his father," Pace said. "He seemed like such a nice man. This will be awfully difficult for the Arnold family to deal with."

Courtney nodded, then she had another thought. "Why is this all erupting now, a year after the event? Why was Dash killed? Why did someone take a shot at you?"

"All that was my fault," Pace said. "Styles thought he was home free. He didn't have a care in the world— until that night at Tommy Jacob's office when I mentioned to him how appreciative I was of the Long family's generosity. I remember mentioning to him that, since I was a big guy, I needed a heart from a large donor. Prior to that moment, I'm certain it had never occurred to Styles there might be some sort of size requirement.

"As soon as Styles heard that, he knew he was sitting on a time bomb. Now that I knew that my new heart had supposedly come from Ted Long, it might be only a matter of time before I tumbled to the truth. Then Styles would have to explain how he could have made such a mistake, and that was bound to lead to even more questions."

"So Styles wanted to kill you before you put two and two together?"

"It looks like it."

"And Dash for the same reason?"

"As far as I know, Dash didn't have any insight into any of this until I mentioned it to him yesterday afternoon. I don't know if he went to warn Styles or to blackmail him. Either way, Styles wasn't taking any chances."

After a few moments' silence, Courtney said, "I'm trying to think how much of this we can prove. If they find a bullet in what we presume is Ted Long's body, it can be checked against the gun that was taken from the car the night of the accident. And it should be pretty straightforward to test Styles' DNA against DNA from the Lovett rape."

"And you can use the material from my heart biopsy," Pace said, "to do what amounts to a paternity test—check DNA from the biopsy against samples from Dean Arnold's parents. That would tell us whether or not my transplanted heart came from Dean."

"You've got this all figured out, haven't you?" Courtney said.

"I'm just glad it's finally over," Pace said.

—49—

By the time they were zipping through the countryside, halfway to her house, Joan had shed all her concerns about Charles Styles. He was gracious and charming. He was articulate—a gifted conversationalist really—but then she supposed that was what he did for a living, talked.

So when, in the middle of a particularly desolate patch of road, he suddenly took his foot of the accelerator and said, "Uh-oh, I think we're out of gas," Joan was more annoyed than anything else. How puerile! She made up her mind that if he made a pass at her, she'd just get out and walk the rest of the way home.

The car rolled to a stop, but she could still hear the engine running. Who did Styles think he was fooling?

"Give me your hand," he said.

"Okay, that's it," Joan said. "I'm out of here." She turned toward the door and reached for the handle.

"Don't make me have to shoot you," he said, his voice suddenly feral.

And in that instant, Joan understood exactly what was happening. She was nauseated. She felt like her temperature was 106. Then why was she shivering so? She thought she was going to be sick right there in the car.

Instinct told her that her only chance was to get out of the car—now! Risk the gunshot. It would likely be a far better end than what Styles had in mind.

But she hesitated. And then Styles had her wrist in his clammy grip, and it was too late.

He reached around and grabbed her other hand, then roughly pulled both arms behind her back and began taping her wrists together. He did it all so efficiently, so effortlessly, Joan had no doubt he'd done it before. She had never felt so utterly helpless in all her life.

When he was done with her wrists, Styles slapped a piece of tape across her mouth. Then he opened the glove compartment and pulled out a knit ski cap which he placed on her head and rolled down over her face. He put a band of tape around the lowered edge of the ski cap, turning it into an unremovable hood. She couldn't move her arms. She couldn't talk. And now she couldn't see. She was totally defenseless against what she was certain was about to happen. Her only hope was that someone would happen by in a car and discover them.

Then suddenly Styles jumped out of the car and slammed the door behind him. She was alone! An indescribable sensation of relief washed through her body. The car that had been her prison was now her sanctuary.

But in only a few seconds, the door was pulled open beside her.

"Get out," his voice now a hoarse, savage whisper.

Joan made her decision. She would not cooperate.

Styles didn't bother to repeat the command. He merely grabbed her by the collar of her dress and pulled her out of the car and onto the ground.

"Stand up," he ordered her in that same chilling

voice.

She refused.

He simply dragged her to the back of the car.

She heard the gruesome sound of Styles opening the lid of the trunk.

"Get in."

She lay motionless on the ground.

Styles grabbed the ski cap and a handful of her hair and began to pull. When she didn't respond instantly, he gave her a fierce kick in the area of her right kidney. She climbed into the trunk.

Before he closed the lid, Styles issued a warning. "When I open the trunk, if you've managed to take the hood off or worked the tape from your mouth, I will strangle you very, very slowly."

Then the lid crashed down, and he was gone. If she had been able, Joan would have screamed. As it was, she could only sob. More than anything, she grieved for David, knowing how devastated he would be at losing her. And then she passed out.

Joan was in and out of consciousness. She had no idea how long she had been in the trunk. During her waking moments, she worried carbon monoxide might accumulate in the trunk, then she decided carbon monoxide poisoning would be a blessing.

She awakened for the last time as Styles yanked at her arms, pulling her from the trunk. She managed to get her feet under her and was half walked, half carried by Styles as he steered her over a short distance into a building. The brief respite brought by the cool night air was quickly traded for a new kind of suffocating confinement—trapped once again at close quarters with Styles.

He dragged her up a short stairway, then threw her

onto a bed. He pulled the hood from her head. It was dark in the room, but she could see Styles—which was of course exactly what he wanted.

He did something with his face. In the dark, it took Joan a moment to understand what had happened. The beard was gone.

And then he took off his suit coat and loosened his tie, all the time making eye contact with Joan.

Here it comes, she thought.

But it didn't, not yet. Styles was waiting for something. He kept going to the window and checking. He was nervous. Or excited. But it looked like nothing was going to happen soon.

Outside, Senator Edward Long sat in his car. He too was waiting.

—50—

Courtney called Detective Marks on her cell phone while they were still at the restaurant. He said she'd given him more than enough to bring Styles in for questioning—probably enough for an arrest. Marks said they'd pick up Styles immediately. Then—would wonders never cease—he actually thanked Courtney for the call.

Pace and Courtney shared a long hug outside the little restaurant, then Courtney headed back downtown. She said she had a couple more hours of work to do but would catch up with him later. They still had their hotel room and figured, since they were going to be billed for it anyway, they might as well stay there one more night.

With Courtney headed for her office, Pace saw no reason to rush back to the hotel. He'd bought a few necessities since their hasty departure the night of the shooting, but there were things he needed from home. Now was as good a time as any to drop by and pick them up.

Parking his car on the street, Pace passed a large, late model sedan parked on the opposite side. The dark silhouette behind the wheel seemed vaguely familiar—a neighbor, Pace thought, putting the man out of his mind.

As he tread the familiar walk leading to his front door, a wave of nostalgia hit Pace, a need for this place that had been his home for so many years. If he hadn't planned to meet Courtney back at the hotel, he'd move back in tonight.

The evening was cool and pleasant—perfect for a nice long jog with Max. Pace felt more than a little guilty that he hadn't been able to keep his promise to see the dog today. He made an irrevocable pledge to see Max in the morning, no matter what. Then he thought, maybe I could still see him tonight after I collect my things. The veterinary hospital is open twenty-four hours a day. If they're not too busy . . .

He subconsciously began the tried and true maneuver required to open the front door. With his right hand he turned the key clockwise. With his left hand he lifted the handle while simultaneously depressing the latch with his thumb. When he heard the gratifying click of the lock, he pushed. Pace smiled to himself. The quirky front door was one of the many friendly eccentricities of the house that warmed his heart and made him feel at home. Not unlike, he imagined, the familiar idiosyncrasies of a spouse of many years. And that made him think again of Courtney and his increasingly confident belief that yes, she was going to be the one for him and, he hoped, vice versa.

Pace stepped inside and flicked the light switch. Nothing happened.

"Stay right where you are," a voice ordered out of the darkness. "I have a gun."

Pace didn't recognize the voice, but he had no doubt who it belonged to. And in that same instant, Pace understood his mistake. *Pace* knew that Styles was finished, but Styles hadn't yet received the word.

Styles was like a lone Japanese holdout on some godforsaken dot of sand in the middle of the Pacific. World War II was over, but the poor guy hadn't heard the news. Well, Pace could remedy that.

"You're done, Styles," Pace said. "The police know everything."

Styles considered the information in silence while Pace weighed his options. His eyes had not yet adjusted to the darkness. In all likelihood, Styles could see him a whole lot better than he could see Styles. Still, it was dark, and Pace might be able use that to his advantage.

There was no percentage in simply charging across the room and trying to overpower Styles. Styles would shoot him before he made it halfway. But there was another possibility. Pace didn't have to stand around and wait for Styles to put a bullet in his head. The front door was just inches away, not even completely closed.

But Styles read his mind.

"If you try anything," Styles said, "it will go very badly for Dr. Bennett upstairs."

Pace heard the words, heard the threatening tone with which they were rendered, but their import did not immediately register. Dr. Bennett? And then he understood—Joan! And with that came the broader understanding of what Styles was trying to accomplish. He was eliminating anyone who might be able to put together the events surrounding the transplant. Only a couple of days ago, it might have worked. If Styles' bullet had killed Pace instead of wounding Max, Styles' crimes might never have come to light.

"Why don't we just head upstairs and check on Dr. Bennett?" Styles said.

Pace now had no choice. He couldn't consider escape for himself and leave Joan behind in the hands of Styles. Could Styles be lying? Perhaps Joan wasn't really upstairs. Pace knew that was only wishful thinking.

Pace's eyes were slowly adjusting to the limited light. He could see Styles more clearly now, see the gun in his hand. Styles stepped back to keep Pace at a distance, then motioned with the gun for Pace to move up the stairway.

Pace hesitated, considering what options remained. He could sprint up the stairs and try to get a door between him and Styles, but no door upstairs could stop a bullet. And he didn't know for certain which room Joan was in or what condition she was in.

Then Pace remembered the car parked across the street and instantly knew who that dark figure was behind the wheel. He had to work out what that meant. For now, he had no choice but to give every appearance of meekly submitting to Styles' demands.

Pace turned and silently climbed the stairs.

Joan was on her knees on Pace's bed. A piece of insulation tape was plastered across her mouth. Her hands were taped together behind her back. Her eyes were filled with terror.

Pace put his arms around her and pulled her to him. Ignoring Styles, he gently pulled the tape from her mouth, signaling to Joan that she should remain quiet. Then, without pausing or seeking permission, he began to slowly remove the tape from her wrists. While he worked at the tapes, he also tried to work on Styles' mind. As understanding came to Pace, he knew what he had to do.

"Now that the police have you as their number one suspect," he told Styles, "it's a simple matter for them to check a sample of your DNA against DNA from the Lovett rape. Killing us isn't going to get you anywhere."

"You're lying," Styles said. "I've got to admit, you're a pretty quick thinker, but I don't believe you put this together until you walked in the front door and found me waiting for you."

"The police also know that it was Dean Arnold who died that night in Ted Long's car. They'll be charging you with that murder as well."

Styles began to violently shake his head. "That wasn't me. That was that idiot Ted Long. He got drunk and beat the hell out of Arnold with a baseball bat, then he expected me to come and clean up his mess."

This was a new piece of the story for Pace, the final piece. "And when Ted called and ordered you to come and clean up after him, you had no choice but to obey."

Styles was silent.

"Because Ted knew you were driving his car the night Francine Lovett was killed, so he also knew you committed the murder, and he was holding that over you." Another thought occurred to Pace. It all seemed so obvious now. "This wasn't the only rape he was holding over you, was it?"

Styles remained silent.

Charles Styles, chief of staff to the state's senior United States senator—and serial rapist. Pace remembered that Melissa Gardner had said Ted always had a way to get money when he needed it. He'd probably been blackmailing Styles for years.

"So when you arrived at the Dean Arnold murder scene," Pace said, "you saw a golden opportunity. Kill Ted, then make it appear that Arnold had died in a car crash. Take the gun you'd used to kill Ted and put it with Arnold in the car, along with Ted Long's wallet—to make it appear Arnold had stolen it. Melissa Gardner was so drunk, just leave her in the car and throw in a kidnapping to boot.

"Then Sheriff Dash came along and messed up all your plans by assuming Ted was the man who'd died in the crash. At first you thought Dash had ruined everything, then you realized that the misidentification and transplant scenario might just be the luckiest thing that ever happened to you."

Pace was watching the other man closely. Styles was becoming increasingly agitated. He had a demonic look in his eyes. It wasn't difficult to imagine that it was in precisely this climactic state that Styles killed.

Pace began to edge slowly, carefully away from Joan—to remove her from the line of fire.

"You cannot imagine the pleasure it gave me," Styles said, "to put a bullet in Ted Long." He raised the gun in his hand and pointed it at Pace's head.

Pace saw that the gun had a silencer. It was undoubtedly the same gun Styles had used when he shot poor Max by mistake.

"Make peace with your God, if you have one," Styles said. "It's time."

Joan gasped. Pace felt the urge to go comfort her, but didn't dare. He had to do something. He needed to stall just a little longer.

The gun was pointing directly at his head. At this range, there was no possibility that even an agitated Styles could miss. Pace imagined that Styles was beginning to put pressure on the trigger. It was now or never.

Pace lunged, and, in the same instant, he heard the shot.

The sound of the pistol's discharge reverberated